DEATH IN THE FAMILY

DEATH IN THE FAMILY

Tessa Wegert

Berkley Prime Crime

New York

BERKLEY PRIME CRIME
Published by Berkley
An imprint of Penguin Random House LLC
penguinrandomhouse.com

Library of Congress Cataloging-in-Publication Data

Names: Wegert, Tessa, author.
Title: Death in the family / Tessa Wegert.
Description: First edition. | New York: Berkley Prime Crime, 2020. |
Series: A Shana Merchant novel; book 1
Identifiers: LCCN 2019026827 | ISBN 9780593097892 (hardcover) |
ISBN 9780593097908 (ebook)
Subjects: GSAFD: Mystery fiction.
Classification: LCC PS3623.E422656 D43 2020 | DDC 813/.6—dc23
LC record available at https://lccn.loc.gov/2019026827

First Edition: February 2020

Printed in the United States of America
1   3   5   7   9   10   8   6   4   2

Cover art: *Isle with house on lake* © Michael Trevillion
Cover design by Judith Lagerman
Title page photograph: Shutterstock/Sarah Mika
Book design by Elke Sigal

For my family, who gave this story life

Acknowledgments

There are many brilliant and generous people without whom this book would not exist, and while I can't name them all here, I hold them in my heart. Thank you, Marlene Stringer and Grace House, for your inestimable contributions, and for loving this story as much as I do. To Sheriff Colleen O'Neill, thank you for allowing me to pick your brain about life as a BCI senior investigator. Thank you to Martin Karlow, Dorinda Bonanno, and Michelle Sowden for reading, and also to John and Carol Repsher, for introducing me to the Thousand Islands all those years ago. To Karl, Leila, and Karel Wegert, your encouragement means more to me than I could ever express. Finally, thank you to Remi and Schafer for your boundless enthusiasm (never give up!), and above all, to Grant. I couldn't have done it without you.

PROLOGUE

It was late September, the kind of morning that turns orange when you close your eyes, weather so sweet everyone on the sidewalk gulps fresh air like kids drinking soda. I got off the subway at Woodhaven Boulevard eager for my share, but as I made my way up the avenue it wasn't the incandescent day I saw but weeds pushing up through the cracks in the sidewalk, ugly blotches where spilled coffee defaced the pavement. In spite of its flaws, Queens was drenched in autumn beauty.

It all looked cheerless to me.

My plan was to tolerate him. I figured it was the best I could do. Like my walk to 1 Lefrak City Plaza, though, the man I came to meet was confounding. With his sky-blue shirt and recent trim, his neck still ruddy from the clippers, he looked the part, yet the socks peeking out from the cuffs of his pants were patterned in spectacled kittens, and he smelled like he'd been cooking with sage though it was 10:00 a.m. on a Tuesday. When we made our introductions his tone oozed pity like I knew it would, but his folksy accent—Rhode Island or Mass was my guess—softened the blow.

"So," Dr. Carson Gates said as we took our seats. He folded his hands. "You're here. That's good."

"Is it?" My own hands were clasped in an impenetrable ball. It was the only way I could keep them from twitching.

"I bet there are a dozen places you'd rather be. The DMV. A dentist's office, needle hovering above your gums." He shivered, not just for effect. "But you came. So yeah, it's a good start."

It's a requirement, I thought, indignant, but I didn't hate this guy with the clear eyes and wacky socks. For what it was worth, the delicate fern on his desk appeared to be thriving. *Go through the motions*, I told myself. *Give him what he wants and you can go home.* At the same time, I felt like my head was filled with bees. Talking was easy, except when it wasn't.

"You don't think I can help," said Carson. "No, it's okay—I get that a lot. I want you to know something, though." He leaned in, studying me. "I won't give up on you, Shana. You can do this. Start at the beginning. Just take it slow."

The beginning. Where was that, exactly? Nowhere I wanted to take a stranger, even if he did smell nice. But maybe I could go back partway, just far enough to make him happy. Back to a limestone building on East Fifth Street, and a day that grabbed me by the throat and still hasn't let go.

I was shoulder-deep in a fatal hit-and-run when my NCO supervisor called me into his office and told me to brace myself. *Change of plans,* he said. *This has you written all over it, Shana.* I figured he was talking about my investigative method—upending people like stones in a garden to find what's lurking underneath is kind of my thing—but that wasn't it. They needed me, and me alone, in a way I could never have imagined.

The guys from the Seventh Precinct were investigating a series of murders below Houston. Another body had turned up, this time in the East Village—my domain. They knew some things about their suspect already, and it was their latest intel that made the sergeant yank me from my desk and send me down to Pitt Street, where the case was laid out like a map on a table: in the span of four months, three murders, all women. *Becca Wolkwitz. Lanie Miner, Jess Lowenthal.* There was no evidence of abusive relationships, no history of drugs or run-ins with bad crowds to explain why they'd been plucked from the street and turned into statistics. The only common thread was all three women used the same dating app, and all had dated a man named Blake Bram.

Bram's profile picture, I explained to Carson Gates, showed a Caucasian male in his midthirties with dark hair and blue eyes. Hair dye, colored contact lenses, and photo filters were a given; it's witness-based composite sketches, not manipulated photos, that tend to get us our guy. Still, something about his picture tugged at my gut. His face evoked a memory, dog-eared and soft from use but long ago misplaced. I'd seen Bram before, but couldn't say where.

The guy's bio claimed he liked airport novels and Bill Murray movies. More lies. Historical data from the app's administrators told us he updated his profile often, no doubt trying various combinations to see what stuck. There was just one constant among the write-ups, a line of text present every time. Blake Bram was from a town called Swanton, Vermont.

"Swanton. Sounds pretty as a picture, right?" I said as Carson listened with parted lips. "Back in the sixties, the Queen of England gifted Swanton with a pair of Royal Swans, and swans still swim in the town's Village Green Park. To the west, you'll find Lake Champlain; to the north, Canada. The 2010 census put the population of Swanton at 6,427. I know this because Swanton is where I grew up."

There it was. It took an embarrassingly long time for me to go on. "When I heard the killer claimed to be from my hometown, I understood why the sergeant asked me to drop everything for this case. There was a two-week time span between the disappearances, and no reason to think Bram's spree was done. We were roughly the same age, he and I, and six thousand people wasn't a lot."

Carson waited, cupping the back of his baby-smooth neck with both hands.

"They were hoping I could ID the guy," I went on. "Surely you know him, they said."

What I didn't tell Carson, or anyone else, is that they were right.

ONE

Thirteen months later

M urder," I repeated, the word clumsy on my tongue. The last time I spoke it, I was in another world.

Tim rocked his office chair, testing the bounce on springs sticky with dust, and raised his empty coffee mug. "Murder *on an island*," he said. "If it didn't make me a heartless creep, I'd call this your lucky day, Shane."

It was a nickname I hated, but I was still trying to reconcile Tim's news with the water coursing down the window behind him, so I let it slide. *Shane!* Tim said my first day on the job. *Don't tell me you've never seen* Shane! *Old western movie? Gunfighter with a mysterious past? Get it?* I didn't, hated westerns with their drama and dust, but Tim was convinced it was funny.

That morning, no one was laughing. Tim took the transfer call from dispatch while I was putting a second pot on to brew, listening to the thunder rattle the panes and expecting nothing more from the Saturday than dry skin from the electric heat. As much as I wished the call was a joke, too—Tim needling "the new guy" or a prank by some bored townies—I knew it wasn't, for three reasons. The first was Tim's face. He had cartoonish eyebrows, so wide and straight they might have been drawn with a Sharpie. I'm not saying I'm perfect. Most people, when they look at me, see only my scar. But I wondered if in spite of Tim's athletic build, perps saw him as a hapless clown with no sway. As I watched him ask the routine questions on the phone and scribble notes on a lined yellow pad, Tim's face got hard as stone. It was an entirely new look on him. At least, it was new to me.

The second reason was the timing. I'd been told prank calls in the fall were unicorns, rare enough to be the stuff of legend. We were smack in the middle of October and the exodus was nearly complete. The majority of the seasonal residents, even the stragglers who tried to eke out a few more days of summer, had packed up their water trampolines and put their garish red-and-yellow cigarette boats in storage. The short-term tourists were back where they'd come from, too: Manhattan, Toronto, Montreal. This was the off-season in the Thousand Islands of upstate New York, nobody left but the locals. Just us.

Above all, though, I knew the call was legit because of the rain, sideways and lashing at that window by Tim's desk. On the morning news the local weather guy—Bob? Ben?—said it was a nor'easter. The storm had started the previous day with lethal-looking green clouds that plunged the village of Alexandria Bay into premature darkness. It dumped freezing water on us all night and was expected to last forty-eight hours in all. Nobody wanted to be out in that weather, helping to dock a police boat. I couldn't imagine anyone setting foot outside if they had a choice.

No, this call was the real deal. It was my first murder case in over a year, since the one that convinced me to trade Manhattan for total obscurity. I glanced around me. We weren't the only investigators working out of our station, but we were the only ones present today, and now, somehow, I had to get to an island. "Grab your coat," I said, watching Tim's eyebrows inch upward. "We're going for a ride."

I used to think of boats differently, which is to say I rarely thought of them at all. A ferry to Ellis Island when my parents were in town and wanted to see the Statue of Liberty. A dinner cruise a few years back that ended with my date vomiting his shrimp cocktail into the East River. That was it for getting my sea legs. I hoped my inexperience wouldn't be an issue today, but I knew it probably would.

It was a three-minute drive from the station to Keewaydin State Park, a straight shot up Route 12. I relished the warmth of the cruiser, savored the feel of my dry clothes while I had the chance. "What do we know?" I asked, flexing my fingers on the wheel. They were tucked into gloves I wished I'd thought to make toasty on the heaters before we left the station.

"That we'd rather be back inside with that coffee?"

I doled out half a smile. The coffee would've gurgled to the top of the pot by now. I could picture it steaming in the break room. By the time I saw it again, it would be cold, pungent sludge. "Besides that," I said.

"White male age twenty-six, gone missing from a summer house. He was up from the city. It was the estate's caretaker who called it in, noticed the guy's absence first thing this morning."

"Whoa," I said, swiveling my head. "Missing? I thought you said murder." Those weren't the same thing at all. Had Tim been playing me in the office? Joke's on Shane?

"Murder's what the family wants to call it." Tim shrugged, making it clear he didn't put much stock in that claim. "There's no body," he admitted, way too late for my liking. "The man's just gone."

A missing persons case that may or may not involve a murder. Suddenly my hands were too hot. I peeled off the gloves, jammed them in the center console. "Name?"

"That's where this gets interesting."

"It's interesting already."

Tim grinned. "The guy? He's Jasper Sinclair."

I gave him a blank look.

"The Sinclairs are a New York family. In the fashion industry, I think," he said. "They're kind of a big deal. And this morning Jasper's girlfriend woke up to an empty bed and the sheets soaked with blood."

"But no body," I said. "Huh, that's . . . different."

"Yeah."

"So they're pointing the finger at her?"

"Not clear on that," Tim said. "I don't see how a young woman could transport a grown man's body through a house full of sleeping people without waking anyone up."

"Trapdoor in the floor?"

He laughed. "Maybe so."

"That's assuming the attacker worked alone."

"Attacker," Tim repeated and winced.

I knew what he was thinking. Murder on Tim's turf was a personal affront. "How many people in the house?" I asked.

"Eight, including the girlfriend. The missing man made nine. They all slept through the night, so the caretaker says, despite the storm."

I squinted at him. "And it's all family over there?" No crime was easy to stomach, whether the body was on-site or not, but family stuff? That was the worst. I've seen the terrible things fathers, mothers, brothers, cousins are capable of. Blood ties can be bloody.

"Family, the caretaker, the girlfriend, and a couple significant others. Like I said, full house. No sign of an intruder, apparently, but the caretaker seemed a little funny on that point."

"Funny how?"

"Like maybe he was holding something back."

We took a left off the highway and sailed through a puddle the size of a lily pond. The dock and slips were just ahead.

"I asked them if they've done a search," Tim went on. "Figured there was a good chance the guy's licking his wounds in the bathroom or a cupboard under the stairs. A big house like that, you never know."

"How do you know the house is big?"

"They all are, Shane." He tacked on an eye roll. "But this place is really something. I used to dream about living there when my dad would take me fishing nearby as a kid. No sign of Jasper, though. Not yet."

"Other than his blood, that is." I tapped my fingers on the wheel. "We'll have to do a proper search. If it's an island, there could be cliffs and stuff, right?"

"Plenty of places where people could tumble into the river in the dark," Tim agreed.

"We'll need forensics, too. For the blood." It was worth pointing out. This was A-Bay after all, and I couldn't be sure what I'd get. There were six investigators in my unit, and the region had twenty troopers—plus Sheriff McIntyre and the deputies in Watertown overseeing all of Jefferson County. That was sufficient manpower for a hundred thousand law-abiding citizens. The issue was the island. I noticed Tim didn't question my decision to bring him along. BCI Investigators, even senior ones like me, largely worked alone, but if ever this job warranted a partner, it was today.

"'Course we will," Tim said, sounding offended. "With island crimes, it's closest car—or in this case, closest boat—but the others will be along. I'm sure they'll all want a look. This kind of thing doesn't happen much. Nobody around here even locks their doors. This isn't New York City."

I cut my eyes at him again, unsure of what I'd see—the trace of a smile, maybe, or a smidgen of quiet glee. Tim was downplaying the situation. A murder, even a missing persons case, on one of the islands was unheard of. McIntyre made that clear when she hired me. So I guess I thought Tim would be excited. I know plenty of cops in the city who'd get a big thrill from a case like this, in a place where they happen every day. If Tim was pumped, he didn't show it. His expression was solemn, his lips a neutral line.

I turned the wheel, trading the easy swish of the highway for the hard crackle of gravel road, and there was the river. Damn, but the water was high. The summer had broken all kinds of records for flooding, the water level three feet higher than the norm. I'd read it hadn't been like this since 1973. The damage was already bad, and now, with a nor'easter, it was going to get much worse.

I pulled the car onto a patch of grass waterlogged with rain and peered dubiously at the sky through the windshield one last time. Tim's eyes were on the boat. The folks at headquarters, Tim included, had been more excited about the police vessel's arrival than about mine. We came at the same time: the new plaything courtesy of a special fund administered by the U.S. Coast Guard, me courtesy of a fiancé and a need to get the hell out of the city. I guess I couldn't blame them. Even I could appreciate the boat's tantalizing, new-toy shine. When Tim saw the size of the waves on the river, the loving look on his face was replaced with a frown.

"Okay, then," he said brightly while baring his teeth. "Ready?"

"Now or never," I replied, and we stepped outside. Puffs of breath lingered ghostlike in front of us as we splashed toward the reedy edge of the St. Lawrence River, where the waves smacked the boat against the dock. The thing was small and exposed with a flimsy navy canopy—Tim called it a T-Top—that snapped in the wind. I pulled the hood of my rain jacket over my hair, kinky from the humidity. Acres of naked fields lay to the south of us, endless water to the north. The isolation of the place was jarring.

Upstate New York. I'd pictured it as nowheresville, a mishmash of farmers' fields and dilapidated barns, and I wasn't wrong. The towns are small, the people as down-to-earth as they come. It's a patriotic part of the country, but every American flag looked as if it had been flying since the thirties, abandoned to the elements, bleached out and threadbare. Something about those flags seemed vulgar, like Lady Liberty's been subjected to an upskirt. I keep that opinion to myself. Both Tim and my fiancé are locals, born and bred on the river, so I also don't tell them it still comes as a shock when I wake up in the morning and find myself here. Instead of investigating homicides with the NYPD on the Lower East Side,

I'm fighting crime for the New York State Park Police in a place where violent crime doesn't exist. Until, one day, it does.

"Weekend on the river's what the caretaker said," Tim called from on board the boat. "They're cutting it real close."

Manhattan's chilly in October, but I'd been told it could get arctic in the Thousand Islands. Even a weak fall system's likely to be nasty. Past the boat the bay was the color of thunder, and rain ricocheted off the water's surface with such fury I could barely make out Comfort Island a quarter mile away. It was the closest island to that part of the mainland, one of the few I knew by name. Comfort Island looked the opposite of comforting in the stormy morning light.

"Guess you wish you'd taken that trip to see your parents," Tim said, exposing the boat's controls and seat cushions, tucking covers into storage bins. Now that I was living closer to my home state, I'd been driving to Vermont on a regular basis. If not for the storm, I'd be there now.

"And miss all this?" I said as a gust of wind doused my face with cold rain.

Tim dug into his pocket and came out with a key attached to a red float. "Flip you for it."

"Funny. The lines?" I knew what to do with those, at least. Tim started the engine as I waded across the dock, which was six inches underwater, and freed the boat from the cleats. I huddled inside the tiny console and stayed out of Tim's way while he nudged us out of the slip. Only when we were off did I realize I'd left my gloves in the car. Rain hammered at the T-Top and stung my face as we lurched forward and sped across the water toward the island.

The very first thing my fiancé told me about the Thousand

Islands was that the label's a lie. There are actually 1,864 rocky patches of land along the stretch of St. Lawrence that divides Ontario from New York State. A century ago the area was as posh as the Hamptons, the go-to summer getaway for millionaire titans of industry and the upper crust of New York. Many of them still own property on the river. According to Carson, the proprietor of the Waldorf Astoria once commissioned a hundred-and-twenty-room mansion for his wife only to watch her die before it was done. If the legend's true, the man never returned to it again. What strikes me isn't that he lost his bride, but that he didn't see that outcome coming. He named the place Heart Island. Some ironies are too tempting for the universe to resist.

It was rougher out than I expected, and I'd expected rough. Under the water, shoals lay in wait, their teeth big enough to tear through boats as if they were made of matchsticks. When we entered the channel I felt the current's fierce pull. The channel was for freighters bringing Canadian wheat and iron ore from the Great Lakes over to Europe, but there were no tankers on the water today. No other boats at all.

We were halfway there before Tim revealed our destination. Tern Island, on the U.S. side. This island wasn't open to the public like Wellesley (American) or Wolfe (Canadian), but privately owned.

"You told them to stay put, right? Not to disturb the scene?" I shouted over the shriek of the wind. In my old job, the scene of the crime was never more than ten minutes away. The fact that our cruiser could scream out of the parking lot and bully its way through the streets like a tank was a source of pride to me, but getting to an island isn't something you can rush. Thinking about all the things the people on it could get up to before we arrived filled me with dread.

Tim laughed. "They've only got one boat in the water, and it's a skiff—a little motorboat for getting back and forth from shore. It'd take three trips to transport everyone to the mainland, and they'd be crazy to do it now. Don't you feel it? The swell of the water?" he said. "The currents are insane. Anyway, it's just up here, past Deer Island."

Deer Island. That was another one I'd heard about from Carson. It had once been a retreat for a Yale secret society called Skull and Bones; now its dense trees and derelict lodge made it look as sinister as a horror-movie set. A chill danced up my spine as we raced past it, but the landmass quickly disappeared, sucked back into the fog.

I'd been bracing myself against the knocks and jolts of our boat in the choppy water, but wasn't prepared when Tim shouted, "*Shit! Hang on!*" He jerked the wheel to dodge a near-invisible shoal, and I barely managed to avoid tumbling overboard as a wave breached the gunwale, dousing me with icy water. The skin on my thighs burned and my pulse pounded in my ears. Along with the storm, the sound was deafening.

"Not a great place to take a life if you hope to keep your freedom." I dug my fingernails into the back of Tim's leather seat. "Why here? Why now, when it's so hard to get away?"

"You're thinking suicide, then," Tim said.

Like me, he was remembering the caretaker's report. How the missing man's family was tucked in bed all night. Now, I'm not prone to churning out conjecture like assembly-line muffins. I like my theories fully baked before I share them with a partner. But this guy's disappearance, and the caretaker's call, and the timing of it all was strange, and I wanted to know what was going on inside Tim's head. "Stabs himself next to his girlfriend and stumbles over a cliff? It could happen," I said.

"There are easier ways to kill yourself on an island."

"And why risk alerting someone to your plan?"

"Unless he wanted her to know," said Tim. "Who's to say what kind of relationship they had?"

"Some people are messed up," I agreed. "But the caretaker said murder."

"And if they aren't suggesting suicide, there's a reason for that."

"Eight people." I rubbed my nose, numb now from the cold. "This is going to take some time."

"We'll have help," Tim reminded me as the boat arced left. "We'll need it. Made it. Whew."

I didn't know what Tern Island would look like. I wouldn't have been able to find it on a map. When it finally emerged from the mist, it was like the peak of a mountain had busted through the water and rumbled skyward.

"Would you look at this place?" Tim said as we tipped back our heads to take it all in. Though he'd seen it a million times before, he was as awestruck as I was.

Tern was all jagged gray rock crowned by a massive Victorian house with a jumble of stories pockmarked by windows of various shapes and sizes. A turret thrust into the sky like a fist. The siding was forest green, as if the house was trying to blend in with the thick trees that surrounded it. As if it could. There was a matching boathouse at the river's edge, and the entire island was bordered by a high stone wall that might as well have been painted with the words *Keep Out*. A staircase so steep it was nearly vertical extended from the boathouse all the way to the island's summit. The house's foundation was stonework, too.

A nor'easter was no match for this place. No storm was. Someone had invested a fortune in masonry work to make sure Tern Island could withstand anything. But from that house a man was missing, possibly dead. I wasn't sure the island would withstand that.

TWO

There's history here—real-life aristocracy. This is where America's elite come to play.

These words, Carson's words, swam to the surface of my memory as Tim navigated the boat toward the island's shore. My fiancé hoped the romance of the place and its extreme wealth would woo me. He wanted to make sure I was on board with the idea of moving here, so he kept trying to convince me, even as I rode next to him in the rental van that contained everything we owned. "It's peaceful," Carson said, squeezing my knee and flashing a smile. When I twined my fingers with his he added, "You'll love it, Shay. People come here to leave their worries behind. We can do the same. You'll see."

If only it was that easy. We'd been here a handful of months, he and I, and already I was causing Carson more consternation than I had throughout the whole of our relationship. *If he knew what I was about to do*, I thought as I craned my neck to see the house atop Tern Island, *he might wonder if coming upstate was such a good idea after all.*

A voice reached us through the wind in increments and I spotted a man in a heavy rain poncho standing at the end of the island's dock. This dock was underwater, too—the whole thing plunged below the surface of the river, and the sight of him on its slick, algae-coated planks so far out in the river made me feel ill. *One big swell and he's a goner*, I thought, but the man seemed surprisingly steady. He opened his canvas-clad arms, and for an eyeblink he was Christ the Redeemer guiding us to port.

"Looks like he wants us docked in the boathouse," Tim said, wiping rain from his eyes with the back of his hand. "Should be plenty of room if there's only the one other vessel."

I looked to the left in time to see the boathouse doors lift and expose a cavernous space. My parents' whole house in Swanton would've fit inside, with room to spare. There was an empty slip next to the skiff Tim said they used to ferry guests to and from the island. The little vessel looked toylike, way too small for a boathouse of this size. On the building's interior wall I spotted a wooden sign decorated with curly gold script. It was the kind of thing you'd affix to the back of a yacht or a sailboat, the equivalent of vanity plates for your car.

"*Loophole*," I read. "Either these people have a sense of humor or they found an awesome tax attorney."

"I wonder where *Loophole* is now," Tim said as he glided our boat inside. "The owners of this place come from old money. They're what the guides on tour boats call a family of the Gilded Age. It's weird all they've got is this puny skiff."

Just as we were about to get out of the rain, one last manic gust of wind blasted me from behind. It was as violent as a shove. "What else do you know about them?" I lowered my voice before asking. In the shelter of the structure it was quieter, and the man in the poncho waited nearby.

"Not much, but this island's always been one of my favorites. The house was built in the late 1800s, I think. I've seen old photos of it in shambles, but it was bought and fixed up in the forties. Far as I know, it hasn't changed hands since. Islands rarely go up for sale," Tim added. "When they do, it's a feeding frenzy. Can't wait to see what the house is like inside."

I didn't question Tim's knowledge about an island he'd only ever seen from the water or the people he'd never met. Tim could tell you which Canadian newspaper mogul just embedded a man-made waterfall into his island's cliff face, and which nineteenth-century tobacco tycoon's family funded the expansion of the area's most prestigious golf resort. Carson thought of himself as the authority on the region, but my colleague had him beat. Part of that's because of Tim's job: a small-town investigator gets around. The few times I mentioned Tim's expertise to Carson, Carson got testy and changed the subject. Nobody likes being told they don't know the lay of their own backyard.

Inside, the boathouse smelled of wet wood with an undercurrent of rotting fish. The thump of our fenders as Tim flipped them over the side of the boat, the slap of water against the interior walls . . . noises fell in a way that made me uneasy. The place was too empty, too quiet. Quickly, I disembarked.

"Thank God you're here, I was worried you wouldn't make it. Philip Norton," the man said as he tied up our vessel, yanking the lines tight with ease. "I'm the one who called."

"You're the caretaker?" I asked.

"Caretaker, cook, housekeeping staff. I do it all."

"I'm Investigator Tim Wellington," Tim said, his eyes lingering on Norton's face. "And this is Senior Investigator Shana Merchant."

Even with his hood up, I could see Norton's bald head and neck blended seamlessly. I suspected that underneath the poncho his body was similarly bare and square. Eyebrows and lashes so blond they were almost white disappeared against his skin. His cheeks were pudgy and his eyes too small, like raisins in an underbaked bun, but the effect was endearing. "No remote," Norton explained as he hit a button on the wall to close the boathouse door. Then he grimaced in my direction and said, "Please excuse the smell."

I came across men like this sometimes, older guys who couldn't fathom how a woman could be a cop, or that I'd come to this work willingly and was better at it than most. I got the sense it was my femaleness that brought the color to Norton's cheeks, but it could just as easily have been my scar. "Mink trouble," the man said apologetically, and it took me a second to catch up. He meant the smell, but when I heard *mink trouble* all I could think of was a rich lady's fur coat, a stain the cleaners couldn't get out.

"Ah," Tim said. "Those buggers can make a real mess. As long as they're leaving their leftovers down here and staying clear of the house, though."

"Isn't that the truth. We had a trapper up here yesterday, just in case."

Tim said, "A trapper, huh?"

A stranger on the island. So that's what Norton was holding back when Tim asked him about intruders on the phone.

"Local guy I found in town. Shifty fella, I didn't like him," Norton said. "He disturbed the nests—the ones made by the geese. Nothing in 'em now, of course, but the birds'll be back in spring and they like the sunny side of the island. He should have known that."

"How long was he out here?" Tim asked.

"Oh, hours. Morning to midafternoon."

"Did he have any luck? I'm surprised the flooding didn't chase the mink out of here."

"Maybe it did," replied Norton. "He looked and looked, but he couldn't find them."

"Mr. Norton," I said, getting antsy. "What can you tell us about last night?"

From the corner of my eye I saw Tim flinch. We were still trying to get a read on each other's methods. I had a feeling he'd prefer to ease into it, keep the small talk going, knowing a relaxed witness is likely to let something slip. But a man was missing, and there was a crime scene inside that might be getting more contaminated by the second. The trapper would stay on my radar, but we needed to move on, and questioning Norton right there on the dock was about simple math. Up in that house there were seven other people, all of whom would need to be interviewed. I saw my chance to get a head start, and I took it.

"I still can't believe it," Norton said. "I've known Jasper since he was six years old. It just doesn't make sense."

Murder rarely does. "This must be tough, then," I said. "Try to think back. Anything out of the ordinary happen yesterday?"

"Well, the family did their own thing until cocktail hour. Everyone was together for that, I know. After dinner they had some more drinks. A couple of 'em went to bed on the early side—Miss Beaudry was one of those. Jasper stayed up, I'm not sure how long. I turned in pretty early myself. It was a long day for me, prepping to welcome Miss Beaudry and the others, and I slept like the dead. Like a log," he said quickly, mortified. "Next thing I know, it's morning and she's screaming her head off." He scrubbed his temples as if trying to dislodge the memory from his mind.

"And Miss Beaudry is . . ." I pulled a notepad and pen from the pocket of my coat.

"Abella Beaudry." Norton spelled it out and watched my hand glide across the pad, making sure I got it right. "She's Jasper's girlfriend," he said.

"And you heard her screaming this morning?"

"Shrieking at the top of her lungs. Camilla—Mrs. Sinclair—was right behind me when I got to their room. She saw everything. God, I wish she hadn't." Norton's frown sank deep into his skin and stayed there as water trickled down his face.

"What's 'everything'?" I said, leaning in. "What did she see?"

"The bed. The . . . blood."

"Who else was in that room this morning?"

"Nobody."

"Not even to take a peek?"

"No. Just Miss Beaudry, Mrs. Sinclair, and me. I thought it would be better to keep everyone out so you could . . . well, do your thing."

"Thanks for that." Three people leaving footprints, fingerprints, and DNA in the room wasn't good, but it sure as hell was better than eight. I ran down my mental checklist. "Any blood on Abella? Body or hands?"

"A little on her clothes, maybe. I'm not sure. By the time we got there, she was across the room, hiding in the corner like a mouse."

"What happened next?"

"She—Mrs. Sinclair—sent me to call 911."

"You called as soon as you noticed Jasper missing," I said. Paraphrasing drives some witnesses crazy, but it's crucial for re-creating the scene. "That means you found him at, what, eight a.m.?"

"No." His mouth twisted and a dimple appeared in the center of his clean-shaven chin. "I didn't call right away," he said. "I told Mrs. Sinclair and Abella to stay inside while the rest of us went looking for Jasper. Everyone was hoping there was a simple explanation. We thought we'd find him. Injured, maybe, but . . ."

"But alive."

Misery is a master of disguise. I've seen beauty buckle under its weight, unsightly faces turn sublime. Norton's grief manifested itself as an anguished, misshapen smile. "We looked everywhere," he said. "All through the house, all over the island. Down here by the river. In the woods."

"Did you see any blood along the way? Any indication of where he might have gone, or . . ."

"Or where he was taken," Tim said, staring hard at Norton.

"No," he replied. "Nothing at all."

"Did you search as a group?" I asked.

"We split up."

"Ah." I didn't like that. Assuming they weren't all in it together, which seemed unlikely, splitting up meant someone had the chance to cover their tracks or finish what they'd started during the night without being seen.

Tim asked him to describe the search parties, and I recorded them in my notebook. Camilla Sinclair, Jade Byrd, and Abella Beaudry—the girlfriend—stayed together inside. Flynn and Barbara Sinclair, along with a man named Ned Yeboah, searched the house, while Philip Norton and Miles Byrd combed the island. I didn't yet know who those names belonged to. They were strangers to me, strange. I made a point of memorizing the composition of those groups, though. There was a reason they broke out the way they did, and I'd have to find out what it was.

By Norton's account, the search lasted forty-five minutes. I thought about my drive into work that morning and how grateful I'd been for my nice, warm car as I listened to the caretaker describe circumnavigating the island in fifty-mile-per-hour winds. I wasn't surprised they didn't find anything. Much of Tern appeared to be forest, and it was late autumn. The leaves were down. This was no immaculate lawn we were talking about, but a contained wilderness with plenty of places to hide. I'd heard some of these islands had natural caves down by the water's edge.

If Jasper left the house during the night, whether under his own power or by force, I thought, *he might still be out here.* To do this right we'd need a proper search party, maybe even a dog. Norton's efforts, while valiant, weren't nearly enough.

The storm battered the near-empty boathouse like a drum. "I have to tell you," I said. "We find it strange you called this in as a murder."

Norton blinked. "How do you mean?"

"It sounds like a missing person situation. No body, and all. So why phone it in as murder?"

His mouth made a downward turn once again. "Well," he said, "that wasn't my idea."

"Whose idea was it, Mr. Norton?" Tim said.

"You know, I'm not actually sure. Everybody was upset. There was a real panic going on, chaos, like, and when I went to the kitchen to make the call they were shouting it." He swallowed, looking green. "Jasper's been murdered, they said."

"I see. And you don't agree?"

"I guess there's a chance he could have left Tern on his own." As soon as he said it, Norton reached out and knocked on the boathouse's wooden wall. "For luck," he explained when I gave him a look. "God knows we could use some."

"But the boat's still here," I said. "How could Jasper leave? Unless . . ." I glanced up at the mounted nameplate. "*Loophole?*"

Norton said, "No, no, Mrs. Sinclair sold her a while back. There are no other boats on the island."

"Someone could have picked him up," said Tim. "Last night, when everyone was asleep. The dock's a long way from the house, I doubt anyone would've heard it. There are boats out on the water at all hours around here, people coming back from a late dinner, night fishing. Even if someone did hear, you get used to the sound of a motor. Learn to ignore it."

"I guess that's true," Norton said.

"So maybe the question we need to be asking," I said, "is whether Jasper had a good reason to leave without telling his family and friends."

"Like did he go to a hotel, or drive home," Tim said. "He lives in New York, right?"

"Yeah, but leave without telling anyone?" Norton repeated, testing the idea. "He came with Miss Beaudry, and she's still here. I don't know why he'd leave. Everyone's here for the weekend, the whole family. That doesn't happen often. You know how families are."

Another look passed between me and Tim. "It seems to me," I said, "a person wouldn't call a disappearance a murder unless they thought there was a chance the missing person was in danger of being hurt."

"Oh," Norton said, flustered. "I guess you'd have to ask the family about that."

"We will. In the meantime, what can you tell us about Jasper?" I wasn't interested in the man's gender, age, or race. That was information we already had. What I wanted was to look under Jasper Sinclair's bed and comb through the boxes at the back of his closet, where the secrets are kept. "You say you've known him his whole life. If you had to describe him—character, temperament, relationships—what would you say?"

"Well," said Norton, "I'd say he's a good man. Everyone likes Jasper."

It always bothers me when a victim's family and friends describe them as perfect in every way. What's the implication there, that their beauty was too much for the killer to handle? They brought violent death on themselves? I hate that, hate everything about it. Perfection enrages some people, can raise their hackles something fierce, but isn't motive for murder.

"Where are they now?" I asked. "His family?"

"Inside. Waiting for you."

"If you remember any more details, you'll let us know?"

Norton said he would. I expected him to make a move toward the house, but while his hooded head pivoted in that direction, he didn't budge. To my horror, I realized he was tearing up.

"I'm sorry," he said. "It's just . . . he's a kid, really. Still so young."

"Don't apologize. Shock affects people in different ways," I said, thinking, *I should know.* "You and the family must be close."

"I've worked here a long time. The others don't come out to Tern often, but Mrs. Sinclair stays all summer, every year. She's a wonderful lady. She doesn't deserve this. You'll find him, won't you?"

"We'll do our best."

"When you see her, please tell her that. She needs to hear it. Okay," Norton said, breathing deep. "All right, then. Follow me."

We stepped out of the boathouse into the rain. Tim's eyes swept the landscape, lingering on every brush pile and fallen tree, and we started up the long set of stairs. The climb to the house was brutal, and I was winded inside of three minutes. Those beautiful stone steps were even steeper than they'd looked from the water, and impossibly slick. All three of us wore rain boots with minimal tread. Tim's a gym rat, and I stay in pretty good shape. But when we got to the top and crossed a wraparound porch to the house's double entry doors, only Philip Norton wasn't panting.

"Cam— Mrs. Sinclair is still upstairs. The rest are through there."

"How's she holding up?" I asked. "It's a terrible thing, not knowing what happened to your son." I kept my go-to line at the ready: *No parent should have to outlive a child.* I know how to make it sound unrehearsed, like I'm delivering it for the first time.

"Oh no," Norton said. "Camilla Sinclair is Jasper's grandmother." My gaze flicked to Tim—*how did you miss that?*—but he was stoic, taking it all in. "Jasper's parents," Norton said, "passed on."

"When was that?" I said.

"Almost two years ago."

"Is she the owner of the house? Camilla Sinclair?"

"Yes, ma'am. Has an apartment in the city, too. Please, this way."

Norton pushed open the door to reveal a wide entry with impeccable wood floors framed by a geometric border. The scent of the pine cleaner he'd used to make them shine like glass hung in the air. Somewhere on the main floor, a woman was crying. Her rhythmic sobs echoed down the hall.

The moment I'm about to start investigating a homicide, even a nebulous one like Jasper Sinclair's, is a moment like no other. I can't explain how it makes me feel, and believe me, I've tried—for Carson especially. It's somewhere between the sick feeling of waking up to find a day you've been dreading for months is here, and a slap you don't see coming. It's physical, visceral, gutting.

For me, the moment doesn't come when we get the call, but when I'm about to step into the crime scene and see the horror du jour. It's my last chance to feel like an ordinary human being, sometimes for a long time, because I know the crime's going to seep into my pores and cling to me like a nerve agent, slowly eating away at my body, mind, and resolve. It always does.

And the thing is, I can't shake it unless I get a solve. The cases that get away from me, that I nearly get killed trying to crack and fail to get a conviction on anyway? The biological effects of those don't go away. They're an eye twitch I can't contain. Seeping blisters on my lungs that burn with every breath. By the time I told Carson about Bram, on that bright fall day in Queens, my cuticles itched inexplicably and every morning my pillow was soaked with cold sweat. I didn't want to believe this would hinder my ability to do my job, but it sure as hell made me uneasy.

Before I followed Norton over the threshold, I turned and took one last look at the river. From that height I should have been able to see for miles, but the storm erased the view. It felt like the island wasn't one of thousands, but the only one, all alone on the wide, wild river. The family I was about to meet might as well have been the last people on earth. For the next twenty-four hours, they would become my everything.

THREE

It wasn't how things were supposed to be done. If Jasper Sinclair went missing on the mainland, and that bed looked the way it did, the crime scene would have been hopping by the time I walked in. An EMT known for his gentle touch would be wrapping a heat-conducting blanket around Mrs. Sinclair's shoulders and steering her away from the distressing sight. Folks from CSI would pull disposable booties over their shoes and pinch evidence bags between their gloved fingers as they walked the room. Tim's job would be to neutralize lingering threats while I zeroed in on the witnesses. In other words, we'd have support.

We had none of that today. The minute I set foot in Jasper's bedroom I was no longer a plainclothes detective with the Bureau of Criminal Investigation but captain, crime-scene manager, and evidence tech. Until we got some help, it was all on us to secure the scene and interview everyone in the house. All I had to work with was Tim, and a bed that made clear why the Sinclairs called this murder.

A bed that would haunt my dreams.

It was made of reclaimed wood, a rustic yet modern look that must have cost thousands. Silky linens were bunched by the footboard, like someone kicked them off in a hurry. My God, but the blood. There was more than I'd expected—a lot more. On the side closest to the bedroom door, the fitted sheet was saturated with a dark stain that, to my revulsion, assumed the vague shape of a heart. If Jasper was average height for a guy, the stain would map with his abdomen. This was no nick; he'd been the victim of a calculated bloodletting. It looked to me as if someone eviscerated the man while his girlfriend dozed peacefully at his side.

Camilla Sinclair, Jasper's grandmother, watched from the doorway as I made my way around the room. She had to be in her nineties but she had great hair, white and glossy, cut in a bob. I could tell she'd been tall once, but now Camilla leaned on a cane in a way that made the vertebrae of her spine tepee the back of her shirt. Her free hand trembled as it gripped a framed photograph of her grandson, but her expression was stoic, her eyes watchful and dry.

I'd already asked her about Jasper and how he'd spent the previous night, and while she'd been forthcoming with her answers, her story, like Norton's, was conspicuously uneventful. Cocktails. Dinner. Bed. When the interview was done, I invited her to join her family on the main floor. Yet here she stood.

"Mrs. Sinclair," I ventured for the third time. "Ma'am? I need you to go downstairs. Sit down, let Mr. Norton get you a cup of tea." If I'm being honest, I was worried about her health. Her skin was like old newspaper, flaky and gray. "I have to insist," I said.

I'd expected her to leave the room when we got to the island. I could understand why she'd stayed before that, but most people perceive the police's arrival as a transfer of responsibility. We take the situation out of their hands, along with a heaping portion of the proximate horror, and they're happy to let us. Not Jasper's grandmother. She stayed put.

I'd be lying if I said I didn't have preconceptions about what these people in their floating ivory tower would be like. I thought I knew what I was dealing with, assumed they'd be collectively cold, or so shattered they couldn't get a word out through the sobs. People with that kind of wealth often feel untouchable, and it's a shock when they discover they're not. So far, Camilla Sinclair had maintained an unflappable demeanor, but I found it odd she'd made an effort to look presentable. Her crisp white shirt and pink-checkered slacks were tailored to complement her thin frame, and she'd dabbed on pink lipstick to match. Maybe it was habit for women of her generation to put themselves together no matter what. Either she'd roused herself very early, before the screaming started, or she'd left Jasper's room after all and, despite her grief, took the time to do herself up.

"My grandson has vanished," Camilla said, her gaze still on the bed. "And you're suggesting that I have a cup of tea?"

"I know how upsetting this must be." I stepped into her line of vision. The woman had stared at that bloodstain long enough. "But we need to find out what happened here, and there are procedures I have to follow. I'm sure you can appreciate that."

The crinkled corners of her mouth dipped downward and her blue eyes flashed. "That's your job," she snapped. "I expect you to do it. My presence has no bearing on that."

"I'm afraid you're mistaken. Until we're able to determine

otherwise, we're working under the assumption that a crime has been committed here. Even the slightest misstep could disrupt the scene, a scene that may be contaminated already." I paused to let her picture Abella and Norton stomping around the room before our arrival. "It's important we get this right. If your grandson is hurt—"

"If!"

"—then we have to make sure we do things by the book. There'll be attorneys involved here, down the line. If Jasper was attacked, whoever did it will be represented by someone determined to identify every mistake we make and use them against us to dismiss our findings. To dismiss the charge."

Bulldog attorneys and gainful justice. I suspected this was language Mrs. Sinclair could understand, and immediately saw I was right. "His things," she said. "He has a beautiful gold watch that belonged to my husband. A silver-plated lighter from my mother. I don't want you taking them. Tell the others. Everything belonging to Jasper stays here."

"I can promise nothing will leave this room for now. There are other officers on the way, but I'll make sure if they need to remove anything they talk to you about it first."

"I'm not referring to your colleagues," she said. "I want you to tell *them*."

"Your family?" I frowned. Why worry that a family member would take Jasper's stuff? Then again, her grandson was nowhere to be found while the rest of the Sinclairs sat warm and dry downstairs. "I'll tell them."

She nodded and looked down at the framed photograph in her hand. "Where is he, detective? Where has my Jasper gone?"

I said, "I'm going to have a closer look in here, all right? As soon as I know anything, anything at all, I'll come down and tell you."

For a moment I thought she might collapse. I hurried over, prepared to catch her if she fell, but Camilla shut her eyes and drew a deep, yoga-style breath. When her eyelids lifted, she shooed away my hands and turned to leave, somber yet self-possessed once more.

At the door, she stopped. "You'll find him," Camilla said. It wasn't a question.

Remembering Norton's request, I said, "I'll do everything I can. That's a promise."

She turned her gaze back to the bed and her eyes went glassy. "Grandparents aren't supposed to have favorites."

He's special. That's another thing people say when somebody goes missing. I've heard relatives declare it about lost loved ones many times. The one who was taken is always the best. It's a philosophy that highlights the injustice of what's happened, and heightens the drama of it all; humans are hardwired for storytelling, and every good story needs drama. I doubted Jasper was the snowflake his grandmother thought him to be—but I had to admit in the looks department, he was remarkable. The man in the photograph Camilla had showed me, a candid shot taken in sparkling sunshine, might have been Jude Law in the nineties. Jasper's hair and eyes were threaded with gold and his straight teeth generated a leading-man smile. His nose had a slight bend, a lacrosse or football injury from his teen years no doubt. It only added to his mystique.

"*Special* doesn't begin to describe him," Camilla said. "Do you know Jasper's the only one who visits me? Three times a week in the city, just to keep me company. We play cards. He's a young man with an important job and a busy life, but he always makes time for me, and never asks for anything in return. Most grand-children don't do that. Believe me. I know." When she shifted her meager weight, the floorboards didn't so much as whisper. "He deserves better. I've always thought so."

I wondered what she meant by that last bit—*better than gold watches and private islands?*—but by then Camilla had moved into the hall. I watched her descend the staircase, each step a painstaking struggle. Only when I heard Tim's voice greet her on the main floor did I go back into Jasper's room.

Tim was getting nothing done down there beyond chatting up our witnesses and keeping them calm. I knew this, sure as I knew I had little time to assess the scene before I'd have to barricade the door and get downstairs myself. There was no way to conduct the interviews with other witnesses listening in, twisting the story to serve their own needs. We'd have to separate them, but with every minute that passed, the killer—if there was one, if that person was even still here—had more time to think the situation through and prepare their next move. More opportunity to gain the upper hand.

Early in my law enforcement training, one of my instructors said it's nearly impossible to convincingly fake an alibi without first re-creating it step-by-step. Plan to tell the cops you were out getting wine at the time of your lover's death? You better drive to that liquor store and browse the aisles for the elusive Australian Shiraz that supposedly brought you there. You couldn't have killed your boss because you were at the gym all evening? Unless you follow through with that fictional workout, a cop's not going to buy it. Only by living the lie can guilty people deliver believable accounts. It's scary to know it can be done at all, but there's some-thing scarier still. Despite everything I'd been told, I've seen killers pull alibis out of a hat neat as a magician, no false bottom in sight.

And I had no desire to give these people the chance to show us what they, too, could do.

Snapping on the fresh pair of latex gloves I'd hurriedly stuffed in my pocket—my cuffs and tactical flashlight I'd clipped to my belt—before leaving A-Bay, I pulled out my notebook again. Over the years I'd gotten in the habit of making my own analysis. It's a game I play to keep my skills sharp. I like to compare my conclusions to those of the forensics team. My training included some crime-scene investigation and management, but just as you wouldn't expect a liberal arts grad to be an authority on psychology based on a couple of courses, I'm no pro. Look, don't touch: that's my motto. Otherwise there'll be hell to pay with the guy or girl who gets to the scene next.

Blissfully alone, I walked the room a second time imagining Jasper and his girlfriend settling in the previous night. I peeked in the dresser and under the bed. The two of them had shared a suitcase. They'd unpacked and stuck the empty luggage in the closet. Did they live together back in Manhattan? I'd need to find out.

Aside from the sheets, which would have to be bagged and tagged, there were several other objects worth collecting. Two iPhones were charging on a nightstand. Wherever Jasper was, he'd left that lifeline behind. We'd need someone to have a look at e-mails and messaging apps. I spotted a little blood on Jasper's pillowcase that made me scratch my head. Blood on the sheets and a smear on the pillow, but everything else was clean. The long, dark hair beside it presumably belonged to Abella, but it would have to be analyzed all the same. I pictured her resting soundly while someone sank a blade into her boyfriend's belly, just inches from her own, and frowned.

If she wasn't directly responsible for whatever happened to Jasper, I thought, she had help getting to dreamland last night. It was the only way I could see her sleeping through the attack; hell, with the number of pills it takes me to drift off some nights you could tap-dance on Carson's body and I wouldn't flinch. And if Abella was in the habit of popping pills, maybe Jasper did the same. You don't need a history of drug use to go overboard or make one lethal, ill-fated match.

On the other nightstand, I found something else peculiar: a water ring, the kind you get from forgetting to use a coaster. It was faint—I had to get in close to spot it—but it was there. Already I'd seen enough of the house to know Norton kept it immaculate. Why not buff away the stain? True, the mark could be fresh, but there was no glass in sight, nothing to collect for testing. Abella Beaudry would be an important interview. She had some explaining to do.

When I was done with the area around the bed, I took note of the location of the windows. Three of them, close together, bowed outward from the house. The screens were all intact, the windows shut tight against the storm, and as a result the room retained its smells. I picked up the sour tang of sweat, but it was almost completely overpowered by the sharp, metallic stench of blood. Aside from the windows, the room also had a glass door that opened onto a Juliet balcony. There were no stairs leading down to the ground, but I wondered if someone could have climbed up another way. The floors were pristine—no messy footprints, no debris from outside. These observations I marked in my notebook, filing them away for later.

With one more sweeping appraisal of the room, I was done. The doors in the house were old with antique hardware. I found the key to Jasper's room in the keyhole and locked it behind me. In the gloved palm of my hand, before dropping it in my pocket for safekeeping, the key seemed to emit a low-frequency vibration that zipped through my body like a shock. At home I never lock interior doors, not even when using the bathroom. Not anymore.

It took twenty minutes to search the second and third floors of the house. On the outside the place appeared huge to the point of obscenity, but its warren of hallways made the interior feel unnervingly cramped. I couldn't get my bearings. There were doors everywhere, closets that turned corners to go on forever. Some were lined with fancy dresses and suits zipped into storage bags. The Sinclairs must have held parties out here years ago, Gatsby-style. The staircase to the third floor, which was entirely occupied by a master bedroom that clearly belonged to the house's owner, spiraled upward to a dizzying height. In good weather, Camilla would be able to see all the way to Canada.

Throughout my search there was a knot in my stomach and a tightness in my chest. I knew I might find Jasper's body at any moment. *Here it comes*, I warned myself. *He's hanging from a rafter, bloodless and bloated, in this high-ceilinged bedroom. This is it*, I thought. *He's here behind this door, ready to crumple heavily against me when I give the knob a pull.* Those twenty minutes seemed to last hours, but other than the blood on his bed I found no sign of him. I checked every room but one, which was locked from the inside. When I knocked on its rich, five-paneled door, I got no reply.

Nine people were staying in the house, and most of them were relatives. I wasn't optimistic that fingerprints would reveal much. Close families have few boundaries. Formalities tend to fall away. If this family was anything like mine, their prints would be everywhere, and that would make the interviews I was about to conduct even more crucial.

The thought made me shudder. I knew even then, so early in the case, that the key to this solve wasn't in my pocket or behind Jasper's locked bedroom door. It was downstairs in the living room.

Waiting.

FOUR

wasn't ready to face them, not yet. There was a part of me that still hoped I'd find Jasper alive and break some local records for the fastest solve in history, so I skirted the living room and went straight for the basement, the door to which I found in the kitchen.

Picture a cellar from a horror film, dusty and dank with crumbling stone walls and a criminal air. Old pipes clang and a strange odor hangs heavy, nauseating in its rottenness, meat-sweet. That's how I imagined the basement in the house on Tern Island. In truth it was pretty ordinary, but walking down those stairs gave me a head rush akin to eating too little and standing too quick. It took me hundreds of miles from the island, to a place I never wanted to be again.

I wasted no time getting out of there to do a cursory search of the grounds outside, rain be damned. There was no way I could cover the whole island on my own, but I poked through leaf piles and peered over steep cliffs with gusto. If there were indeed caves chiseled into the rock, they didn't reveal themselves to me. Back inside I checked the sunroom, library, and Norton's room. It was the sole bedroom on the main floor, accessible through a butler's pantry. Predictably, it lacked the old-world glamour of the rest of the house. A single bed, a small chest of drawers, and a nightstand constituted Philip Norton's belongings. There was a framed photo beside his bed that showed him as a much younger man, with a full head of red hair and his arm around a boy about ten years old. I picked up the frame and scrutinized the kid's face. The boy might have been Jasper, but I couldn't be sure.

Only the room where Tim had situated the Sinclairs and their guests remained. I stepped through the doorway and finally got my first look at our witnesses.

They made me think of Bram. Presented with the family and their pristine house at the summit of Tern Island, he would have seen perfection. To Bram, perfection was synonymous with danger. In the context of a murder case it alarmed me, too. Nothing about this place was flawed, and that uncanny fact had preoccupied me throughout my search. Every room I'd entered was magazine-ready, and the living room was no different. On the mantel sat a mindfully arranged autumn vignette of hefty pewter candlesticks, gourds, and pheasant feathers. Fresh-cut mums burst from vases on mirrored tabletops. Heavy valances in neutral tones were shaped like the bustle of a nineteenth-century skirt. Classy. That's how I'd describe the place. And the family fit right in.

Like Camilla's, their clothes were casual but perfectly tailored—dress shirts overlaid with cashmere sweaters, pants with centerline creases sharp as the blade of a knife. A woman with short dark hair and fat diamond earrings reclined artfully on a settee as if gracing the cover of *Vanity Fair*. A handsome man with coffee-colored skin leaned against the window beyond which trees strained against the storm. It was open a crack to let in a wet breeze, and sheer curtain panels billowed around him like smoke. The youngest of them all, a teenage girl with rosebud lips and shiny chestnut hair, looked like she could have been a celebrity's little sister about to make it big herself. An equally striking man who was surely her father sat by her side. Against the high-polish backdrop of the house's antique furniture and the fire that crackled happily in the hearth they were exclusivity personified. There was one exception, one person who didn't belong in this picture of privilege and wealth, and I'd have bet anything her name was Abella Beaudry.

Abella's eyes were ringed in red. Here was the source of the sobs I'd heard earlier. The woman looked dazed, as if she'd taken—or was given—something for the shock. Out of everyone, she alone wasn't dressed. Her hair was a mess, her pink pajamas wrinkled. Even from across the room I could see the fabric on her hip was stained with blood. Jasper's girlfriend had our missing man's DNA all over her, and she hadn't done a thing about it.

Camilla had taken my advice and gotten herself some tea. She was still ashen, but compared to Abella she looked absolutely hearty. Overall, the rest of the family came off surprisingly well. There was a serving tray on the table that held a plate of sliced cake, a coffee urn, and a pitcher of cream. Several of the mugs were in use. Were it not for their voices, kept respectfully low, and the poor, pathetic girl in their midst, it might have been just another rainy autumn day at the river for these American aristocrats.

As I studied the room, a niggling itch formed at the back of my throat. I took a head count. Nine on the island, Tim had said, including Jasper. Norton stood at attention by the living room door. That left seven. There were five people seated, plus the man by the window. Someone was missing.

"Wellington," I said. "A word?"

Tim followed me into the foyer as the others looked on, and brought his head close to mine. "How's it look up there?" he asked. The movement was minuscule, nothing our witnesses would notice from a distance, but I felt him rock on his feet. Whether he was keen to hear what I'd found out or nervous, I didn't know.

"Messy," I said. "There's enough blood to fill a kiddie pool. If Jasper's still alive, he won't be for long."

"Really?" Tim looked shocked. He dropped his gaze to the burnished floorboards. "Wow," he said eventually. "Gotta say, I wasn't expecting that. You thinking drugs?"

How did Abella sleep through the stabbing? How did Jasper's attacker get him out of a second-floor bedroom without a fight? "Could be," I said. "Nothing visible in the drawers or luggage, but we'll see what forensics says."

"So the guy took a knife to the gut and disappeared."

"Looks that way. There's no easy escape route to the ground. The house is all clear and in order, except there's a room upstairs that's locked."

"That would be Jasper's older brother, Flynn Sinclair. I tried to round him up while you were with Camilla, but he's refusing to leave his room. I nearly had the same problem with the kid." He cut a glance at the gorgeous teen on the couch. "She belongs to Miles Byrd—middle-aged guy with the hipster glasses," he said. "Her dad seemed impressed I was able to coax her down here at all. I'm sure she's dying to get back to her busy schedule of Snapchatting and brooding."

"You told them not to use their phones, right?"

Tim nodded. "First thing."

"Good. We don't need folks getting the media all keyed up before we have a handle on the case." McIntyre liked to talk about the era before cell phones, when it took hours for news of a crime to circulate in town and days to reach the rest of the county. Now witnesses could take a murder public in seconds. McIntyre's good old days were my Shangri-la.

Tim chewed his lip. "No ETA on the Watertown team, and these people are getting antsy, Shane. I'm not sure how long I can keep them in the parlor."

"The parlor?" I repeated, amused. "How posh." Nodding at the ceiling, I said, "Guess that settles it. The first interview goes to Flynn." Frankly, I was a little disappointed. My chat with Jasper's girlfriend would have to wait. At the same time, I was eager to get to know Jasper's family, these people who'd allowed one of their own to disappear. Behind us, a man cleared his throat. "Tell them to get comfortable," I said, taking a step toward the room. "It's going to be a long day."

"There's something else," Tim said. "Philip Norton."

His tone stopped my forward momentum short. "What about him?"

"I'm not sure. There's something familiar. I thought so the minute I saw him, but I can't put my finger on it." He shrugged. "Could be he has one of those faces."

"Well, if anything hits you, let me know. You get the name of that trapper?" It was a long shot, but if he'd been on the island in the hours before Jasper disappeared, we'd need to give the man a call.

"Talked to him a few minutes ago, guy by the name of Billy Bloom," Tim said. "He was on the premises for about four hours yesterday and left after the last of the family arrived, like Norton said. I described Jasper. Bloom saw him briefly on the dock. No contact other than that. According to Bloom," Tim said, "he found the remnants of some yellow perch, extra stinky. He went straight home to shower, then to the Riverboat for some beers."

"Any witnesses?" I asked, though I knew the answer. The Riverboat Pub was always jammed on Friday nights.

"Matt says Bloom was in there from seven p.m. to midnight— Matt Cutts, the bartender," Tim said. "Bloom got so hammered Matt took his keys and called his wife. I talked to her, too. Says he was snoring next to her all night and still sleeping it off this morning."

Tim had been busy. There were benefits to his community ties, and I reminded myself to give him a pat on the back about his swift recon work later on. It would have to wait, because behind me I heard another flagrant attempt to get our attention.

"Showtime," I said. "Ready?"

Tim nodded, and together we turned to face the room.

I liked to think we looked intimidating in our dark rain gear and heavy boots. Tim's shoulders were muscled and his hair was slick and black from the rain. I had height and my badass facial scar to offset my freckles and frizzy hair. I wanted to send a message: this is a serious situation, and you're getting a serious response. Only Abella stared back at us with a mixture of wonder and fear. The others looked annoyed and a little bored.

"You've all met my colleague. I'm BCI Senior Investigator Shana Merchant," I said. "I've had a chance to take a look at Jasper's room."

Slowly, their stalled energy sputtered to life. They were interested in what I had to tell them, at least. That was something. "Let me start by saying we appreciate your cooperation. Based on the evidence I've been able to gather so far, it appears Jasper was attacked." A sloppy sob erupted from Abella, and the man by the window rushed to her side. From her settee the other woman shot them both a look of loathing. "I can't tell you more than that right now, but please know we're doing everything we can," I went on. "This is a tough situation, but with any luck we'll find Jasper safe and sound."

"Situation?" Camilla repeated. "You saw that bed. Someone tried to kill my grandson."

"I assure you, we're all on the same page about that."

The lounging woman snorted. "I sincerely doubt we're on the same page about anything. My grandmother is very upset. Who do I need to call to get someone from the city out here?"

To this elegant woman, mainland towns like Alexandria Bay had nothing in common with Tern. Owning an island was like erecting a sweeping, vine-draped manor in the sticks of Arkansas. The river served as a convenient barrier between the haves and the have-nots, and a public reminder of the Sinclair family's worth. Tim and I didn't meet their standards, not by a long shot. I smiled at her, sweet as candy-shop fudge, and said, "I didn't catch your name."

"Barbara Sinclair—Bebe. Jasper's my brother."

Not was, but *is*. Her choice of words didn't mean she knew he was alive, or even that she believed it, but it was interesting all the same. Past tense can be hard for people; I know parents of children lost decades ago who still can't bring themselves to use it. I've also seen it give murderers away. Other than parents most people are quick to adjust, while criminals tend to overthink it. They play the part of the suffering martyr, thinking they know what grief looks like. They don't, though. Until fear and sorrow smother you like a burial shroud, you have no idea how you're going to react, can't understand that you're powerless to change it.

"This isn't going to be easy, on any of you," I said. "I won't pretend otherwise. What I *will* do is promise not to make it more painful than it needs to be. As you can see"—I shot a sideways glance at Tim—"it's just the two of us here right now. We've got other troopers on the way, but with the weather like this I can't say when they'll arrive. In the meantime, there are some things that have to happen, things that can't be delayed."

In the hearth, a log shifted with a thump and the scent of woodsmoke swirled through the air. All eyes stayed on me. The dark-skinned man was busy stroking Abella's hand, but his eyebrows hovered expectantly. Our witnesses could sense it coming, a request they wouldn't be able to refuse.

"I'm going to interview each of you about what happened here last night," I said. "I want you to tell me everything you remember, no matter how insignificant it may seem. This is going to take some time. As Wellington already explained, we're asking that you turn off your mobile devices and refrain from contacting anyone outside this room."

"But *why?*"

How is it that teen girls are capable of infusing two small words with so much loathing? The kid on the couch looked at me like I'd just told her she wasn't allowed to breathe.

"For one thing," I said, "we're still trying to determine what happened. It's in nobody's best interest to start a gossip chain that could spread false information to your neighbors and friends. For another, there may come a time when we need to take a look at those devices. We won't do that unless we suspect they contain evidence related to this investigation, but until then, we need the information on them to remain untouched and intact."

Slowly, the people in the room came to a consensus and there were small nods of agreement all around. Arms folded defiantly over her chest, the teenager continued to seethe, but she didn't fight back. My appeal made sense to them, or they were willing to pretend it did. I didn't tell them they had every right to use their phones if they wanted to. Under the circumstances, I felt I'd be forgiven for taking a few liberties with the law.

"While I'm speaking with you individually," I said without delay, because this was the tough part, the part they'd hate, "I'd like you to stay right here in this room. Wellington will be with you until the state police troopers arrive. Until then, stay put."

There was a beat of silence, and then everyone spoke at once. I caught snippets of what they were saying, all of it standard-issue outrage. I was accused of treating them like naughty children sent to their rooms. The elegant parlor was likened to a jail cell. Somebody threatened to contact a reporter. Someone else—the man in glasses, the teenager's dad—pointed out he was a lawyer and prepared to act.

I didn't respond, didn't say one damn word, and eventually the clamor died down. Only when they were all red-faced and deflated did I go on. "I'm not saying you can't get up to use the bathroom. I'm not cuffing you to a chair. We're here to find out what happened, and this is how we do it. But I want to remind you of something, too. While I haven't seen any evidence of an intruder— no broken windows or busted locks—we can't rule that possibility out. You need to understand whoever did this might still be here, on the island. Your comfort and convenience is not my priority. My priority is to keep the rest of you safe."

The wind blew harder and the house gave a shudder. Against the windows the rain mimicked the sound of a million pebbles falling from a great height. A log split open with a crack like a gunshot, and this time I felt everyone tense. Abella drew in a ragged breath. Bebe Sinclair's jaw hung slack. Her skin reminded me of rubber; there was a shiny, overplumped quality to it that smacked of Botox. A new smell filled the air, mingling with the wood smoke. *Fear.* "Now," I said. "Who are we missing?"

It was the man next to Abella who answered. "Flynn," he said. "We're missing Flynn."

"Flynn Sinclair. Jasper's older brother," Tim told me, blushing hard as he stared down at his boots. "Thanks, Ned," he said, then, back to me, "Sorry. I should have mentioned that."

We were new to it still, to each other, but Tim and I were slowly learning to play the game, and the seamlessness of our exchange thrilled me. Tim, as it turned out, could act. He wore an abashed expression that wasn't lost on the others. Bebe watched with interest and the tiniest of smirks, while Camilla looked slightly offended by Tim's apparent misstep. Her eyes crinkled in a way that implied disappointment. Unlike Bebe, Camilla took us for consummate professionals. Tim had let her down.

I sighed and jutted out my chin in the direction of the hallway. It gave our witnesses a good look at the colorless crease that slashed across my cheek, stretching from my earlobe all the way to the corner of my mouth. The only benefit of having a scar like mine is related to my work. People assume I'm tough. *Good. Let them.* Tim didn't look up as he followed me out of the room.

"The apology was a nice touch," I said, keeping my voice low.

"You sure you want to talk to this guy alone?" Gone was the face of a cop who'd messed up, the face of a performer. Now Tim looked uneasy. I could hear the others conferring, and I couldn't shake the image of the blood on the bed. I'd made our objectives, mine and Tim's, clear. If the Sinclair family had something to hide and hadn't made a desperate, slapdash attempt at collusion already, they didn't have much time left. We had to move fast.

"I'll call you if I need help," I said. I had no reason to fear Flynn Sinclair, not yet. Tim was just being cautious. But my lungs felt like they were in a vise and my palms were starting to sweat.

"I still think Jasper skipped town," he said. "But there's something strange going on here. Is it me, or does it seem like Camilla and Abella are the only ones sad to see that Jasper's gone? Maybe not everybody goes berserk when a loved one disappears, I'll give you that—but what does it say about these people that they don't look remotely upset?" His eyebrows got straighter. "I don't like it. Watch yourself, okay?"

My gaze traveled back to the seven people in the parlor. This island was their territory, and I felt like an intruder. I didn't know what awaited me upstairs, or around the corner, or even in the parlor itself.

"Yeah," I said as I twisted my body to face the stairs. "You too."

FIVE

I didn't like him. It didn't matter that I hadn't met him yet. The eldest Sinclair sibling hadn't bothered to come downstairs to hear what we had to say about his brother's disappearance, and that transported me back to the police boat. It made me feel queasy and ill at ease.

This time when I knocked on the locked door, I got a reply. "Come in," Flynn said at once. I was about to argue—*it's locked, don't you know it's locked?*—but when I tried the knob it turned easily in my moist hand.

He sat on the edge of a four-poster bed all the way across the room. When had Flynn unlocked the door? For a moment I wondered if I'd been wrong. Maybe it was just jammed, or sticky with age. Maybe it was never locked at all. It wouldn't be the first time

I'd imagined a locked door. Usually, though, it was me on the other side.

Flynn Sinclair looked nothing like his name, which had a Peter Pan quality, elfish and light on its feet. He was a large man with simian features, a seventies-style mustache, and dense dark hair. From the shape of his shoulders and upper arms, contained by a gray cashmere sweater like you'd wear to Sunday brunch, I could see there was muscle under his mass. My guess was he played football in college and was killing himself fighting the middle-age spread. Flynn didn't get up to greet me. But he did ask about Jasper.

"We haven't found him yet. We're working on it," I said. There was a needlepoint pillow in Flynn's lap that he held against his stomach like a compress. It made the big man look more vulnerable. I'm sure that was his intent. "We need you downstairs. But let's talk a minute first."

"You saw it? The blood?" He clutched the pillow tighter. "Philip wouldn't let me in there. What happened to my brother?"

I had trouble imagining stubby Norton taking on Flynn. If Flynn wanted to see that room, he'd have done it. "We're still trying to figure that out," I said. "Hopefully we'll know more when the forens—"

Flynn flinched. It was that word; too much crime TV makes the public associate forensic science with death. "When the rest of our team gets here," I said, backpedaling, "we may have more information about the nature of the injury and crime."

"You've got to have a theory. People don't just disappear."

You're wrong, I wanted to tell him. *People disappear all the time.* Instead, I said, "Not every day, no."

"Did you talk to *her*? She's the one you should be talking to, not me."

"You're referring to his girlfriend." I took out my notebook. "That would be Abella Beaudry?"

"Obviously. Christ."

"I do plan to speak with her. But right now, I'm with you. Do you mind if I sit down?"

A muscle rolled across Flynn's jaw. I couldn't tell if he was suppressing anger or pain. He jerked his chin in the direction of a chair and I took some time getting there, seizing my chance to study the room.

The curtains on the windows were open. Rain beat against the glass. This side of the house was closer to the trees, and they blocked most of the dull daylight in a way that made the room feel cold. Some coins and a set of house keys were scattered across the surface of the dresser. Flynn had emptied his pockets of the things one didn't need on a private island. Must be nice, I thought, to have the luxury of sloughing off the burdens of the outside world. Beside the items, he'd placed his billfold-style wallet. But no, that was wrong. There wasn't one wallet, but two.

"Mind if I take some notes?" I adjusted myself on the stiff ladder-back chair. Like the parlor, Flynn's bedroom was sparsely decorated with antique furniture and Adirondack flare. I was pleased to find sitting across from someone with notepad and pen in hand still came easily, as if each step of the interview process was ingrained. It emboldened me; I took it as a good sign. Flynn hadn't answered my question, but it didn't matter. I was taking notes regardless.

"Okay, so. First question. Are you and Jasper close?"

"Of course we're close. He's my brother."

"There's a pretty big age difference between you." I thought of Jasper's photo as I looked at Flynn, whose skin was rough and had succumbed to decades of gravity. His heavy jowls made me think of melting wax. "Ten years?"

"Twelve."

"You were almost a teenager when he was born."

A shadow passed across his face. "What's your point?"

"Not making a point, I just wonder how well you know him—now, I mean. A lot of siblings grow apart as they get older."

"That didn't happen to us."

"Fair enough. So, Flynn. Why don't you tell me what happened last night?"

That muscle again. It slid beneath the surface of his skin like an eel in shallow water. It wasn't just that I didn't like the guy for hiding up here while the rest of his family was downstairs. Something about Flynn's body language made me edgy. "If I knew," he said coolly, "you wouldn't be here."

"Why don't you walk me through yesterday and we'll see what we can turn up?"

"My brother's been gone for hours. There's a goddamn hurricane outside. It's fucking freezing, and Jasper's jacket and shoes are sitting in the mudroom downstairs. You're wasting time. She's *right downstairs*." To make his point Flynn slammed the sole of his shoe against the floor. It was an oil-tanned leather moccasin dyed navy, fine, and out of season. No wonder he'd opted to join the search party that stayed indoors.

I'd been with Flynn ten minutes and already the ridges of my ears were tingling. He hadn't relinquished the pillow, but the vulnerability I witnessed when I entered the room had been replaced with an aggression so intense it radiated from his body in waves. In my academy days, when we were learning to use our firearms, we'd compete to see who was the quickest draw. We would stand back-to-back, western-movie style, while an instructor manned the stopwatch, tapping his foot in wait. He was deadly serious about our reaction time on those drills—in the city, the fastest draw is the one who survives—but we had other motives for winning. Fastest draw was bragging rights, and bragging rights were currency in the academy. Plenty of times it was me who was flush.

It isn't that Flynn's hostility had me worried. I could be on my feet with my weapon trained on his chest in just over a second. What worried me was that this shifty witness would go to scratch his nose and I'd instinctively put a bullet in his big, hairy head. I was jumpier now than I used to be back in the academy. Before Bram.

Like my instructor during those drills, I tapped my foot, and waited. I figured Flynn for a hothead. He'd lash out, lean on his strength to get his way. But he didn't. His shoulders began to relax.

"I was working yesterday," he said at last. "I'm always working. I barely saw Jas at all."

"Walk me through it anyway. The whole day. Give me every detail you remember."

I crossed my legs and leaned back in the chair to make it clear I expected a long story. Flynn glared at me, sighed, then started to talk.

Interviewing a witness effectively hinges on a series of questions designed to draw out the who, what, where, when, and why of a crime. I let them do most of the talking and keep interruptions to a minimum. Some people call that free recall. It's a good way to tap a person's memory of the time frame in question, a kind of stream-of-consciousness exercise that helps me extract the details I need with as much accuracy as possible.

Cooperative witnesses do well with this, and I usually come

out with answers. But here's the problem—I didn't yet know if Flynn was a witness or a suspect in his brother's disappearance. Everything he told me could be a truthful recollection of the events that might help us find Jasper.

On the other hand, the entire story I was about to hear—every word of it—could be an expertly crafted lie.

SIX

By the time Flynn Sinclair arrived at Tern Island on Friday, October 20, his brother was already there. As Norton pulled the skiff up to the flooded dock, Flynn spotted Jasper on the shore. Jasper's arm was around a woman. She was Jasper's height, but her nonverbal cues made her look small. Like a girl with something to hide, Flynn said.

It was Jasper's idea to come to the island. He and Abella had been dating only a few months, but he was eager to introduce her to Camilla. Camilla, in turn, insisted the rest of the family come, too, and what would have been a quiet weekend morphed into a huge family affair.

Abella delivered a practiced smile as Flynn climbed out of the boat. There was a stranger in the boathouse dressed in camouflage, but since getting up in age, Norton sometimes brought on help for the labor-intensive jobs around the island, so Flynn ignored it and offered to help dock the boat.

"I'm heading back to the mainland," Norton said. "One last run to the market before the weather turns."

As he revved the engine and raced off across the water, Flynn clapped his younger brother on the back.

"The elusive Abella, at last," Flynn said as he shook the woman's hand for the first time.

"Call me Abby," she replied with a weak smile.

Jasper explained the English call her Abby, while the French use Bella. Flynn didn't like that. Having two nicknames felt like deceit. Even before meeting her, Flynn wasn't optimistic about his brother's relationship. Jasper and Abella met at the PR firm where Jasper used to work. She was from Montreal and in the U.S. on a work visa, but she'd recently been fired. Without a company to back her, Abella couldn't stay in the country much longer. Her whole life was up in the air, and Flynn mistrusted her instability.

"You're late, by the way," Jasper said with annoyance. "Your better half's already here."

"Some of us have to work." Flynn forced a laugh. "Jasper parties for a living, you know that, Abby?"

"Abby knows exactly what fashion marketing entails," Jasper said, "and that we're operating in a saturated and competitive market. Not as easy as it sounds."

"Parties for a living, like I said. It's freezing out here," said Flynn with a shiver. "Let's go up, yeah?"

An avid indoor cyclist—he pushed a stationary bike to its limits daily while trainers shouted at him over live-streaming video—Flynn shouldn't have had trouble with the steps, but as he ascended the pathway toward the house he felt winded. Jasper, on the other hand, talked nonstop as he climbed, his stories punctuated by Abella's laugh. She giggled in all the right places. The rhythm of their conversation was so smooth it appeared rehearsed. That, too, grated on Flynn. He couldn't stop thinking about what awaited him at the house.

Tern Island was ready for company, meaning the house looked like an interior stylist came through to buff and fluff every object in sight. A long table was set on the enclosed porch, the mule-deer-antler chandelier that hung above it wiped clean of dust and rubbed to a resin-like shine. Later, Norton would light a couple dozen candles and the family would eat while the antlers threw warped shadows across the walls. It would be cool on the porch, and the forecast called for a storm, but Camilla wouldn't have it any other way. Flynn's grandmother believed dining on the porch was the best way for first-time guests to experience the beauty of the island.

Camilla wasn't the only one keen on welcoming Jasper's new girl. The smell of Norton's fresh-baked rolls and something tangy-sweet Flynn later discovered was sour-cream coffee cake wafted through the house. When Jasper flopped down on the couch in the parlor and pulled Abella onto his lap, Flynn excused himself and went upstairs.

"Well, I finally met the girlfriend." Flynn dropped his overnight bag on the bedroom floor and pulled the door shut behind him. "Honestly, what does Jas see in her? She's got the personality of a dead fish and a complexion to match."

Ned Yeboah sat up. He was on the bed with his long legs crossed at the ankles and an iPhone in his hand. "Girlfriend," he repeated. "So he hasn't done it yet."

"Done what?"

"Nothing, just . . . I heard Jas might pop the question."

Flynn chuckled. "The day Jasper settles down is the day Nana sprouts wings and shits rainbows. Where'd you get that idea?"

"Jade will say anything for attention, I guess."

"You should know better than to listen to her." Flynn sat down on the bed and said, "You made it out early." He'd lost track of Ned that morning, having been busy at work. The only contact they'd had all day was the pointed text Ned sent when he arrived at the river. "How'd you manage it?" Flynn asked.

Ned shrugged. "Caught a lift with Bebe."

"Huh. Where were Miles and Jade?"

"They had stuff to do before leaving the city. Bebe offered. I accepted."

"You should have waited for me."

Ned gave him a long, dull look before returning his gaze to his screen. "Your nana's waiting," Ned said. "Better run along."

Knowing Ned was right about his grandmother, Flynn made his way upstairs to see Camilla. But the strained exchange and curt good-bye would trouble him for hours.

"How long have you been dating?" I asked when Flynn paused to roll his neck. His account suggested he and Ned weren't getting along, but this was a one-dimensional view of a two-sided relationship.

"Six months," Flynn replied. "Jasper's the one who introduced us."

I had a vague idea of where the Sinclairs' fortune came from; Tim had mentioned something about fashion, which didn't jibe with the old-money claim for me. But Flynn described Sinclair Fabrics as the largest designer drapery and upholstery outlet in the city, established by Camilla's husband in the 1930s and managed by members of the Sinclair family ever since. When Flynn's father died two years ago, Flynn took over the finances and Bebe was appointed CEO. Only Jasper had held out. He hadn't joined the company until last year, when he became its director of marketing and PR.

It was Jasper who discovered Ned—that's the way Flynn put it, as if Ned was an unknown exoplanet or a distant star. Ned had a YouTube channel where he offered fashion tips to a few hundred thousand subscribers. It was a small audience by social media marketing standards, but apparently Jasper liked Ned's style and felt Ned could connect with the hip young designers that composed the company's target market. Jasper proposed a partnership, and Ned became the face of Sinclair Fabrics. His job was to produce sponsored videos that highlighted the company's products in exchange for a yearlong contract that paid two hundred grand. If Flynn hadn't stopped by their first video shoot to chastise Jasper for spending a fortune on a YouTube star, Flynn and Ned might never have met.

"So you work together. You and Ned."

"Not directly," said Flynn, "but we both work for the business."

"Sounds like joining your family's company was a big win for him," I said. "How's the video stuff going? I've got a teenage niece who's obsessed with YouTube. She talks about YouTubers like they're real-life BFFs. Has Ned's—what do you call it—follower count gone up?" I asked because I needed to find out how the arrangement was affecting Ned's own business prospects. He was making a killing off Jasper at the moment, but his contract was half over, and the man who'd employed him was suddenly gone.

"We have a strong brand," Flynn said. "Associating himself with us has gotten him a lot of attention."

"That's a good thing, right? More exposure for him means more exposure for you."

"Except Ned's getting offers from other brands. Bigger ones."

Bingo. I waited.

"He thinks we're holding him back, if you can believe *that,*" Flynn said. "He got greedy is more like it. And now Ned wants to be released from his contract."

"And you're not cool with that."

"He signed an exclusive agreement with us, so he's legally bound to the company," Flynn explained as I recrossed my legs and jotted more notes. "Everyone knows him as our spokesperson now. It'd be devastating for our brand if he walked away—not to mention a breach of contract."

"A drag for you, too, I bet. Having your hot celebrity boyfriend sashaying around the office is a hell of a job perk."

It was a risky thing to say. Tim and I, alone on an island full of witnesses . . . we had limited tools to work with. We needed these people to open up to us, and we had no hope of achieving that unless we gained their trust.

Flynn fixed me with a cold glare—but he was still in the room, and I counted that as a win. "I apologize," I said. "That was unfair."

"Unfair, and unoriginal. You think Ned's my boy toy. That I dress him up and take him to lavish dinners in the city just to have a gorgeous guy on my arm. No," Flynn said as I began to protest. "I get it. You see wealth and status and equate that with power. Why wouldn't I take advantage of my position to woo a young YouTube star? It's the only way a man like me could ever attract a man like Ned."

Flynn squeezed the pillow in his lap harder, and the silence between us swelled like the belly of a blood-fat tick. Something about him was still making me anxious. I couldn't suss out what it was.

"Ned's got a great gig with us—job security, total creative freedom. That's far from guaranteed if he goes somewhere else. I only want the best for him. He doesn't understand that," said Flynn.

Because he doesn't feel the same way. All at once it was perfectly clear, and I couldn't believe Flynn didn't see it, too. It was Flynn who'd stacked those wallets on the bedroom dresser. Flynn wanted Ned to stay with Sinclair Fabrics. He thought that by arranging Ned's life to match his own he could keep the man for himself. Preserving the company brand might have factored into his desire to keep Ned on the job, but that wasn't what made Flynn so desperate to hold on. Everything he'd implied about the differences between the men's looks and status and age was true. Flynn didn't think he deserved Ned. He was afraid when Ned left the company, he'd leave Flynn, too.

"Did you and Jasper argue with Ned yesterday?" I asked. "About his desire to quit?" An imminent breach of contract and the inevitable legal fallout, an office romance, two brothers and an unpredictable element they needed to control, and now Jasper was gone . . . the scenario spelled trouble.

"I told you," Flynn said, "I barely saw Jas yesterday."

"So it was you who did the arguing, then."

Flynn sighed aggressively. "Look. Ned came to the island without me. When I confronted him, he refused to talk about it and gave me the silent treatment for the rest of the day. I was pissed, okay? We didn't *fight*—I just didn't feel like being social. My inbox was flooded with messages, and work was a convenient excuse for me to be alone, so I dropped in on Nana, took my laptop to the library, and shut everyone out. If I had to guess, I'd say Ned was with Jas and Abby all afternoon. I didn't see any of them again until cocktail hour."

The babble of the others lured him to the parlor then. When he stepped into the room—the same room where his family now waited while Flynn, from the comfort of his bed, walked me through the previous day—he discovered Norton was already serving drinks. Everyone was there. Bebe Sinclair (Flynn and Jasper's sister, the middle Sinclair child) who'd opted to keep the family name. Her husband, Miles Byrd. Miles's daughter, Jade, the teen I'd seen downstairs and the product of a previous marriage, sat on the floor by the fire (Jade Byrd: the name sounded more like a Chinatown trinket to me than a kid). Jasper, Abella, Camilla, and Ned rounded out the group, and everyone was laughing with abandon. It was something Jasper said that set them off; Flynn knew this instinctively. Storytelling was as natural as breathing to Jasper, according to Flynn.

"What'd I miss?" Flynn asked the group, trying his best to sound cheerful. It was only five o'clock, not yet dark, but the clouds had choked the life from the sun and the rain was really coming down. The parlor was bathed in yellow lamplight and an empty crystal tumbler awaited Flynn on the table, but there was no sign of Norton. Awkwardly holding his empty glass while the others drank wine around him, Flynn sat down to wait.

"Jas was telling the story of how he met Ned," Abella said. "I can't believe I never heard it—you boys have been holding out on me. Did you really mistake Jas for the gofer and ask him to get you a sandwich?"

"I'd never met him before! I forgot to eat lunch!" Ned's teeth flashed when he smiled, and the effect was dazzling. "You make me sound like a spoiled brat."

Playfully, Abella said, "If the shoe fits," and got a round of chuckles in reply.

"You're in good company, Ned," said Jasper. "Abby only likes this story because she can relate. Jas, get me a latte. Jas, grab me some water. Get me a—"

"Stop!" She elbowed Jasper in the ribs as she took another sip of wine. When he pinched her waist, Abella wriggled like a tickled child and almost slopped her drink into his lap. "That's not true, I swear," she said. "This isn't the first impression I want to make!"

"You make a great first impression," Ned said. "There's no shame in loving a little attention."

"He should know," said Flynn. "If anyone loves attention, it's Ned."

That was a fact, but Jasper and Abella were too wrapped up in each other to acknowledge it, and Ned was still ignoring him. It irked Flynn that the three of them commanded the room like a main-stage comedy act while he played the role of spectator in the cheap seats.

When Norton finally appeared he was carrying a bottle of Johnnie Walker and more chardonnay, along with a cup of ice. Flynn was first to hold up his glass, but Norton went straight to Abella.

"Ice in wine?" she said as he plucked up a cube with silver tongs. "Is this an American thing?"

"This bottle could be colder," said Norton as he dropped the ice into her glass. "This'll help."

"I don't care if the scotch comes from a kettle, bring it the fuck over here," said Flynn. From her place by the fire, Jade giggled as Norton finally made his way over to Flynn.

"Language," Camilla warned in her creaky voice, and smoothed the blanket draped over her lap. "Now, here's an idea. Why doesn't Abby work for us?"

Bebe snorted. "To keep Jas in line? Lord knows he needs it."

"To help him," said Camilla. "Well, why not?"

The guests fell silent.

"She does have PR experience," Miles said thoughtfully, smiling at the couple. "And you already know you work well together."

"You see? It's perfect." Camilla reached out to take Abella's hand. "You're all so busy, you always say so," she told her three grandchildren. "I'm sure you could use another sharp mind."

"Oh my God," said Abella. "I mean, I'd love to, of course!" Flynn watched her closely, took in her red face and the slur in her speech. *Nice*, he thought. *First time meeting the family, and the girl gets shitfaced.*

"It's an idea," said Bebe, "but—"

"What do you think, Jas?" said Miles.

"Might cramp my style, what with all my office affairs." Jasper grinned as Abella rolled her eyes. "You might be onto something, Nana."

"No more for her," said Miles sharply, his sudden change in tone at odds with the happy atmosphere. Norton had taken the new bottle of wine around the room and come to Jade. The girl held up her glass for her share, but Norton hesitated.

"Aw, let her have it," said Jasper. "It's just a little wine."

"She's fourteen," said Miles. "One is enough."

"Come on, man, it's a special occasion." Jasper winked at Jade and her cheeks went pink. The kid was well on her way to joining Abella in her drunken haze.

"You're such a killjoy, Miles," said Bebe.

"You can give her some of mine, it's mostly water," said

Camilla. "This job idea. Promise you'll all talk it over. I would hate for Abella to have to go."

"No one's going anywhere," said Miles, nodding at the window. "Have you seen the forecast for tomorrow? This is going to be one hell of a storm."

"Welcome to the family," Jasper said, kissing Abella's neck. "Looks like you're stuck with us."

Abella tried and failed to suppress a hiccup and raised her glass to toast the room. "Fine by me. There's nowhere else I'd rather be."

"Forgive me," I said, "but I don't see it."

I'd have bet a month's salary Flynn was going to paint Abella as a murderous vixen prone to fits of rage. Instead, he'd described a girl with every reason to stay on Jasper's good side. The couple seemed to care for each other. Camilla liked Abella so much she wanted to give her a job with the family business.

"Don't you get it?" said Flynn. "She needs Jas, and the feeling isn't mutual. There's no way he'd hire her. She's just a fling."

"But he brought her all this way to meet the family. Norton prepped for days. Ned's under the impression they're getting engaged."

"Ned repeated a rumor he heard from Jade, a kid who stirs shit up just for laughs. Abby—or Bella, or whatever her name is—is a fuck buddy, nothing more. She may be the first girl to come here, but we've met dozens of Jasper's girlfriends in the city. We used to do a family dinner once a month at some of the best restaurants in Manhattan, and he brought a different woman every time. Abella's not his one and only. She's just the only one who realized she's being used."

The implication was Abella wanted more than Jasper was willing to give. As far as motives for murder go, I thought, it was weak. "You don't do that anymore? Get together as a family?"

"It was our mother who organized those dinners. So no," Flynn said bitterly. "We don't."

Two years since the death of their parents meant two years without family get-togethers. It wasn't as if Bebe, Flynn, Jasper, and Camilla couldn't have kept up the tradition. That left me wondering if there was another reason the siblings no longer made an effort to catch up.

"And you didn't hear anything last night?" I confirmed, remembering Norton and Camilla's insistence that nothing happened after dark. "Voices maybe, or loud noises? Seems like you might not have slept so well, given what's going on with Ned."

Flynn bristled. "I'll tell you what I heard. I heard perfect little Abella stumbling around drunk in the hall."

"How do you know it was her?"

"What?"

"How do you know it was Abella you heard and not Jasper, or somebody else?"

He hesitated. "There was a fight. I heard them shouting."

"What time was this?"

"Late, past midnight. Abella must have left the room to use the bathroom afterward. I didn't hear anything else."

Outside, the wind whistled and wailed. Last night past midnight the storm was already in full swing, and I had a hard time understanding how Flynn could be sure of what—or who—he'd heard. I got to my feet. "Thanks for your time, Mr. Sinclair. I'm going to need you downstairs now."

"I'm not setting foot in the same room as that bitch."

"I'm sorry, but you don't have a choice."

Flynn's fury was starting to mount again. It bared itself in the clench of his teeth and the bulge of the blood vessels at his hairline. "You saw his bed," he said in a voice that was low and dangerous. "She slept in that bed with him. She was alone in the room with Jasper all night, and they fought, and the bed's covered in his blood and he's nowhere now, just *gone*." He dug his nails into the pillow and twisted hard. "What's wrong with you? Are you seriously so stupid that you don't see it? She killed my brother. I don't know how she did it, but she did. And if you don't do something about it, I swear to God I will."

"That sounds like a threat." I made a show of noting it on my pad. "Watch yourself, or the next conversation we have will be at the station."

"You don't scare me," he said with a sneer. "If you think you can manipulate me, you're wrong."

"Tell you what," I said, spotting my chance. "You do what you're told, and I'll try to find your brother. When this is all over you can file a complaint against me—here, take my card."

I reached into my pocket and tossed the card into his lap. Reflexively, he raised his right hand from the pillow to bat it away.

It was a quick glimpse, but it was enough to confirm what I'd come to suspect. The knuckles on the hand Flynn was hiding all this time were an unmistakable shade of fresh-bruise blue.

SEVEN

C hange of plans," Tim said.

He met me at the bottom of the stairs, where I watched Flynn join the others in the parlor to make sure he sat as far from Abella as possible. *Ned and your family are down there*, I'd told him. *If you're right about Abella, are you comfortable with that?* Begrudgingly Flynn left his room, but I knew he'd bring his anger with him. He'd thrown a punch at something—or someone— already. I didn't trust the man at all.

"That was the headquarters." Tim waved his phone at me. "You're not going to believe what they said."

A dozen ideas sparked to life in my mind, each more preposterous than the next. *Jasper's a drug addict who owes an inner-city thug a fortune. The Sinclair family crossed the Mafia and it's payback time. Abella Beaudry is Canada's Lizzie Borden, a fugitive on the run.* I was wrong on all counts. My confusion escalated as Tim recapped his call.

"What do you mean, they're not coming?"

"They tried." Tim looked apologetic, and a little embarrassed. To him I was still a cop from the big city, and he wanted to show me his rural operation was the real deal. "The troopers got as far as Heart Island," he explained. "There was another vessel in the water, a Boston Whaler full of teens who thought boating in a nor'easter would be fun."

"Shit," I said, recalling our own harrowing ride. "So they got sidetracked by a rescue. They'll be here once they get those kids back to shore, right?"

"The Whaler capsized in the channel. The timing was lucky—those kids would have drowned. But our guys didn't see it until the last minute. They hit it."

"They *hit* it?"

He shrugged. "Their boat's a mess, and a couple of the injuries are bad. They had to bring in the Coast Guard to help. I put in a request for another boat, but with the flooding in town and the storm getting worse, every deputy's overwhelmed. For the foreseeable future, we're on our own."

Over Tim's shoulder I could see the family collectively straining to hear us. I grabbed the man's elbow and pulled him toward the stairs. "Okay," I said, thinking, *Breathe, Shay. Breathe.* "Let's recap the situation. We don't have a body. The evidence is locked up safe and sound. We're fine on our own for now." I tried to sound believable and ignore the fact that what I felt tugging at my collar was fear.

"Agreed," said Tim. "We're fine. Lots more interviews to do still, and all the time in the world to do them. How'd it go with Flynn?"

"He likes the girlfriend for this, but I'm not convinced yet. I think the family dynamics around here are off."

"You mean these filthy-rich blue bloods from Manhattan aren't the Cleavers? You don't say. In the meantime, I've gathered some useful information."

"Really?" I said, perking up.

"Oh yeah. I've mapped the location of the incision from Bebe's facelift. I can tell you how recently each of the men shaved, whether they file or clip their fingernails, and who didn't eat enough for breakfast. When Ned's stomach growls it sounds like he swallowed a howler monkey."

Tim's humor helped to calm me down. We were both chuckling when I noticed Philip Norton walking toward us.

"It's almost noon," Norton said. "Everyone's getting hungry. Would it be okay if I excused myself to make the lunch? It's chicken soup with fennel and farro, and homemade buns. Jade's favorite."

Audibly, embarrassingly, my own stomach rumbled. I had hours of interviews ahead of me, and I was already as ravenous as Ned. We'd all need to eat eventually, wouldn't we? The kitchen was right down the hall from the parlor, and Norton worked alone. The only opportunity he'd have for collusion was with the deli meat.

"That's fine," I said decisively. "I'm stepping out to make a call." I was still wearing my jacket, and the fire in the parlor had brought up the temperature in the house. Between the heat and my hunger, my head swam. "Wellington will be here to . . ."

"Keep an eye on things," Tim said.

"Right," said Norton. "In case it's the butler in the kitchen with the knife." His entire head went fuchsia. "My God, I'm sorry. I can't believe I said that."

"Don't worry about it," said Tim. "Nerves. Happens to everyone when cops are around."

Norton nodded. "Thanks for your help with this. It's a hell of a thing. We're all glad you're here."

We'll see how long that lasts, I thought as I watched Norton walk to the kitchen and made my way down the hall. In my ten years working as a detective I'd only been popular with one suspect, and that case nearly got me killed.

I wasn't in the habit of calling Carson from work. I didn't want to remind him what I was doing, and he didn't want to be reminded. At the same time, it was clear Tim and I were going to be occupied on the island for hours. The least I could do was let him know where I was.

I pushed open the front door, savored the cold air on my skin, and dialed. Carson, when he answered, sounded distracted. I could hear him typing on his laptop while an industrial cappuccino machine hissed and spit in the background. He was at the coffee shop again, and not likely to be chipper. My timing couldn't have been worse.

When he first brought up the idea of leaving the city, I was as worried about him as about myself. What did Jefferson County have to offer a man like Dr. Carson Gates? What would he do in a little village upstate after the stellar career he'd built in the city? The money he'd been making in Queens was good, the work important. It satisfied him, and that satisfied me—after all, his work was what brought us together. We owed a lot to his job. Yet he didn't hesitate to leave it for me.

Over time I warmed to the idea of him opening his own practice in Alexandria Bay. I imagined I would visit him when he was between patients and we'd share a tuna fish sandwich at his spotless glass desk. Three months into our new life, though, there was still no desk, no office. He was ironing out the details, constantly visiting potential locations. He was arranging meetings with local physicians to lay the groundwork for referrals. He liked that part of the process. But I could tell he was getting impatient, especially on the days he didn't have somewhere to go. That's when he'd head to the coffee shop around the corner from our short-term rental to send e-mails. The place was dingy and crowded, the coffee burned, but it was better than our apartment, which was well below Carson's standards. Whenever I suggested finding someplace better, he reminded me setting up a new business while planning a wedding takes major cash. To do it all right, we had to save a little now. We'd be glad we did later, he explained, once we were settled into a big, contemporary house on Swan Bay.

"Busy, hon?" I asked, turning my shoulder to the wind. Way down by the boathouse below me, whitecapped waves smacked the island's stone wall. Tim was right. The weather was getting worse.

"Always," said Carson. "But I'm glad you called. What is it we agreed on for dinner? I'll take a trip to the market."

"Fish."

"Right. Fish." I could sense him deliberating over sauces—remoulade, dill and lemon, or mustard cream? Cooking was Carson's passion. "We should eat on the early side, yeah?"

"Oh," I began. "I—"

Carson groaned. "Please tell me you're not going to your parents' place again."

"No, no," I said quickly. "But I'm not sure when I'll be home. I'm . . . kind of on a case."

The patter of his keyboard fell away. All I heard now was the cackle of a female patron and the steady thump of coffee-shop indie pop.

I've never had a problem keeping casework at the office when the workday is done. I hear doctors are the same way, especially the ones who treat sick kids or disassemble dead bodies. Bring that shit home and it'll invade your world like a cancer, spreading unchecked until it consumes everyone you love. The darker your workday, the tighter its grip on your heart. For that reason, I didn't want to tell Carson too much.

"It's a missing person situation on one of the islands," I said. "It's weird, but nothing major yet. May take a while, though."

"A disappearance." His awe ballooned into disbelief. "Please tell me you're joking, Shay."

"Hon, I'm *fine*."

"What island?"

"Tern."

I was curious to see whether he'd heard of the owners like Tim had. If Carson knew Tern Island, he didn't let on. Instead, he said, "You're not fine. Fine is not what you are. You're not ready for this, not even close." I could picture him at his coffee-shop table with a finger pressed against his temple, massaging the skin in slow circles like he did when he was stressed. Carson took a deep breath and exhaled loudly. "Shay. When you went behind my back and applied for this job, I humored you."

"*Humored* me? You were furious." I'd never seen Carson so mad as when I told him I was going back to work. He'd likened my decision to a kamikaze mission. We fought that night for the first time ever, didn't talk at all the next day.

"I wasn't furious, I was worried. It was a huge decision, Shay. You should have run it by me first."

"I knew what you'd say."

"Doesn't that tell you something, babe? If it's dangerous—not just to you, but to everyone around you—why do it?"

"Because," I said, not liking how much I sounded like a pissy kid, "this is my career. It's what I *do*." It was the same argument I'd been making for months, and Carson was no closer to understanding. I needed to get back to what I loved. I needed to know if I could.

If Carson had his way, I'd still be a shut-in. And that was what I needed, at first—to be sheltered while I worked through my mental state and emotions. What it all meant. He'd handled everything from the shopping to our finances while I recovered. But more than a year had passed. I'd undergone countless hours of counseling and worked through the trauma step-by-step. Carson couldn't seriously believe I'd be willing to hide forever. What was he doing for all those months if not helping me move on?

"Look," I said, because I couldn't stand his silence or the immense disappointment it conveyed. "I'm taking some statements over here, that's all. This missing guy will probably turn up. Tim's sure of it."

"Tim," Carson repeated. "You're there with Tim."

"Yeah," I said. "Of course I am."

There was a long pause before Carson muttered something I couldn't quite hear. "Listen to me, all right? This is serious. Be careful. Be aware of what you're experiencing, Shay. If you notice any kind of stress reaction, any familiar signs of—"

"I'll call you," I said, unwilling to hear the laundry list of symptoms yet again. "I will."

"Promise?"

"Promise."

"Okay," he said. "Stay safe."

I knew he wanted to help—he was the only one who could, who truly understood. But sometimes when Carson talked about my condition, the seeds of fear and doubt already planted in my mind took me back to the dark place I started in—and once there I had a hell of a time leaving without him. As I pocketed my phone I felt the memories rush forward, a psychological assault that forced my chin to my chest and turned my legs to goo.

I was on the floor of the cellar where the smell of fried meat lingered, hugging my knees to my chest. I watched it happen. Waited for my training to kick in. Knew it never would. There was blood on my hands and a dead man on the floor, his name a sizzling brand on my heart next to the others. *Jay Lopez. Becca. Lanie. Jess.*

The wind lifted the ends of my hair, and I turned to face the Sinclair's house once more. The pain those names inflicted was as fresh as ever, but I forced myself to repeat them. *Jay. Becca. Lanie. Jess.* I chanted them like a mantra under my breath until they blended seamlessly into one long, lilting gasp. Only then did I add another.

Bram. Bram. Bram.

EIGHT

I would have settled for a grilled cheese and a glass of water. Philip Norton was cooking a feast. It was nowhere near ready when I got back inside, but I was glad for the extra time. As Tim entertained the guests-slash-witnesses with stories of how the islands got their names—this one after the British Overseas Territory where Napoleon Bonaparte was exiled, that one for General James Wolfe when the area was under British rule—I spotted my chance to substantiate some of Flynn's hand-to-God account.

"Abella," I said from the parlor doorway. "Can we talk?"

The woman jumped to her feet. Holding it together in a house full of strangers couldn't be easy. With the exception of Camilla, the Sinclairs looked at Abby like she was a pariah. All eyes, Tim's included, were on her bloodstained hip as she left the room.

Even with unwashed hair and a face puffy from crying, Abella

Beaudry was a stunner, all lashes and lips. Whether Jasper saw her as a fling or his future wife, he had good taste.

"How are you doing?" I asked as we sat down in the library. The room was directly across from the parlor. When I'd slid the pocket doors shut behind me they'd made a sound like a dry-lipped kiss.

"I don't know," she said. "I just . . . I can't believe he's gone."

Abella had a slight French accent, but her English was flawless. She could easily slip from one culture to the next, Abby to Bella and back again, but I wasn't as convinced as Flynn that her multiple nicknames were a sign of duplicity.

"Do you have any idea where Jasper could be?" I took out my notepad and inclined my head. Abella looked at me with confusion. "Let me rephrase that," I said. "Has Jasper ever disappeared before? Does he like to go off and spend time by himself?"

"No. He didn't just *leave*."

"But he was in bed with you last night. And then, this morning, he wasn't."

"I know that sounds crazy," she said. "But it's what happened, and that's all I know."

My gaze traveled back to her bloodstained hip. "Did you hear anyone come into your room?"

I could see her picturing it, someone leaning over her sleeping body. Abella shook her head.

"And you were in the room all night. You didn't leave? Not even to use the bathroom?"

"No," she said. "I slept straight through." Abella must have picked up on my doubt, because she added, "I had a bit too much to drink last night. I was nervous."

"Meeting the family."

"Yeah."

"That must have been stressful."

She lowered her head and worked her fingers through her tangled hair. It was looking a little greasy, her body's reaction to the ordeal. "You have no idea," she said.

"Are you and Jasper serious?"

"We haven't been dating that long. But yeah, I would call it serious."

"Jasper's brother, Flynn? He told me Jasper plans to propose."

Her brown eyes went wide. "What? He said that?"

"He also said you were recently fired from your job. Is that true?"

Her mind was still on the proposal, so she didn't answer right away. After a few seconds she blinked and remembered where she was. "I wasn't fired. They were downsizing, and I was happy to leave. They had me working like fifty hours a week for next to no pay. Some days Jas and I wouldn't see each other at all, even if I stayed over at his place. I'd get home from an event at two a.m. and leave again at six that morning. It sucked."

"If you married Jasper, an American citizen, you wouldn't have needed that job." I nodded at the stately room. "You might not need a job at all." *Welcome to the lap of luxury. Get comfortable.* It was the same suggestion I'd made to Flynn about Ned. The odds that the Sinclairs' gargantuan wealth didn't play a part in the family's relationships seemed slim. Just like Flynn, though, Abella dismissed it at once.

"I'm not looking for a free ride. And it's not like in the movies. It can take a year or more to get a spousal visa. I want to work." Her chest rose and fell under her pajama top. "I love him," she said weakly. "I'm not using him."

But is he using you? Flynn claimed his brother was the love 'em, leave 'em type, and that Abella caught him out. I couldn't picture this woman attacking her boyfriend with so many others sleeping nearby, and there was no chance she could relocate a dead man's body alone. "Were you fighting last night? Around midnight?"

"What? No way. I was asleep way before that."

If Flynn lied about hearing an argument, I thought, he was a fool. Voices loud enough to reach him through his closed door would have been heard by everyone else on that floor, too. "Have you ever talked about working for Sinclair Fabrics?" I asked, remembering Flynn's statement. *I'd love to, of course!*

"Work with Flynn and Bebe?" Abella looked appalled. "Not a chance in hell."

Huh. "Ned does it, doesn't he?"

"Not for much longer. He's being considered for a Burberry campaign, and a bunch of others, too. As soon as one of those comes through, he's gone."

"How does Jasper feel about Ned leaving him in the lurch?"

"He's totally okay with it. It's a huge opportunity for Ned, way bigger than what he's got now. Jas wants that for him—I do, too. We're friends, all of us. We care about each other."

"You, Jasper, and Ned."

"Yeah."

"It's weird," I said, "because Flynn made it sound like you were excited about the idea of working with Jasper."

She glanced at the closed library door. "I love Jasper," she repeated. "That doesn't mean I love his family."

"But you've only just met them. How do you know you won't get along?"

I could see her withdrawing, questioning the wisdom of saying more. I'd hit on something with this line of questioning. The moment I mentioned Flynn's name Abella started avoiding my gaze. Through her parted lips I spotted a small gap between her front teeth. It made her look like an anxious child.

"Camilla's great," Abella said. "I wish I could have met her sooner. Had more time with her, you know?"

I nodded. It was a testament to Camilla's stamina that she was still spending the summers on a relatively isolated island. At her age, her days with the family were numbered. The question was whether Abella's were, too.

"What about Bebe and Flynn?"

"I don't really know them."

Again I mentioned the age difference between Jasper and Flynn. "How are things with them, relationship-wise?"

"Not all brothers and sisters get along."

"So you wouldn't say they're close? What makes you so sure? You and Jasper have been together for, what, a few months?"

"Two."

"Two months. You think that's enough time to get a handle on the subtleties of sibling relations?"

Again I sensed hesitation. "It's the way they treat him—Flynn especially. He's an asshole to Jas, and to Ned, too. Don't make me go back out there," she said. "I can't just sit there while they sip their coffee and pretend everything's fine!"

"Abella, if we're going to find Jasper I need your help. You were with him last night, all night. You were here yesterday, too. If you know anything, saw anything that might explain what happened, now's the time to talk."

She brought her thumb to her lip and scraped her teeth along the nail. Abella's fingernails were ballet pink and had the high-gloss shine of a professional manicure. She was in the spotlight this weekend, and she knew it. She'd wanted Jasper's family to be impressed.

The moment she decided to spill it, Abella's chin quivered and her eyes filled with tears. The story I was about to hear was going to be different from the one Flynn recounted, no question. I hoped it would be the truth.

"It's my fault," she said.

My body went rigid. "What's your fault, hon?"

"It's my fault he's gone."

"Did you do something to him? Hurt him, or . . ."

"No." She met my gaze with big, watery eyes. "But I know who did."

NINE

The island was a secret paradise Abella couldn't reconcile with the world she knew onshore. Just that morning she'd been in Manhattan, and now she stood by the water's edge in a heavy fall sweater while Jasper hugged her to his side and whispered dirty propositions in her ear. He was trying to distract her from what was coming, and she appreciated the effort, but they were out of time. Norton pulled the skiff up to the dock, and out crawled Flynn Sinclair.

"Your better half's already here," Jasper said.

"Better at what?" Flynn replied. "Making bad choices, or being an ungrateful prick?" Flynn didn't hug his brother or even shake his hand, and Abella assumed Flynn was in a shitty mood after the five-hour drive from Manhattan. Jasper turned his back on Flynn and offered to help tie up the boat, but Norton waved him away.

"One last run to the market before the weather turns," Norton said.

"Seriously?" said Jasper. "You were just there yesterday. Aren't you supposed to be getting things ready inside?"

Her boyfriend's comment struck Abella as rude, and that wasn't like him at all. Something was grating on Jasper, though she couldn't imagine what it was. Norton's smile, when he managed one, was forced. Abella's was, too.

"Lots to prepare," said Norton amiably. "Won't be long." Pushing off, he revved the engine and headed back to shore.

Flynn stared at his luggage with distaste. The job of lugging it up the steps was on him. "Nice you two could get here so early. Some of us have to work."

"Meet Abby," Jasper said in a way that told Abella he'd taken a ribbing from Flynn before and had no interest in engaging with him again. Flynn didn't leer at her exactly, but his eyes lingered on her longer than was polite. It made her uncomfortable.

Jasper did his best to keep the conversation going as they climbed the steps. By contrast, Flynn moped in silence the whole time. All Abella wanted was to get away from him and flop down on the couch with Jasper to savor their last few moments alone before she was put on parade. So she was thrilled when, as soon as they got to the house, Flynn went straight upstairs.

"There he goes, off to kiss Nana's ass. *Now* do you see why I didn't introduce you sooner? What a prick," Jasper said. "He won't let up."

"On what?" Abella asked.

"On *who*. Flynn treats Ned like shit. I swear, he can't control himself. If I'm not around he immediately goes searching for someone else to abuse. Actually, he does it whether I'm there or not."

Ah, thought Abby. So that's what caused Jasper to snap. He rarely talked about his siblings, and Abella had thought better of prodding. "Is he really like that?" she asked.

"An alpha male? A natural-born sadist? Yeah, he is." Jasper blew out a breath and rubbed the back of his neck. "It's fine, I'm used to it. It's just fucking embarrassing, that's all."

On the mahogany coffee table in the parlor a little clock ticked steadily. Abella could hear the flagpole clinking in the mossy enclosure that stood in for a front yard, the erratic snap of the Scottish and American flags that flew when Camilla was on the island.

"Maybe it's a competition thing?" Abella said it carefully. She didn't want to talk about his family. This was dangerous territory, and they were still in their honeymoon phase, when serious conversations were better kept at bay. "That's how it is with me and my sister. She can't stand it when I win."

She was cautious with her words for another reason. Abella wasn't supposed to know as much about her boyfriend as she did. He wasn't one to brag, but her due diligence on the new man in her life had revealed a highly accomplished individual who excelled at everything, and always had. The Internet divulged that in grade school Jasper was a regular installment in his Westchester County town's local newspaper, three-time winner of the district's geography bee. When his middle school won the statewide math competition, Jasper took the individual first prize. His high school lacrosse team, one of the best in the country, won countless tournament titles. What older brother would be comfortable competing with that?

"Let me tell you a story," Jasper said. Abella didn't like his tone. She could feel his heartbeat through his ribs. His body heat was rising. "Flynn had just finished his junior year. School was over for the summer, and report cards were coming in. My parents called us both to the kitchen. Flynn wasn't good at school. Usually they let that slide, but he was a year away from college and his grades were worse than ever. I guess they figured it was time to get real." He snorted, as if he couldn't believe it took his parents as long as it did, or imagine how Flynn could be such a loser. "They took away his car, gave him a curfew, did everything they could think of. On some level I think they knew it was meaningless, that they'd end up making a huge donation to Dad's alma mater and the school would take Flynn no matter what. But they tried."

Absently, Jasper looped a strand of Abella's hair around his finger and examined its healthy shine. "Flynn was pissed. Then my parents turned to me and said I'd been invited to join the gifted class in the fall. This was kindergarten. I was, like, five years old. I had no idea what they were even talking about, but they looked excited, so I got excited, too.

"Afterward, Flynn and I went outside and Flynn patted me on the back. 'Good job, Jas,' he said. 'You're a fucking genius.' He swore all the time around me, and my parents didn't catch on for years; the first and only time I cussed in front of them, Flynn got the blame for that, too. So we're out in the yard, and Flynn's got this big grin, and I remember thinking, wow, my big brother's proud of me. It felt so good—and then it got even better. Flynn asked if I wanted to toss around the football. He played for the high school, was pretty good at it, but he'd never once played with me. I was so psyched. I was a scrawny kid, but I gave it all I had when I threw that ball because I wanted to impress him even more. Flynn caught it and whipped it back, hard as he could. Straight at my face."

Reflexively, Abby brought her hands to her nose. She could almost feel the crushing blow, the hot geyser of blood and confusion and fear Jasper experienced that day, as if she'd taken the hit herself. She'd noticed the bend in his nose, of course she had. He'd never mentioned how he got it.

"Flynn doesn't deserve excuses," Jasper said. "He's an asshole, yet somehow he always gets what he wants. He slacked off all his life and now he's fucking CFO. Flynn thinks he's my boss. Can you believe that?" Jasper stared out the window, his mouth a fixed line. "It's not about competition for him, Abby, it's about control—over me, and Ned, and everyone else. The only thing that keeps me from smashing his face in is knowing it can't last forever. One of these days, his luck's going to change. And he deserves what he's got coming."

The wind was picking up. Beyond the window tree branches stuttered and swooped upward, buoyed by gusts so strong they shook the leaded panes. Abella sank deeper into the crook of Jasper's arm and used the pad of her thumb to buff a tiny smudge from her pinkie nail. She didn't know how to comfort him, not about this. In the hallway, the staircase creaked. She sensed Jasper stiffen, and a second later Flynn passed by the doorway with his laptop under his arm. He paused to glance disinterestedly in their direction before entering the library and slamming the pocket doors closed behind him.

"I better check on Nana," Jasper said. "God knows what Flynn said to her. I swear her blood pressure spikes when he's in a half-mile radius." He lifted his arm from around her shoulder, and instantly Abella felt cold. "Maybe she wants to play a round of rook with us. You in?"

Abella loved this about Jasper: his thoughtful nature, his devotion to his grandmother. He was everything Flynn wasn't. "Sounds like fun," she said.

"We'll need a fourth."

"Ned?"

"Definitely. Will you track him down? He's probably up in Flynn's room. With everything going on between them right now, my bet is he's keeping a low profile. He doesn't want to stir shit up with everyone around."

Abella felt a twinge of pity for Ned then. She knew he and Flynn were having problems; Ned often talked to her about them, and the anecdotes he shared were almost always negative. After hearing Jasper's story, Abella told herself she'd be both more attentive and more supportive of her friend. Why Ned was still wasting his time on a man like Flynn, she had no idea.

She set off to find him, but Ned wasn't upstairs, or anywhere else Abella searched on the second floor. After Abella met Jasper and Flynn's sister, Bebe, earlier, Bebe had announced she was going to her room to take a nap. Through Jade's door Abella could hear the girl talking to her father. With Camilla on the third floor, Flynn working downstairs, and Norton still at the market, the rest of the house was quiet. Where could Ned be?

Wandering the Sinclairs' home alone felt like an invasion of their privacy, but Jasper had asked Abella to find Ned, and she intended to do it. Back on the main floor she checked the kitchen. A full wall of windows framed river and sky, and the white cabinets and marble counters were bathed in a ghostly, colorless light.

There was a door nearby that concealed stairs to the cellar, but it seemed unlikely Ned would be down there. On the far side of the kitchen she found a mudroom that led outside. Abella could see a shed, the outbuilding teetering on the edge of a high cliff about fifty yards from the house.

Based on its size and shape, she imagined the shed was used to shelter lawn-care equipment, possibly firewood. It was a miniature version of the house, with the same siding and custom windows. Through one of these windows she caught a flicker of movement. A dark shape shifting behind the glass.

A smattering of raindrops hit the door, and Abella shivered. Without Norton around to make a fire, the house was freezing. It seemed possible Ned could have gone to the shed to get wood. She peered through the glass. She wasn't mistaken. Someone was out there. Inside that shed.

She turned the handle and a gust of cold wind slapped her in the face. A dozen oilskin jackets and raincoats pressed in on her from both sides of the mudroom. She chose a long slicker from a hook at random and buttoned it over her clothes. Abella mentioned she'd spent an hour straightening her hair that morning, and she wasn't about to let the rain ruin it now. Pulling on the hood, she stepped out of the house and began to traverse the yard.

As she walked, she thought of nothing but finding Ned. This weekend was crucial for Abella, a chance to prove to Jasper she fit in his life like a key in a lock. They'd been dating only a handful of weeks, but she was hopeful he saw her as more than a fling. He'd invited her here, hadn't he? That had to count for something. Her job situation and status in the country, that stuff would resolve itself. In the meantime, she couldn't risk a misstep that might make him question how he felt. Her every move had to look effortless.

She needed her presence to feel natural, not just to Jasper but to all of the Sinclairs. She wanted them to feel like she'd been there all along.

Slippery moss coated the rocks and the wind thrashed her from all angles. It made Abella move like a kid on a balance beam, arms windmilling ridiculously, on the verge of wiping out. The closer she got to the shed, the more convinced she was that she was right. Ned had gone to get firewood. A fire would be nice.

She reached the door. Should she knock? No, that would be weird. Instead, she put her hand on the rusty latch, the iron so cold it felt hot to the touch. She squinted through the window at the darkness inside, and felt a zing of horror whiz down her spine.

It couldn't be. She couldn't believe what she was seeing. There was clutter everywhere, dangling garden tools and rope and wood-working instruments with mean edges that glinted in the pale light—and in the middle of it all stood Ned. His pants were a puddle around his feet. In front of him a woman leaned over a sawhorse, Ned's hand a dark tattoo on the creamy skin of her hip. Behind a wave of dark hair, Abella could just make out the pinched-eye, openmouthed expression of ecstasy on Bebe Sinclair's face.

With her heart beating wildly in her rib cage, Abella stared at Ned and Bebe as their bodies bucked and swayed. The scene in the shed was horrible and hypnotic and she couldn't look away. What she was witnessing was dangerous, and Abella knew it. She couldn't win. If they saw her, she'd no longer be Jasper's girlfriend but an infectious disease that could spread throughout the house to compromise the health of countless relationships. Flynn and Ned, Bebe and Miles, Abella and Jasper . . . all were at risk. If anyone else found out what she now knew, she'd be the one blamed. Abella was a stranger, the family would say, only there to spread rumors and cause trouble. They were Jasper's blood relatives. When they urged him to cut her from his life, he'd listen.

The raincoat's hood trapped the heat of her body and Abella felt as if she'd stuck her head in an oven and was waiting, fearful and frozen, for the gas to take effect. *Go,* she thought. *Go now.* With a burst of adrenaline she turned and sprinted back to the house. The wind screamed across the open land, shoving her left and right. She was almost at the mudroom door, so close she could see the jackets hanging inside, when the heel of her shoe slipped and she went down on the rocks with a grunt, her pulse thundering in her ears.

She didn't need to look. Sprawled on the ground with her cheek against cold stone, she could feel their eyes on her back. Inside the shed, Ned and Bebe were watching. Abella knew this sure as she knew what it meant. She'd seen them. And they had seen her.

The next few minutes were a blur. By the time she found herself hobbling down the hall toward the parlor, Jasper had set up the game and settled Camilla into a chair. In the hearth a newly laid fire sparked to life. There was firewood in a basket by the wall, there all along. Panting, she stumbled into the room.

"Where'd you go?" Jasper asked with a note of concern. He surveyed the jacket, her crimson cheeks, the wide stripe of mud on the thigh of her jeans. She'd panicked and come straight back inside without even taking off her muddy shoes. A look of disapproval rolled across Camilla's face as her gaze followed the muddy footprints down the hall.

"Just . . ." Sweltering, Abella shrugged off the hood. "Outside," she said. "To get some air."

If he picked up on her fear, Jasper didn't show it. "My jacket looks good on you." He said it with a wolfish grin. Abella wearing nothing but his too-big T-shirt on a lazy Saturday morning. Abella tucked into one of his threadbare college sweatshirts as they sat on Jasper's couch drinking good wine. The images he was trying to convey with those words and that playful expression were meant to be prophecies, but they were as painful to her as torn skin. They were what Abella thought she wanted, and what she'd now never have. "No luck with Ned?" asked Jasper.

Abella took off Jasper's jacket and draped it over her arm. She stared at it for a long time before meeting his gaze again. "Sorry," she said. "I couldn't find him anywhere."

TEN

"B ebe and Ned," Tim repeated slowly. "She's absolutely sure."

I'd seen the shed Abella was talking about. It was visible from the library window where I'd listened, unmoving, to her story. Where Tim and I stood now, alone. "She's sure," I said.

"Flynn's boyfriend and his sister. Man, it's like . . ." Tim paused. "Like a bad soap opera or something."

Together, we glanced over at the parlor. I'd questioned the wisdom of sending Abella back in there with Jasper's family, but isolating her could tip off the others to what she revealed in her interview, and I needed to hear their side of things without that kind of interference. Tim had implemented a mandatory bathroom break, which meant he was on break, too. While the Sinclairs took turns stalking down the hall muttering about the absurdity of the routine, Tim and I took the opportunity to regroup.

"If it's true," I said, "they'd want to keep their affair secret. That, right there, is motive. Picture it—they're in the shed while Flynn's working here in the library—"

"That's a hell of a risk to take," Tim interrupted.

"But for whatever reason, they take it. They're hyperaware of their surroundings. They had to know there was a chance that they'd get caught—and then, suddenly, they hear a sound and see someone running back to the house. The yard's wide open, nothing to obstruct their view, and the someone they see is wearing Jasper's raincoat. They assume it's him and realize he saw them smack in the middle of . . , you know." I tried not to blush. I hadn't worked any sex crimes with Tim yet, so talk of lewd misconduct and inappropriate hookups was brand-new, but the fact that I felt like a teenager in an awkward conversation with my dad was downright embarrassing.

"Bebe is Jasper's sister," Tim said. "She couldn't tell the difference between him and a girl she just met?"

"They were distracted. The shed windows are covered with cobwebs. I can see how Bebe could make that mistake."

Just to be sure, I'd grilled Abella about the scene and what came afterward. It took until she looked down at Jasper's raincoat in her arms for the horrible realization to sink in. They were close in height, and both she and Jasper wore jeans that day. Tim had a point, but I found myself wanting to side with Abella. There was a good chance Ned and Bebe believed the Peeping Tom was Jas.

"What kind of person cheats on her husband at her grandmother's house with the whole family around?" Tim looked at me like he thought I might know the answer, what with all my years living in New York with a mixed bag of human garbage.

"The kind that kills her brother when she thinks he's caught on?"

95

Tim's eyes widened. "You think?"

"Could be. Ned has reason to freak, too, but Abella's pinning the blame for the affair squarely on Bebe. She says Ned's a close friend. They hang out together in the city—her, Jasper, and Ned. If you ask me she's giving Ned a lot of credit, considering she caught him banging his friend's sister, but she insists he's innocent."

"They hang out in the city," Tim repeated thoughtfully. "Does the happy group include Flynn?"

"I got a hard no on that. It's Ned, Jasper, and Abby who fraternize, no asshole brothers allowed. Flynn made it sound like he and Jasper are pals, but Abella says they hate each other. According to her, Flynn's got a history of aggression. You should have heard the story she told me about Flynn torturing Jasper when they were kids. Way worse than your typical sibling stuff."

"So does Flynn know about the affair, too?"

"Abella doesn't think so. If he did, and he's as violent as she's suggesting, it'd be Ned or Bebe missing, not Jasper." I paused. "You've had a look at Ned. He take a fist to the chin?"

"The fresh bruises on Flynn's knuckles," Tim said. After talking to Flynn, I'd texted Tim a truncated report of what I knew so far. It wasn't as good as sharing my findings in person, but I wanted to keep him in the loop without having to constantly pull him off guard duty. It was kind of like backing up critical data. Tim made a useful hard drive. "No sign any of them took a punch."

"Maybe there's a wall somewhere missing some plaster?"

"Or maybe it was Jasper who got hit," Tim said. I started to speak, but he cut me off. "You know, I bet that's it. Jasper got in a fight with his brother and took off. Out here, so close to the border, he could easily make a dash for Canada. There are lots of places where he could have crossed, where the border's just an invisible line in the river. You're supposed to check in with your passport on the other side, but it's an honor system. Agents don't patrol the border area much this time of year. Even if he went over without letting them know, it's not so easy to slip into another country unnoticed if you plan to stay awhile. If that's what happened, we'll find him."

"This doesn't feel like a runaway situation," I said. "Jasper's phone is still charging upstairs. What twentysomething guy leaves the house without his phone? I think Jasper's in trouble." It was such a huge understatement; saying it out loud sounded stupid to my ear.

"We'll find him," Tim said again. "I know we will."

"These people." I shook my head. "This isn't a soap opera, it's a shit show."

"They're not from around here. So."

I hadn't meant the comment as an attack on the Thousand Islands and their residents. Tim was fiercely loyal to his community. It was my community now, too.

"Right, of course," I said. "Wonder what the parents were like? Abella never met them, but she told me a little about their deaths. Car accident while on vacation."

"Shit, I think I remember that," Tim said. "Didn't put two and two together—but yeah, the deaths would have been in the paper up here on account of their island connection. Google?" He reached for his phone.

"Already done," I said with a smile. We were clicking in a way I'd hoped we would months down the line. Tim had worked at the state police Alexandria Bay station a long time, so while I was technically his superior, I'd come to rely on him to indoctrinate me in the ways of the North Country. The ease with which we could bounce ideas off each other, his ability to read me and gauge where I was going next—those aren't guarantees in a colleague, and finding it so soon with Tim was a nice surprise. "The accident was big news farther south. *New York Textile Tycoon and Wife Killed While Vacationing in the Caribbean.* Two years ago, Baldwin and Rachel Sinclair went on one of many quick getaways to Antigua and never came back."

Tim sighed and dropped into an armchair. There was a second chair nearby, so wide and plush I wanted to curl up in it and reset my brain, but I knew neither of us should get too comfortable. I could see Abella nervously watching us from across the hall, and I was itching to talk to Bebe and Ned.

"Both parents in one shot. Can't have been easy on the kids," Tim said. Then, "Where's the money?"

"Excellent question. It went to the three of them, most likely—Jasper, Bebe, and Flynn. We need to confirm that. I'll ask Camilla."

"This girl, Abella," Tim said. "You believe her?"

I'd asked myself the same question multiple times since sitting down with her. My gut told me she was innocent. But could I trust it? "Right now, at this moment? Yeah, I do."

"Because the girlfriend has every reason to lie. She was in a bed stained with blood. There's blood on her clothes. She could be making the whole thing up: the affair, Flynn's bullying, all of it."

"She could be," I agreed, "but I still can't imagine her rolling over to stab her boyfriend and going back to sleep." Someone else had done that, and I was increasingly sure that someone was still in the house.

"Know what I think? I think Abella knows exactly what happened." Tim interlaced his fingers and clasped the back of his neck in a stretch. "The fight Flynn overheard last night was probably them breaking up, and Jasper didn't feel like sticking around to deal with the fallout in the morning. I know lots of guys who don't have the balls to face an ex. Abella's pissed and embarrassed by the fact that he left, and as for the blood, couldn't it be . . . you know . . . female trouble?"

I gaped at him. "What?"

"Bleeding all over the sheets at an ex-boyfriend's house is even worse than the boyfriend taking off in the middle of the night. The family called it murder, and she didn't want to fess up, so she let it snowball. From where I'm standing—sitting," he amended with a grin, "this seems like a simple misunderstanding that got way out of hand."

I contemplated Tim's straight eyebrows and the evenhanded character I'd come to know. Between the two of us, I was the only one who seemed certain Jasper Sinclair was dead. Tim was considerably more optimistic about the man's fate, even when faced with evidence to the contrary. As he rolled his neck and relaxed his shoulders, it was clear he thought he had it figured out.

It occurred to me I might be the victim of self-sabotage. Could it be that my subconscious was trying to trick me? I have too much history with gruesome homicides to assume everything's flowers and rainbows when I find blood all over the walls, but what I was feeling wasn't just healthy skepticism: it was a bone-deep belief this missing person was dead. There were parallels to the horrors I'd left back in New York. Memories circled me like hungry dogs. The sooner I solved this case, the sooner I could get off the island. I wanted to be there, but I didn't. Thought I could do what needed doing, and doubted myself at every turn. It was a push and pull between my head and my heart. Either way, I lost.

I was willing to consider Tim's theory. Of course I was. But when he winked at me and said, "It's not as complicated as you think, Shane," all I heard was "Listen, sweetie, get a grip. This isn't *Law & Order*."

"What's that supposed to mean?" I said.

His eyes got marginally larger. "Just . . . I know you're used to crazy cases in the city. Around here, the explanation's usually pretty simple."

"A missing person and a ton of blood. You think that's simple?"

"Not *simple*," he said, flushing. "*Simple*'s not the right word. But this *is* a missing persons case."

"That was called in as a murder. Everything I've seen so far leads me to believe that's what we've got. So I'm thinking we should take them back to the station." I said it quick, knowing my resolve wouldn't last. I didn't know if I could trust it, but if my intuition about these people was right, I didn't want to be alone with them on the island for one more minute. "We've got the two boats. You drive one, Norton will take the other."

"Take them all in? In this weather? Shane, come on. It's rough on the water, getting worse all the time. We have to question them here. On the off chance we need to make an arrest, *then* we can—"

"A man is missing without a trace! We've got critical evidence up there that's deteriorating with every passing second!"

"We've got no body," Tim said. "He could still show up—what then? Do you want to be the one to explain why we're clogging up headquarters with eight witnesses to a nonexistent crime?"

"You know as well as I do that murder and a corpse aren't mutually exclusive. We don't need a body. We don't even need the murder weapon, not if we've got a confession or enough circum-stantial evidence. It'll take hours to question everyone, and it's already nearly noon. We'll be here all day. If we stay, we could get stuck."

"Yeah, but not, like, *forever.*" Tim showed me the side of his face and looked at me from the corner of his eye. "You're acting weird. What's this all about?"

Shit. Pull yourself together, Shay. "It seems like a bad idea, us against them."

To my absolute horror, Tim laughed. "There are two of us, and we're both armed. I think we can handle them for a few hours, don't you?"

He looked tickled, like this wasn't a homicide investigation but some sort of weekend team-building retreat. I wondered why he didn't share his theory with me sooner. Was he humoring me all morning? Did my efforts to probe our witnesses amuse him? So much for the two of us being on the same wavelength. "You're a BCI investigator," I said, suddenly furious. "You were trained to solve murders. Why does it feel like you aren't doing your fucking job?"

The smile melted from Tim's face. After a beat he said, "No, that's fair. I should have prepped you better. That's on me. Look, I've been working for the New York State Police in this region for seven years. You want to know how many homicides I've seen during that time?"

I already knew the answer. When I applied for the job, McIntyre dangled the data in front of me like a fishing lure, and I'd bitten greedily. I didn't see the point in playing his game. "I'd rather know how many times you've found a bed soaked with blood and it turned out a woman ran out of pads. Don't you get it?" I said. "We don't have the team we need to do this right. We have to be on the same page, and that page has murder written all over it. This is entirely about protocol," I told him. "I'm not okay with straying from procedure, and you shouldn't be either. It's sloppy, Tim, and sloppy is dangerous. You understand that, right? Please tell me you get that."

Over the few weeks that I'd known him, I'd challenged myself to learn Tim's tells. I was getting pretty good at extracting information from the most neutral of expressions. If Tim doubted what he was hearing, whether from a witness or suspect, his mouth shifted a hairsbreadth to the right. When he was nervous, he swallowed twice in quick succession. If I was ever in doubt, I could always rely on his eyebrows. But as he sat there in that comfy chair, staring up at me, his face was as indecipherable as a book written in a foreign language I was trying to read upside down.

"Sure, Shana. I get that," he said.

I thought about explaining myself. I didn't think about it for long. It was an asshole move, attacking him like that, but I figured Tim and I had years of thoughtless remarks and regrets and makeup sessions ahead of us. He'd stumbled across a trip wire. In time he would learn to sidestep those, just like I would circumvent his.

Silence. His eyebrows were a steady line. "So what now?" he said when he tired of waiting for an apology that wasn't coming.

The question was rote. What came next couldn't be answered with a word or a three-point plan. I was still in the middle of preliminary interviews, and there would be follow-up questions, hours more of exploration as I searched for a crack that would give me a sure foothold on the case. What Tim actually meant was *you're acting crazy, and I don't know you well enough to understand why, so can we please move on?*

"I'd like to check in with McIntyre," I said. She'd have heard about the case by now, and I should have called her sooner, had been putting it off. I knew what McIntyre would say when she found out where I was, and after talking to Carson, I didn't feel like listening to another lecture.

"Yeah, okay," Tim said, faking cheerful. "But first, let's see if Norton's done buttering his toast points and spooning the caviar. I'm starving."

ELEVEN

Tim and I broke bread with the Sinclairs while a grandson, brother, boyfriend was missing, possibly out in a historic storm, dead already or fighting for his life. I couldn't help but think about how, just that morning, I'd sat at the breakfast table with Carson and reached for his pumpkin-spice creamer believing it was the most excitement I'd see all day.

The in-box on my iPhone had been crammed with messages from brands—reminders to update the wedding website Carson built for us, e-mails from Crate & Barrel and Williams-Sonoma warning me their sales were going, going, gone. I scrolled through them while sipping my too-sweet coffee. After I got my scar, getting married wasn't something I thought I'd do. God knows planning a wedding wasn't something I expected to enjoy; the fashion and extravagant frivolity were lost on me, a woman who used dollar-store shampoo and owned exactly three pairs of pants. But Carson kept signing me up for newsletters, hoping I'd come around. He said it would be cathartic, and it was true I'd found some comfort in ticking off a to-do list. My ability to be methodical about unresolved issues means organization comes naturally. Plus, planning the wedding kept my mind off the marriage itself.

It wasn't that I was reluctant to wed this handsome and successful catch, just that everything was moving fast. I'd already pushed back the date once because of the move, so Carson was more eager than ever to "tie the knot and get on with our lives." For him, the big day couldn't come soon enough. As I deleted a message promising to reveal my bridezilla ranking on a scale of one to ten, he brushed my cheek with his hand and asked if I'd thought about inviting Tim to the wedding.

"Hon," I said. He'd brought up the idea twice already. In fairness to Carson, I couldn't stall any longer. "I've thought about it a lot, actually. I know you'd like him there. The thing is, it's awkward."

"Why would you think that?"

"It just *is*." I flipped my hand on the kitchen table and the diamond on my engagement ring, an obscenely large cushion cut I'd drop in a box on the dresser before leaving for work, struck the wood. A spark of pain whizzed up my arm like a shock. "For one thing, we barely know each other."

"All the more reason for him to come."

"For another, we can't invite him and not McIntyre and the rest of the troop."

"Timmy's your partner. It's different."

"BCI investigators don't have partners," I said, though I saw his point. Compared with Tim, the time I'd spent with the other investigators was negligible. "Timmy," I repeated with a half smile. "Did he really let you call him that?"

I thought I'd seen blue eyes before I met Carson, but his were next level. Shards of sky and slate twinkled and flashed at me when he smiled in response. "We used to be best friends, Shay. I helped him blow out the candles at his fifth birthday party. After the summer we learned to water-ski? When he sprained his wrist? I took notes for him in class for a month. I was there when Timmy set fire to a porta potty at a construction site in town and landed himself in jail." Carson scratched his salt-and-pepper goatee and laughed. "I thought his dad was going to lose his mind."

"When I told you we were going to be working together, you said you hadn't talked in years. All that stuff you just described happened a long time ago. Be honest," I said. "Do you have anything in common now other than being from the same town?"

"Sure we do," Carson said. "We have you." He tilted his head and studied me. "Okay, so we're not exactly besties. But let's look at this another way. You've got some random grandma on the guest list who you met in a kung fu class you stopped taking six months ago."

"Karate," I said, "and Sueanne's in her fifties. She doesn't have grandkids yet."

"I stand corrected. Tim's local, and we both know him. Inviting him makes sense. So what's this really about?"

Carson was always analyzing, always two steps ahead. Watching him think reminded me of riding the subway. To pass the time and hone my investigative skills, I used to observe the other commuters and try to read their body language, their minds. I'll never know if I was right, but it was a fun challenge. With Carson, there was no point even trying. When he looked at me, my fiancé could have been devising a new name for my condition, considering disclosing his darkest secret, deciding whether to have a second bagel, or all of the above. That fascinated me, and it never got old.

"Work is work. This is personal," I said. "I don't feel comfortable blurring the lines."

"How long has it been?" he asked.

"Thirteen months." As if I needed reminding.

"Thirteen months since it happened." He used his thumb to remove a smear of cream cheese from his plate. Carson had mild OCD, which I thought was ironic given his profession— or maybe it made perfect sense. He couldn't stand it when things were a mess. "Thirteen months since I found you, and every day I worry— every single day. And now, at last, you're going to be my wife." He glanced at my hand, at the ring, and paused. "It's my job to protect you. It's why you hired me." He waited for me to laugh, but the joke was old and inaccurate. I never hired Carson; he was assigned to me. "I love you, you know that," he said. "So sue me if I want to make damn sure the guy I used to cut school with, and who now spends ten hours a day by your side, isn't another deranged piece of shit."

My vision blurred and the room turned white. We had a rule: Don't talk about Bram. We'd long since picked apart what happened between me and him. I'd rehashed my time in that cellar until my throat was raw. The day Carson finally suggested we shift the conversation from Bram to me in an effort to help me heal, I was ecstatic. And here he was comparing my colleague to the man who stabbed those women. *Becca. Lanie. Jess.*

I took a breath and willed my palpitations to diminish. *Carson's worried about me. That's all.* For a second I considered telling him he didn't need to be, because I didn't expect to be with Tim for long. I was sure McIntyre would still change her mind and drop me. When we first got to A-Bay I didn't unpack my clothes for weeks; why bother, when I wouldn't be staying? If I blew my chances at the only detective gig around, we'd have to relocate, no question. My apathy toward living out of boxes had driven Carson crazy. He wanted me settled in his hometown. The whole point was to leave New York—and what happened there—behind. Carson would feel better knowing I'd be his again, all his, very soon.

I could have put his mind at ease, but I didn't. I decided against it, because what if—*what if*—I was wrong? What if I was a better investigator now than ever? What if Carson was mistaken about my going back to work?

What if I was healed?

We stared at each other across the table. Sometimes, when I got tired of revisiting the worst experience of my life and projected my frustration onto him, I told myself his eyes were too close together. The color made up for that. They were the clear, cool pool I always found relief in when I needed to loosen my muscles and mind.

Carson slid back his chair far enough for me to see his socks. He'd picked Bob Ross today, the painter's face and iconic puffy hair encircled by the words *Happy Clouds*. The socks made me smile. "You're gonna be late," Carson said. "We'll talk about it over dinner. Let's just do takeout. I'll pick up some Thai food."

"Not Thai," I said. "Anything but that."

"Fish, then," he said as he kissed the crown of my head and strode off to the bathroom down the hall. The place where his lips met my scalp felt as bright and hot as a flame.

108

Lunch on Tern Island was more refined than my breakfast with Carson by a mile, but there was just as much tension in the air, and just as much unrest. Aside from Camilla, who was still trying her best to be a perfect hostess, everyone stared unsmiling at their plates.

Tim and I planned to eat in shifts—one of us would supervise the Sinclairs while the other wolfed down only the most filling components of Norton's meal. Camilla had other ideas. She insisted we all sit together in the dining room while the rain streamed down the windowpanes. Naturally, she took the head of the table. Flynn sat at the opposite end. Tim and I were elbow to elbow with our fellow interlopers, Abella and Ned, but Tim did most of the talking, beaming at the others while praising the food. One thing about Tim is he doesn't like awkward silence. If there's a chance to talk, he's going to take it.

As for me, I tried to be invisible. It was my first opportunity to study our witnesses' faces without looking like a creep, and I intended to make the most of it. Maybe it was because I had Carson on the brain, but I found my eyes lingering on Miles. Looks-wise he reminded me of my fiancé—cool glasses, dark hair with a smattering of gray. If I saw Miles Byrd on the streets of New York, I'd definitely turn my head his way. As I ate, he looked up from his soup and met my gaze with a shy smile.

What was this guy's relationship with his brother-in-law? Men as good-looking as Miles and Jasper often stuck together. From my place on the periphery I've observed that beautiful people travel in packs. Then again, Jasper was an eligible bachelor while Miles was married, a man in his forties with a daughter to think of. He didn't appear to be devastated by the day's events. He didn't look afraid that a dangerous criminal might be lurking on the island either.

Next to Miles, Flynn reminded me of a circus bear. He ate noisily and didn't bother to wipe the soup from his mustache, but his facial hair and clothing were lavish enough that I suspected he, like Ned, enjoyed standing out. When Flynn and I made eye contact, he radiated anger. I noticed he wasn't trying to hide the bruises on his hand anymore. Nobody else at the table gave his swollen knuckles a second glance.

I set down my spoon to wipe my own mouth, and was surprised to see it quiver in the bowl. Glancing to my left, I saw Abella's eyebrows knotted in concentration as she tried to lift a spoonful of broth to her lips. On the other side of her, Ned whispered something in her ear and took her hand under the table.

If Abella had lied to me, she was a convincing actress. While her boyfriend's family slurped chicken, fennel, and farro soup all around her, the girl's knees shook so violently I thought she might fall off her chair.

TWELVE

There was no question as to what Tim and I would do when Norton cleared the table. Tim immediately escorted the family back to the parlor, where he would tackle the dual challenge of distracting an increasingly impatient lot and counting the stylized flowers on the Persian rug. Buoyed by a full belly—the Sinclairs' caretaker was an excellent cook—I retraced Abella's footsteps to the kitchen, out the mudroom door, and across the yard.

The October air was raw and cold and the rain pummeled me from all sides. If I didn't have a slicker of my own, I'd have been soaked through in seconds. High above me the treetops thrashed like barbed whips and I heard the telltale crack of a splitting branch. I picked up the pace, careful on the dicey rocks, and hoped a falling tree wasn't about to cleave me in half.

As I trudged through the muck with boots squelching and mud

splattering the backs of my knees, I thought about Jasper. I imagined him beyond the island's stone wall, bleeding and battered by ice-cold waves. I saw him lying pale and still among tall trees as rain pooled in his unseeing eyes. In my mind, Jasper was no longer breathing. Thinking of him like that kept me going. No way would I get lazy or careless if I invited that image to haunt me today.

My destination was the shed, but as soon as I got far enough from the house to see all three stories, I pivoted and planted my feet. Counting windows, I figured out which ones were Jasper's. I hadn't been wrong about his little Juliet balcony. Not only was there no staircase, ladder, or tree nearby, but the first-floor roof wasn't close enough to give someone a leg up either. Whatever his condition when he left his bedroom, Jasper did it through a door.

I walked on, around the perimeter of the house over squishy moss and blue rocks that stuck up like fangs. There were no other access points to the second floor, no signs of forced entry to the cellar door, which was almost invisible, flush with the ground.

Back where I started, I returned my attention to the shed. Earlier, when I'd gone looking for Jasper, I'd taken a peek inside. The building looked just the same now. Strapped to its exterior wall on the west side was a thirty-two-foot aluminum ladder, but it looked as if it hadn't been touched in years. I pushed up the latch, and the door to the small building swung open without a sound.

The inside of the shed was as Abella described it, sawhorse and all. Rakes and hoes and coils of rope hung from hooks on the walls. She'd been right about the woodpile, too. Firewood was stacked floor to ceiling in the corner and there was a general odor of sawdust and wet bark. Crouching, I examined the floor and found a cluster of footprints in the dust. They could have belonged to Norton, Bebe, Ned, Jasper, or anyone.

I shrugged deeper into my coat and dialed McIntyre's number. It wasn't much warmer in the shed than outside, but it was dry, and private. Given the conversation I was about to get roped into, I needed that.

When I accepted this job, it was partly because of Maureen McIntyre. A twenty-eight-year veteran of the state police, a former senior investigator with the BCI in Alexandria Bay, the first-ever elected female sheriff in the history of New York State . . . the woman was a legend. I'd met her once before, years earlier. Shortly after she was first elected, she visited NYPD headquarters and the chief of the Community Affairs Bureau gave her a tour. I made sure to be there that day. A lot of female officers did. It wasn't long ago McIntyre was one of just ten women in her State Police Academy class. We ladies like to support our own.

McIntyre's law enforcement career was impressive on every level, but what she was doing now to clean up Jefferson County was more remarkable still. Watertown, where she was stationed, was embroiled in controversy—four former town officials had just been indicted on charges of misconduct and corruption. Half the town was convinced the accusations against the longtime officials were false, while the others felt so betrayed they wanted them convicted on the spot. McIntyre had her hands full. Couple that with weeks of flooding that led to multiple drownings, damage to public facilities and roads, and countless other hazards, and I wasn't surprised it took her a few rings to answer my call.

"Tough morning?" I asked, checking my watch. With a start I realized it was coming up on 3:00 p.m.

"Neither snow nor rain nor a goddamn nor'easter," McIntyre said. "How's by you? Your first big case on the river and it sounds like a doozy. Everything going okay?"

I'd hoped against all hope there would be no trepidation in her tone, and to my relief she sounded as collected as ever. "Still no sign of our missing person," I said. "The interviews are taking some time. Seems like some of our witnesses have reason to want Jasper Sinclair gone."

"Huh."

"Yeah. We'll figure it out, though."

"I don't doubt you will. Gotta say, this is an unusual situation for us."

"So I've heard."

"You should try to get this thing resolved fast."

"Thank you," I said, "for acknowledging this is a serious case and not a goddamn game of Clue. Don't worry, Mac, I'm all over it."

"Because it can't be good for you to be out there. Fact, it might be pretty bad."

Ugh. In all of Jefferson County, McIntyre was the only person besides Carson who knew what happened in New York. It isn't like I could hide the details from her. They were all right there in my file. No matter how much physical distance I put between myself and the city, no matter how much time has passed since those days that changed my life, I'll never be able to keep it entirely to myself.

A few weeks ago, I stumbled onto my story—funny to call it a story, as if it's something comforting to share at bedtime—online. A lawyer working on behalf of my former department got the press to omit my name from all public reports, but even seeing the words *undisclosed female officer* felt like an invasion. When I mentioned the old article to Carson, he made me read it to him out loud, as if I were a kid and he were the teacher checking I got the intonation right. He said I had to own it, which I thought was odd advice considering we just ran away.

Unless someone knew what to look for, they couldn't easily connect me with the case. I don't know why I chose to tell McIntyre the extra bits that weren't in my file, or even in news stories like that one. That was stuff no one could get anywhere else, the behind-the-scenes footage hardest of all to share. I guess I felt a kinship with her. Maureen McIntyre's a sheriff, but I had also come to consider her a friend.

Shivering in that shed, I wondered if I shouldn't have been so quick to open up. "It's not a problem," I said firmly, my ears uncomfortably hot. "This isn't the same thing. Not even close."

"I know it's not. But it is a missing persons case, and it's your first since you started working again. I heard there's blood on the scene. Cause of injury?"

"We think he was stabbed." *At least I do.*

"Stabbed." Coming from her, the word oozed meaning. "With the troopers held up and this weather"—as if on cue, a sheet of rain assaulted the shed window—"the reality is you're going to be there on your own for a while. So I'm wondering if it might make sense to have a private chat with Tim."

If it was me, well . . . I would tell him. That's what McIntyre meant, and it disappointed me. After I opened up and asked her to keep my truth to herself, she'd made this same recommendation. She respected my decision, meaning she hadn't gone to Tim herself, but she didn't agree with it—and so I hadn't hurried to unpack my boxes in A-Bay. My abilities . . . those McIntyre trusted. It was my judgment she questioned. And in my line of work, judgment counts for a lot.

It's not that I didn't understand where she was coming from. Tim was the closest thing to a partner I had out here. In order to work together effectively, we needed to be in sync. Offset each other's weaknesses and play off each other's strengths. Many days after I started coming to the station and sitting at the desk next to Tim's, I visualized what it would be like to bring him some sludgy, too-hot office coffee and ask for a few minutes of his time. In my mind, the scenario always ended with him giving me a sorry look that mutated into bottomless concern. If by some miracle he heard my story and didn't immediately start questioning my mental state, he would surely see me as a charity case. Assume I was hired because of some obscure office policy that required damaged officers be given a chance to prove they're healed. I'd always be broken to Tim.

As an experiment, I reversed the situation in my head. What would I do if my new colleague and informal adviser recounted a story like mine right after we met? The fact is, I wouldn't trust him. And I deserve to be trusted, don't I? There's more to me than those dark days spent in the East Village, clawing at a cellar door until my fingernails bled. Screaming under the city in the land of rats and rust, and carving objects out of the kind of dark so full and rich it has texture. What happened with Bram doesn't define me. It was Carson who taught me that, though I can't say I was a quick study.

Telling Mac and telling Tim were two very different things.

Tim wasn't a self-imposed mentor like McIntyre, but a peer I'd have to see every day. He was someone Carson knew—hell, Carson wanted him at our wedding. If I allowed that to happen, Tim would meet my parents and see the everlasting shame and sadness in their eyes. There was no way he'd understand.

"This is entirely your call," McIntyre said. "I'm just saying you should give him a chance. Tim's a good man, Shay."

"I know he is." In the three months I'd known him, Tim hadn't done a thing to suggest he lacked empathy. About everything else, in every situation, he'd been sympathetic but strong, compassionate without being feeble. That was part of the problem. I liked the guy. Tim's opinion of me mattered.

"If you need help out there, he can give it to you."

"Speaking of help," I said, anxious to change the subject, "have you got a few minutes to do some recon work on our witnesses?"

McIntyre missed her detective days, and I knew she'd love to pitch in. With a smile in her voice she said, "What do you need to know?"

I gave her every name I had and asked her to poke around for anything peculiar. Assault charges, divorces, bankruptcies.

"I'll text you when I've got something, see if you're free," she said.

I thanked her and quickly hung up. The walls of the shed were quaking. Through the back window I could see the river raging like an open ocean. If Jasper was unlucky enough to end up down there, then down there he would stay.

Tell Tim. I pressed my hands over my eyes. Where would I even begin? There was no way I could tell him, not now. Maybe not ever.

My conversation with McIntyre still fresh in my mind, I flipped open my notebook and started to map out the case. Back at the Ninth Precinct, I'd have an interactive whiteboard or touch screen to help me picture the connections I'd made. All I'd get in A-Bay was a communal bulletin board.

Out on the island, pen and paper would have to do.

There were links all over the place. Our witnesses all had ties to Jasper and to each other. They interacted in the city, on the island, at work. By the time I was done with my preliminary visualization, the notebook page was filled with scribbles and lines and I was staring at what looked like a distorted family tree.

When I stepped back outside I could swear my nose hairs frosted up. The house loomed tall before me as I struggled against the force of the wind. The rain was relentless, painful on my exposed skin. I was dying for a hot coffee and desperately needed to pee, and I wasn't sure how to go about resolving either issue. Being at the Sinclairs was like visiting a great-aunt's house when you're a kid. You tiptoe around without touching anything, and deep down you just want to go home.

My gaze returned to the second-floor windows. Flynn and Ned's bedroom was on the other side of the house, and Camilla's was upstairs. Norton's sleeping quarters were on the main floor, so the rooms on either side of Jasper's must belong to Bebe and Miles, and Jade. In one of the windows a curtain twitched and a pale flash caught my eye. I squinted up at it. *What on earth?* Jade was in her bedroom, and damned if she wasn't smoking a cigarette. Behind the pane she took a drag, looked down at me, and smiled.

I watched the teenager, and she watched me. Jade hadn't factored into my investigation yet, but this wine-guzzling, cigarette-smoking child would need to be vetted just like everyone else. After a minute she broke eye contact. She'd grown bored with me, I guess. Funny how she didn't seem bothered by my presence on the island, let alone the fact that she woke up this morning to find her fun-loving uncle was gone.

Jade disappeared behind the curtain, but I stayed put. What was it Tim said earlier? Jade spent a lot of time brooding in her room.

And from that room, she had a perfect view of the shed.

THIRTEEN

I was the kind of wet that wraps you in gooseflesh and blast-freezes your bones. Dripping all over the mudroom floor, I did my best to clean off my boots and shivered out of my jacket. Then I crouched down on the tiles.

I'd noticed something about the Sinclairs. Aside from Abella, who was in stocking feet today, they all wore house shoes. Apparently, going shoeless in the house was gauche—and based on Camilla's reaction to Abella's dirty footprints in Abella's story, so was wearing street shoes. It explained why Flynn was in summer shoes in October, and the disapproving looks Tim and I got when we sullied the family's floors with our boots. Personally I'm a fan of thick socks indoors, but the Sinclairs' custom was fine by me. It gave me a chance to examine the discarded shoes lined up along the mudroom wall.

One by one, I turned each shoe over to inspect the sole. I was looking for one thing in particular: dried mud. The rain started late afternoon on the previous day, and everyone in the family had arrived at the house by then. The shoes were a way to corroborate Abella's story and find out who else was wandering around in the storm on the night Jasper disappeared.

It was easy enough to match the shoes to their owners. Jade's sneakers were the smallest, while Flynn's, an expensive designer brand, were huge. The wing tips had to belong to Miles the lawyer. Ned's loafers were as long and lean as he was, and Camilla wore pretty boat shoes, sensibly flat. Bebe's were Italian, also designer. The filthy rubber boots could only belong to Norton. That left Abella's kitten-heel booties and the shoes that, somehow, Jasper left behind.

Between Norton's walk down to the boathouse to greet us and his trips outside to restock the parlor basket with firewood, he had an excuse for the wet mud that caked the bottoms of his boots. The state of the other shoes was what concerned me. Aside from Camilla's and Jade's, all showed traces of mud and yellow, tender bits of leaves. Bebe's and Ned's included a dash of sawdust; they'd been in the shed, no question. Miles's were especially messy, but that could be because he'd searched the grounds with Norton that morning. Strangely, Jasper's shoes were also tainted with dried mud. That meant five of the guests, plus Jasper himself, spent time outside between the previous afternoon when it started to rain and our arrival that morning on Tern Island.

My pants felt like spandex against my legs as the wet fabric pulled tight over my thighs. Leaving the shoes the way I found them, I rose to standing and stepped into the kitchen. At the apartment, I always keep a pot of coffee on the counter. I can't say it's always fresh and hot, but that's not the point. It's strong, and ready when I needed it. There was no coffee in the Sinclairs' kitchen, at least none that I could see. Norton probably hid the machine away in a custom cabinet, cleaned and prepped for morning. The kitchen was completely deserted. But something wasn't right. I sensed movement. A whisper, slow and steady, source unknown.

The baby-fine hairs on my neck lifted as my eyes darted around the room. What was that sound? More important, why did every muscle in my body strain back toward the door from which I'd come?

The realization hit me all at once. Across the room, a burner on the gas range flickered blue. The flame licked the underside of a small pot. I ventured closer, images of boiled bunnies racing through my mind. Bracing myself, I looked inside. It was water, nothing more. Nearly all of it had evaporated and the cup or so that was left sizzled softly, trying to disappear.

"Um, can I *help* you?"

I'd already turned off the burner and was holding the hot pot by its handle when Jade swept into the room. I could have left the water where it was, but the disembodied quality it brought to the kitchen unsettled me. I wanted it gone. I was already jittery, and Jade's voice made me jump. "Give it," she said, and made a grab for the handle, upending the scalding water onto my hand.

I yelped and clutched my hand to my chest as the empty pot clattered across the floor. The pain was exquisite; every cell in my body shrieked. I ground my teeth so hard I thought I might crush the enamel into dust. A world away Jade was babbling excuses. I tuned them out and chanced a glance at my hand.

I was of sound mind when I entered that kitchen. Thinking about Bram in the shed hadn't impaired my judgment. I'm not saying there haven't been times when it did. A string of words spoken just the right way or the clang of old pipes can take me back. But in spite of what Carson thinks, the memories don't rattle me. If anything, they make me more vigilant. They remind me people can turn on you faster than an eyeblink, and that the smart ones will make sure you never see them coming.

I was of sound mind, yes. But when I looked at my palm, pink as a boiled Easter ham, it wasn't a burn I saw, but blood. Blood, slick and glossy, gluey and thick. Blood between my fingers and coating my nails. It was like those thirteen months and the distance they put between me and Bram never happened. The walls pressed in around my body, and I found myself thinking, *Please don't let this blood be his. Oh God, I'm too late.*

Fear, dazzling in its intensity, coursed through me. The flashback was so convincing I wanted to cry. My chest exploded with pain and I realized I'd been holding my breath. I closed my eyes, and when I opened them again, the imagined blood on my hand was gone.

It was a second-degree burn, real bad. Soon it would puff up, then blister, then leak, a full-course dinner of pain. Studying the injury triggered a sinking feeling in my gut. It was my right hand. The hand I needed to fire my gun.

"What the hell." It was the best I could come up with. I was incensed. I couldn't prove it, but I was sure Jade burned me on purpose. This was no accident.

That's ridiculous, I told myself, *she's just a kid.*

As quickly as the paranoid thoughts arrived, logic drove them from my mind. *The memories don't rattle me. They only make me stronger. Believe it, Shay.*

"What are you even doing in here?" Jade said.

"*Me?*" The girl's oblivion left me slack-jawed with awe. "What about *you?*"

"*I* was making tea."

"You're supposed to stay in the parlor."

"I don't need a fucking babysitter." She ogled my hand with repugnance. "But maybe you do."

At fourteen, she was nearly as tall as me, so when we glared at each other we were eye to eye. I turned and strode off toward the sink. Cold water from the faucet slapped my raw skin and I sucked in air through my teeth. "I saw you. In your room."

"So? I needed a break. Everyone's so fucking serious in there, it's exhausting. Anyway, the other detective said I could go."

I didn't believe her. If she'd voiced a desire for tea, Norton would have made it for her. Tim had corralled everyone and monitored them all day. He wouldn't invite Jade to wander off now.

"Go get your dad. Right now," I said. *I need a witness so I don't wring your neck.* "Tell him I have some questions for you both."

Jade leveled her gaze. The corner of her mouth twitched. "I know what she did."

I was still occupied with my hand, opening whisper-smooth cabinet drawers in search of a first-aid kit, so her statement caught me off guard. My blood got viscous in my veins, damned up. Which *she* was Jade talking about? Abella? Bebe? Camilla? Or someone else?

"What who did, Jade?" I stepped in closer. "If you know what happened to Jasper, you need to tell me."

She was outfitted with those trendy invisible braces, though her mouth didn't appear to need fixing. When she smiled, the teeth she flashed between candy-gloss lips were perfection. Teenage girls aren't supposed to have Jade's confidence and polish. This kid was growing up too fast. If Jade no longer considered herself a child, that could elicit a whole world of trouble. I'd seen it happen before, and I feared Jade was on her way down the same path.

"Who's *she*?" I repeated. "What did *she* do?"

Jade batted her lashes. "I honestly have no idea?"

There were a dozen things I could have said, a dozen ways to make her talk. But just then, from somewhere on Jade's body, came the unmistakable chime of a mobile device.

"That you?" I asked, cocking my head. "Nah. How could it be, when Wellington told you to turn off your phone?"

Jade blanched. "I—"

"Did you contact anyone with that device after we got here? And don't bother lying," I said, "because I'm about to check for myself."

Her expression darkened. "It's notifications. I didn't talk to anyone."

"Friends from school? Classmates?"

"I said no, okay?"

I wasn't buying her story—what kind of teenage girl doesn't reach out to her friends when her life's turned upside down? Jade was hiding something.

"Unlock the phone and hand it over."

"What? No way."

Her cryptic words—*I know what she did*—were gaining mass in my mind, elbowing everything out of their way. "Failure to comply with a criminal investigation is obstruction of justice," I said, because I was suddenly sure her device was the key to figuring this family out. "Remove it from your pocket and unlock it. Now."

For a few seconds she didn't budge. Then she lifted her T-shirt high enough for me to see her flat, white stomach and slid the phone from between her waistband and the sharp bone of her hip.

I stuck out my good hand and said, "Give it to me." I had no right to seize her phone as evidence, no proof it contained anything that was pertinent to the investigation. All I had was a feeling and a profound yearning to teach the kid a lesson. At the time, it felt like enough.

Jade pressed her thumb against the home button to unlock it, but her hands were too sweaty. I watched her type in her passcode. Even then, the phone stayed in her grip.

You know that game kids play where they pass a hand over their face and change their expression—happy, sad, angry—like the hand controls their mood? That was Jade, except her mood swings were real. "Fuck you," she said as she wagged the unlocked phone in my face.

"It doesn't matter if it's text messages or goddamn emojis, you're withholding critical evidence related to Jasper's disappearance. That's a misdemeanor, Jade, punishable by up to a year in jail." I was improvising. I was desperate. "I'm not kidding about this, not even a little."

Jade went inert. Then, just as quickly, her expression changed again. I should have seen it coming, but I didn't. "God, *relax*. Here, it's yours," she said—and it was. The palm of my left hand was open, waiting. But when Jade finally thrust the phone at me, she went for my right. The girl aimed straight for the burn. Smacked the device against my boiled hand with so much force that I cried out in pain.

"You little . . ." I gasped. The pain was dazzling.

Another flawless smile. "You asked for it."

"What the hell is going on in here?"

Bebe stood in the kitchen doorway, her jaunty hairstyle at odds with her downturned mouth. "Jade? I thought you were using the bathroom. What are you doing with *her*?"

"You were all asked to stay with Wellington," I said, trying to pull myself together. "But since you're here, you should know Jade intentionally evaded his request and concealed a device that could be integral to our investigation." *You want to play, Jade? Let's play.*

"Jade's a fourteen-year-old child," Bebe said. "You can't take anything she says seriously."

"It was a flat-out lie. Deliberate disobedience."

"Jasper's missing. Jade's very upset."

"She has my phone, Bebe," Jade said suddenly. "Make her give it back."

"As I said," I repeated, "I have reason to believe this device—"

"Wait a minute, were you *questioning* her?" Bebe's nostrils flared. "You can't do that, she's underage! You can't question a minor without an adult or guardian. Everyone knows that."

Witnesses don't usually refuse to be questioned unless they have something to hide. I wondered what Bebe didn't want Jade to reveal. "All right," I said. Not *I haven't arrested her, so I can question her all I like*, not *she's the one who came to me*. Just *all right*. I needed Miles and Bebe to give me access to the kid so I could find out what she knew. If Jade shut down at their behest, nothing I said would open her up again. "Let's talk, then. All of us."

"I don't think so," Bebe said. "You should know that when this is over and done I'll be issuing a formal complaint."

Over and done. Like her brother's disappearance and the blood-soaked sheets he left behind were a minor inconvenience that would soon be sorted, laughed about for years to come.

Without another word Bebe grabbed the girl's arm and hauled her from the room. Before they were out of sight Jade looked over her shoulder at me and sneered.

This time I smiled back.

Jade's phone was still in my hand.

FOURTEEN

M y God," said Camilla Sinclair. "You're a mess."

Word for word it was the same thing Norton told me minutes earlier in the kitchen, when Bebe and Jade left and he found me wet and injured staring down at the phone in my hand. I'd long since forgotten the discomfort of clothing that slurped when I moved. I had full access to Jade's phone. Without knowing how quickly it would auto-lock again, though—my own phone was set for the standard five minutes—I didn't have much time to nose through it before it would be rendered inaccessible. I needed to be alone. And now here was Norton.

Deep creases formed on his forehead as I told him what happened, and he apologized for my burn so profusely you'd think he caused it himself. Grabbing some ointment and gauze from a cupboard, he insisted on bandaging my hand. He was efficient, and soon the burn was wrapped tight. I waited for him to be on his way. Instead, he ushered me out of the kitchen and down the hall to face his boss.

"Detective Wellington," Camilla said, turning to Tim, "will you permit me to find your associate some dry clothes?" She lifted her chin, and for a second the pleats of skin on her neck were as taut and smooth as Bebe's. The firelight gave Camilla some much-needed color, but all in all she looked worse than when I saw her last. "We're about the same size, she and I. She can accompany me upstairs, if you like."

A lot of women Camilla's age talk to men as if they assume the guys are in charge. I guess that's because in their day the guys usually were. I'd introduced myself to Camilla as a senior investigator, head of my unit, but she didn't think to ask how I felt about her plan even though it involved me stripping down in a stranger's bedroom in the middle of a case.

But Camilla was also a matriarch accustomed to taking charge, a woman who compelled people to obey. She was adamant that I go upstairs with her, so much so that Tim didn't object. He tried not to stare at the gauze on my hand. Tim knew better than to ask what happened in front of our witnesses.

"That's very thoughtful of you," I told her, "but I'm fine." *Five minutes, if that.* My window of opportunity with Jade's phone was closing.

Camilla sighed, gripped her cane, and stood up.

Out of everyone in the room, only Norton came to her aid. The lines on his forehead deepened as he rushed to her. I noticed Abella studying the two of them with an inquisitive expression, but I was so focused on the phone I didn't give it a thought. "I can get her something from your closet," Norton offered, towering over the old woman.

"Helping a lady choose an outfit is my department, and I could use something to take my mind off of this . . . situation," said Camilla. "Thank you, Philip, but I'm fine." It was decided. Defeated, Norton helped her to her feet.

How long had it been? Two minutes? Three? In my pocket the phone felt like a bomb about to blow. Jade, Bebe, Flynn—all were watching. Camilla moved toward the door, her progress excruciatingly slow. What could I do? I followed.

On the staircase, she took caution with each step. At her age it was a miracle she could maneuver those stairs at all. I could hear her panting lightly as I walked behind her, close enough to deter her from pausing to rest. Her neat white bob, smooth as plastic, seemed frozen in space and time, and I realized for the first time that Camilla wore a wig.

On the third floor of the house, Camilla Sinclair's massive bedroom smelled of some essential oil that made my nose itch. I hadn't paid much attention to the decor during my search, but now I was struck by the sparseness of it. Every object, and its placement, was deliberate. It could have been a period room in a museum. Camilla would have had issues with my own grandmother's disorderly, overly knickknacked house.

"I don't suppose you'll want something too casual." She eased open the closet doors to reveal hundreds of options and tapped a finger against her thin lips. "Let's see. What shall we choose?"

For the love of God, hurry up. "Honestly, anything is fine."

Camilla selected her blandest ensemble, a white dress shirt and beige pants. "Go ahead, dear," she said, crossing the room to sit down on the bed. She twisted a quarter turn away from me and folded her hands in her lap. "I'll wait."

It was the best chance I was likely to get. In the woman's bedroom, just a few feet from where she sat, I quietly pulled out Jade's phone. Holding my breath, I clicked the home button. No passcode screen. It hadn't locked. I navigated to the phone's settings, switched the auto-lock from five minutes to never, and sighed with relief. Five minutes. I must have had mere seconds to spare.

Placing Jade's phone on the floor along with my notebook, belt, cuffs, flashlight, and gun, I struggled out of my wet clothes. I'd bought myself some time, and Bebe couldn't be bothered to help Jade reclaim her device, but how long would it be before Jade told her dad I took it? I had no right to hold that phone. When Jade found that out it would be gone. I'd have to sneak away again before that happened.

"I have a confession," Camilla said.

My head snapped up. "You do?"

"Yes. I have my own reasons for bringing you up here. I'd like you to tell me what you found out about Jasper's disappearance. In private."

"Oh." *Crap.* "Well, Wellington and I are still—"

"Please. Don't toe the line and tell me you can't reveal what you've learned. My grandson was attacked. He's been missing for hours. The time for decorum is done."

"I'm not being evasive," I said. "I need to speak with everyone in the house before I can draw any conclusions." My wet clothes made a slapping sound when they hit the floor. "I will say, Mrs. Sinclair, that everyone I've interviewed so far has a different theory. I'd love to know yours."

The curled-under ends of Camilla's wig shivered as she breathed. "There was a man here yesterday. A trapper Philip hired. He thinks we have a problem with mink."

I pulled on the pants, listening closely. "Norton—Philip—mentioned that. Do you think that man has something to do with this?"

"Philip's convinced he does. I trust his judgment. I wish my family did as well."

"You seem to think highly of him. Philip, I mean."

"Oh, absolutely. Philip is a dear friend, I don't know where I'd be without him." She thought for a moment and shook her head. "But if he's right and Jasper was kidnapped, shouldn't there be a ransom note demanding money?"

"You'd think so, but it's early. Could be a demand's still coming." I tried to sound convincing. Some years ago, I came across a public survey that showed four in ten Americans would murder someone for money. Forty fucking percent. Still, it was a struggle for me to resist offering my condolences on her grandson's death. This didn't feel like a ransom situation. "It's true that where there's money, there's usually someone who wants to take it."

Camilla sniffed. "They're a little late."

I fumbled with the buttons on my newly acquired dress shirt. Let my gaze travel over the sumptuous room. "I'm not sure I understand, ma'am."

"I suppose it will come out eventually," Camilla said, lifting her chin. "The business isn't doing well. Not well at all."

"Sinclair Fabrics? Is this a recent development?"

"I believe things started to go downhill two years ago."

"When Flynn and Bebe took over?"

"When Baldwin and Rachel passed. It isn't entirely Flynn and Bebe's fault. The American textile market isn't what it used to be," Camilla said, though she didn't sound entirely convinced.

My mind went back to the boathouse and *Loophole*, the conspicuously missing yacht. I hated to do it, but I had to ask. "Exactly how are your finances looking?"

She'd been expecting this question. "I have a little money set aside. And I still have my island."

The way she said it, the multimillion-dollar estate might have been a crisp fifty pulled from a birthday card. "When your son and daughter-in-law passed away, what happened to their fortune?"

"It went to the children, of course."

"Flynn, Bebe, and Jasper. So Jasper has some savings?"

"Oh, most certainly," Camilla said. "He's very careful about his finances. He'll be absolutely fine."

Of course he will, I thought. *To you, Jasper's perfect in every way.* "Has he ever had to borrow money from anyone? An acquaintance, maybe?"

"Not Jasper. Jasper's very responsible."

"What about loaning money to someone else?"

"Not that I know of, no."

"Earlier," I said, "what did you mean when you said he deserves better?"

If Abella was sincere, I could guess Camilla's answer. Jasper had a brute for a brother and his sister was a heartless shrew. Still, the noise of the storm dropped away as I waited for the woman's response. "It hasn't been easy for Jasper, growing up with Bebe and Flynn. The age difference has always been a problem. They side against him. Poor Jasper is never included. Oh, he doesn't let that stop him from doing what he wants—he's a very determined person—but it often leads to jealousy."

"Sounds like a lot of siblings I know."

"It doesn't help that he's so accomplished," she said. "Things come more easily to Jasper than the others, in everything. It puts a strain on their relationship, those three, especially now that they work together."

"That's fairly new, isn't it? Jasper joining the business?"

"He came on to help them last year."

I returned the phone and my things to my pockets and holstered my gun. Between the burn and the bulky gauze it wasn't a painless task. "How's that going?" I asked.

She hesitated. "It's been a challenge. He has a lot of cleaning up to do. I'm as eager to see the business bounce back as anyone, but it isn't Jasper's duty to make things right when he had nothing to do with them going wrong." Again Camilla paused thoughtfully. "Do you know how old I am? On my next birthday, I'll be ninety-two. I've had a fair amount of life, wouldn't you say?"

"We should all be so lucky."

Her laugh was dark. "It isn't luck that got me here. I worked hard for what I have, and I expect the same exertion from my family. But I've learned there's more to life than padding your bank account. Money comes and money goes. Jasper knows that. It's why I'm so happy to see him with Abella. She's lovely, don't you think?"

"I'm sure she is."

"Let me tell you something I told Jasper," she said. "Whatever happens in this life, you have to put your own needs first. There may come a day when you wake up and discover you've been pressed into a mold. You're stuck."

"Stuck how?"

"Stuck is stuck. And when something is stuck, Detective Merchant, what do you do? You apply force. Forge a path to your own destiny." She gave a small shrug. "It's really the only way."

I had a million more questions for this woman with her sphinx-like riddles, but before I could ask them, Camilla turned. "All set? Ah. That looks like a fit to me."

The fabric was uncomfortably tight over my hips, the pants several inches too short. On me, Camilla's button-down shirt insisted on playing a game of peek-a-boob. "They're perfect, thanks," I said. "When you say you need to apply force—"

"You should get back downstairs. Would you mind," she asked feebly, "if I stayed? I think I should lie down for a while. It's been a day."

I didn't point out there was much more day to come. The woman looked worn to the bone. The idea of leaving her didn't sit right, but neither did herding her back down those stairs. After Bram, Carson helped me learn to manage my emotions, but I've always worried I might be too ruthless and uncaring now. To do my job well I *needed* to feel. So I disregarded the voice in my head and reminded myself this was an elderly woman under a lot of stress.

"Of course. Stay," I said.

"Thank you." Camilla nodded at the wet clothes under my arm. "Give those to Philip. He'll take care of them. Anything you need, just ask Philip."

At the door, I looked back to see Camilla Sinclair sitting where I'd left her, staring at nothing at all.

FIFTEEN

When I finally got a chance to look at Jade's phone again, this time in the privacy of the empty library, I was surprised by what I found. While Tim and I were getting to know her family, Jade had been getting to know us. A series of open browser windows showed she'd googled our names and the location of the A-Bay police station. She'd even pulled up contact info for the local sheriff. What did Jade want with McIntyre when she already had Tim and me?

I moved on to her photos next, navigating awkwardly with my left hand. I've got a teen niece, my brother's kid, so I know the kind of nonsense girls get up to with their phones. Jade's photos were different. There weren't many images of her with friends. She didn't use filters that turned her into an animated cat. Most of her camera roll captured Manhattan's historic architecture, and there were some nature shots that weren't half-bad. The girl had an eye for composition—and an audience. Her Instagram account, dedicated to her photography, showed two thousand followers.

I knew I wouldn't be so lucky as to find an image of a bloody butcher's knife, but I got the next best thing: pictures of Jasper with Jade. One shot showed them standing in front of a restaurant in the city. In another they were at a photography exhibit in the sort of sparse white space native to pop-up galleries. Both photos were selfies, and young Jade's father was nowhere to be seen.

As I scrolled I found images of Jasper on his own, including a large collection that, according to the dates on the camera roll, were from July 4. Some were close-ups, but others had a creepy stalker quality. I felt sure Jasper didn't know Jade was taking them.

The most recent photos had been snapped the previous day, and they were the only pictures of Jasper with Abella. Given the angle, I figured Jade took them from the house's winding staircase. The couple stood face-to-face in the hall, between the library and the parlor. The first photo showed Norton in the background, moments after he passed by. I zoomed in to the second. By then Jasper and Abella were alone, and it was obvious from their expressions they were arguing.

When I asked Abella if she and Jasper had fought last night, she'd denied it. So what the hell was this? And why was Jade spying on them through the spindles of the stairs?

Jade and Jasper were twelve years apart, but Jasper was the youngest of the Sinclairs, and I could see them being friends. Flynn said the family didn't get together much anymore, but Jade had been on Camilla's island with Jasper for the Fourth of July weekend. Who else would she hang out with here if not him?

Back in the kitchen, when I demanded Jade's phone, she insisted she hadn't contacted anyone—and sure enough no e-mails, text messages, or calls had been made since our arrival. She'd been honest, but in a way that bothered me more than finding out she had lied. What kind of fourteen-year-old who finds herself in a situation like this doesn't text her friends for sympathy and some attention? *The kind who's got a crush on an older guy*, I thought grimly. Jade didn't text her friends or spend time with them in the city because she was preoccupied with our missing man.

I looked down at my bandaged right hand. If Jade *had* intentionally burned me—and that was still a big if—the kid was seriously messed up. Did the photos mean she was obsessed with Jasper? Was Jade just a girl with a crush, or were she and Jasper having some kind of twisted affair?

"Detective Merchant?"

Abella approached the library's open door. Right away I noticed her perfect manicure had taken a hit. The polish was flaking and her cuticles were red from where she'd nervously gnawed the skin. "Can I talk to you?"

I motioned for her to come in. "Jade's phone," I said when I caught her staring. "She and Jasper spend a lot of time together, huh?"

Her pillowy lips turned downward. "What do you mean?"

"Jade has pictures with him. Lots of Jasper alone, too."

"Well yeah, he's, like, her uncle." Abella drew in a breath. "Oh my God. You're not saying you think she and Jas . . ."

Jasper's girlfriend looked shocked, but I couldn't be sure the reaction was authentic. She'd omitted a key event from her account of the previous day. I pondered the possibility she and Jasper had argued about pretty little Jade. Was Jade trying to split them up? She knew Jasper planned to propose. Jade was the one who divulged it to Ned.

"Hey," I said. "I need to clear something up. After you saw what you saw yesterday, did you and Jasper get in a—"

"Might I offer everyone some coffee?"

Norton's presence behind Abella made her jump. "It'll just take a minute to brew," he said, looking from Abella to me, and back again. "I'd like to take some up to Mrs. Sinclair, too, in case she's up from her nap."

"Did someone say coffee?" Crossing the hall, Tim squeezed himself between Norton and Abella, and grinned.

"Go ahead," I told Norton. As he peeled off toward the kitchen, Tim glanced down at my hand. I didn't like that he'd left the others alone in the parlor, or that he was encroaching on my conversation. I had more questions for Abella, and she clearly had something she wanted to say.

"Can you give us a minute, Miss Beaudry?" Tim said.

"I was going to ask the same of you," I said to Tim.

Back in the parlor Bebe let out a hearty laugh. The sound of Jasper's sister enjoying herself on a day like today sent a bracing shiver down my spine. I glanced at Abella. Her eyes were round as plates.

"I just need a sec," I said to Tim.

"Likewise," said Tim, trying not to look baffled by my suggestion that he take a hike. He turned back to face Abella. "Merchant will be right in to get you."

Abella took a step backward. "No," I said quickly. "Stay."

Tim put a hand on my witness's shoulder. "We won't be long. Okay?"

Abella's gaze ping-ponged between us. Eventually, she nodded and walked away.

"What the hell?" I said when she was gone. "Have you forgotten who answers to who around here? She was about to tell me something! It might have been important!"

"It'll keep. What happened to your hand?"

I dragged my fingers down my face. What was he thinking, interrupting when a witness was about to open up? Was this how village investigators operated? With no respect for the hierarchy of the agency and its people? "Jade happened," I said, reconciling myself to revisiting Abella when Tim had whatever assurance he needed that I was fine. "She poured a pot of scalding water on me."

"Poured, or spilled?"

I hesitated. *Not deliberate*, I reminded myself. I didn't want to sound paranoid, but the time I'd spent with Jade left me leery. "I don't know, but it hurts like hell. Why did you let her leave the parlor?"

"What?"

"Before she scarred me in the kitchen, Jade was smoking a cigarette up in her room."

Tim's eyebrows tilted. "No," he said. "She was in the bathroom."

I chuckled. "Thought as much. Watch out for her, that one's smarter than your average bear—and she has a thing for our leading man."

"Jade and Jasper? Come on. Christ, she's a kid."

"Age is just a number, Tim. Obviously Jade didn't schlep Jasper's body out of the house by herself, but I feel like she's involved somehow. She's been reading up on us online."

"What? When?" Tim's face was getting red.

"No doubt she's had plenty of practice surreptitiously texting in the classroom. Don't worry about it. I checked her social feeds and texts and she hasn't shared how she's spending her Saturday at the river."

"You confiscated her phone?"

"She said something that bothered me." I relayed the words she'd spoken in the kitchen as my eyes traveled to the parlor, where Jade now lay curled up on the sofa with her head in her dad's lap.

"*I know what she did*," Tim repeated. "Does she mean Bebe, or Abella?"

"Didn't get that far. But she's got a good view of the shed from her bedroom window."

Tim rubbed his chin. What I needed from him was encouragement. I wanted to hear him agree this was all extremely fishy and warranted caution—to admit at least one of the people on the island was likely a dangerous criminal. What Tim said was, "That might be relevant, if Jasper's actually hurt."

"If?"

"We still don't have proof the blood's even his."

"We've been over this," I said, louder than I intended. "The blood is in his bed. The man is missing. The storm—"

"Okay." Tim showed me his hands. "Just playing devil's advocate. I've gotta do it, you know?"

"No, I don't."

"Knock knock."

Miles, who seconds earlier was in the parlor, now loitered in the hall. "Sorry to interrupt," he said, "but can I have a minute of your time?"

After my altercation with Bebe, I fully expected Miles to give me hell. Hours earlier he made sure to let me know he was a practicing lawyer. I had no doubt that after Bebe barged into the kitchen, she went straight to Miles to recount all the injustices Jade endured by my hand. I should have gone after Abella, but my desire to know more about the inner workings of this couple's relationship kept me rooted in place.

Miles said, "I hear you had a talk with my wife and daughter."

"If you can call it that."

"They weren't cooperative?"

"Not in the least," I said. "Your daughter was surreptitiously using her phone, despite the fact that you were all instructed not to."

Miles nodded. This news didn't surprise him. "Did it interfere with your investigation?"

I wasn't sure what to say. Jade hadn't told anyone about Jasper going missing. So far her worst offense was inflicting my burn. "That's not the point, Mr. Byrd."

"No, of course not." Miles sighed. "Teenage girls."

"Bet she's a handful. Where's her mother?" said Tim.

"We divorced when Jade was five."

"And you got custody?"

Miles gave Tim a sharp look. "Full. I was raised by a single parent, and I turned out just fine. My ex-wife, on the other hand, left us for a prick with a production company in L.A. She was a terrible influence on Jade, obsessed with money and status."

"No offense," I said, glancing back at the parlor, "but I'm not sure you traded up."

My intention was to hack away at his relationship with his cheating wife and wild daughter, a task that shouldn't have been easy. To my surprise, Miles laughed. "You're telling me. If Camilla hadn't insisted, we wouldn't be here this weekend."

"Camilla, or Jade?" I said. "I get the impression Jade and Jasper are pretty close."

Miles blinked at me. "She's a child. He's a twenty-six-year-old man, not to mention her uncle. If Jade told you they're close, I assure you that's wishful thinking. He humors her because he's a nice guy. Maybe she likes the attention—I won't pretend to understand girls this age—but that's all there is to it. Believe me, Jade has plenty of boys her own age chasing her back home."

"Got it," I said. There was no way I couldn't. In a single breath Miles had used three different arguments to make his point. There was absolutely, positively nothing weird going on between Jade and Jasper. *Talk about wishful thinking.*

"You have to remember she's upset," Miles went on. "Something like this can do a real number on a kid—especially with everything else going on. We're moving next week."

"Oh?" Tim said.

"Bebe and I are separating."

All of the emotions I'd expect from the delivery of a statement like that were present and accounted for. Miles looked equal parts confused and pissed off. I kept my eyes off Tim, didn't want Miles knowing this was news we could use. "Sorry to hear that," I said. "Can I ask why?"

"Sure thing. My wife is cheating on me with Ned Yeboah."

I couldn't help it—my eyes went wide. Miles adjusted his glasses, and despite his matter-of-fact delivery I noticed the bridge of his nose was shiny with oil. "That's why I came in here," he said. "I know Bebe doesn't want to talk to you, but frankly, I don't give a shit. I think you should interview her. I'd like to be there when you do."

It was all I could do not to poke Tim in the ribs and hiss, *Are you hearing this?* in his ear. "Mr. Byrd, do you think Bebe knows something about Jasper's disappearance she isn't telling us?"

"I know she does. And for the sake of Jasper, my daughter, and everyone else on this island, it's time she came clean."

If Bebe was concealing information, I didn't see why she'd open up to us with Miles in the room, especially given they were breaking up, but I was happy to oblige this man if it meant we might finally get somewhere with finding Jasper. "That works for me," I said. "Why don't you bring her in?"

"Good," said Miles, and left the room.

Tim and I traded glances and he whistled, low and slow.

"That was weird," I said.

"Can't hurt to try. What are the odds she'll talk?"

I shrugged. "Slim to none, but I'm dying to know what she says."

"At least there'll be coffee, right?"

I didn't return Tim's smile. I couldn't stop thinking about Abella. I had my choice of interviews, both of which could be vital to our search for answers—but I also had time. What had Tim said? *It'll keep.* With that in mind, I sent Tim back to the parlor and prepared to turn my attention to the unhappy couple.

SIXTEEN

I prefer to interview people alone—no distractions, no intrusions. There are times, though, when tackling witnesses as a group has its perks. You can learn a lot from watching people interact. Some witnesses egg each other on, and I was hoping for that from Bebe and Miles. No, I was counting on it.

I knew interviewing Jasper's sister would be a challenge. She gave off an air of superiority that implied she did what she pleased and gave zero fucks about anyone else. On the library's butter-soft leather couch Bebe crossed her legs and stared at me with revulsion. When Miles sat down he left a foot of space between them. The energy in the room felt lethal.

I had just closed the door when my phone buzzed in my pocket. McIntyre. Had to be. She probably had something to report about our witnesses. I was dying to check the message, but with Miles and Bebe right in front of me and Abella waiting across the hall, it would have to wait.

"I'd like to make it clear I'm here under duress." Bebe shot a glance at Miles as she said it. Before we sat down Norton had brought us each a coffee, and while Bebe's sat on the table untouched, Miles took slow, noisy sips while eyeing her over the rim of his cup. "I have no interest whatsoever in speaking with you about my brother."

"Duly noted. This is all standard stuff, Mrs. Sinclair. We need to get some timeline details for his file. So." I tapped my lip like I was thinking hard. "Yesterday. Miles and Jade arrived at the island first, but you came later. That right?"

She sighed emphatically. Bebe's foundation, two shades too light and applied with a trowel, wasn't looking as fresh as it once had. When she spoke, deep pleats formed at the sides of her mouth. "What an amazing display of deductive logic." Bebe's voice was as rough as a jazz-club singer's, all smoke and sex. As she spoke she tucked a lock of short, shiny hair behind her ear and I thought, *No dollar shampoo there*. Rather than Jasper's fine features, Bebe's face mirrored Flynn's, with oversized lips and a bulbous nose. One could argue Jasper had his siblings beat in the looks department, too.

"And you came here with Ned?" I said.

"He happened to be in the office picking up his check. We were both ready to go, so we went. Believe me, I would have loved to be here sooner to spend more time with Nana, but I had to work."

I hadn't seen Bebe so much as acknowledge Camilla, let alone engage her in conversation. "Let's move on to last night. You had cocktails. What was that like?"

"Refreshing."

"Try to be more specific."

Bebe sighed again. "We did our duty and chatted with Abby. Philip served roast pork with dried prunes for dinner and pie for dessert. It was a typical night up here."

"Your chat with Abella included throwing around the idea of her coming to work for you, yes?"

Bebe laughed, but her expression clouded. "Please. Nana was kidding. It's never a good idea to mix business and pleasure. I'm sure Abby knows that."

It was an absurd statement coming from a woman who was currently sleeping with an employee, but I let it go. "What about after dinner?"

"I went to bed."

"Together?" I said, eyeing each of them in turn.

She set her jaw. "I went up first. Dealing with him is exhausting."

Miles shrugged.

"Did Jasper seem normal to you yesterday?" I asked. "Did you see anything that seemed out of place?"

"This is a complete waste of time. I have nothing to do with Jasper's absence."

Absence. Another odd choice of words for a sister with a missing kid brother. She was acting like Jasper went home to watch Netflix and chill. "Where do you think he is?" I said.

"If I had to guess, I'd say he got sick of Abby and went back to the city."

"With a serious wound? Without telling you?"

"My brother's a big boy. He can take care of himself."

"Then why bother calling us?"

"That was Nana's idea. She worries too much."

"You aren't worried about your brother?"

"No," Bebe said, "I'm not. Are you even sure that's real blood up there? My brother has a flare for dramatics."

I inclined my head. "Hang on. Are you suggesting Jasper staged that accident himself?" The idea was almost as cracked as Tim's theory about Abella's female trouble. I glanced at Miles, who leaned back and smiled. He seemed to be enjoying himself.

"How should I know what he did?" said Bebe. "I wish you'd leave us alone to deal with this for ourselves."

"We're investigating Jasper's *absence* as a missing persons case. But Norton called it in as a murder."

"Again, that was Nana's idea. Philip just does what she says."

"Everyone else I've talked to seems convinced Jasper fell into some kind of harm. You don't agree?"

"How many times do I have to say it? No, I don't agree. It's totally feasible he'd take off and leave us to sort out his mess. Jasper gets a kick out of tormenting us."

"Us?"

"Me," said Bebe. "Flynn. I wouldn't be surprised if this was Jasper's idea of a joke. He's probably waiting until we feel good and guilty before he shows up laughing. What a lark. Ha, ha."

I contemplated what she was saying. Norton reported Jasper missing that morning. The nor'easter arrived the previous afternoon. The skiff was still in the boathouse. Could Tim be right? Could someone have ferried Jasper to shore before the weather got bad? Was it actually possible the man was hiding out somewhere, right as rain? Again my cell phone vibrated, another text message coming through. Again I forced myself to ignore it.

Back in the boat on our way to Tern, Tim had said there were easier ways to take your own life on an island. There were easier ways to fake your own death, too. That didn't mean it was impossible—but if all this was a ploy designed to goad Bebe and Flynn, why would Jasper bring his girlfriend along for the ride? Why set the scene in the bedroom and risk Abby getting the blame?

I gave a small shake of my head to clear my mind. There were buckets of blood upstairs on that bed, and it was the real thing. The smell of it hung in the room like a fog. Of course it was Jasper's. Wasn't it?

I reached for the mug Norton had left for me. Earlier, he'd served the family coffee with a side of cream, but to mine he added the cream in the kitchen. It lay on the surface of the coffee, refusing to blend in, and when I took a sip I found it oddly bitter. Flustered, I set it down. I didn't know Philip Norton. Why should I trust him? What if the drink was spiked?

I tried to chase the idea from my mind. It wasn't logical. I'd already eaten an entire meal cooked by Norton and was fine, but that didn't matter. It was happening again. This time the flashback was physical, moving like a worm under my skin. I was lightheaded and itchy. My skin crawled, just as if there really was a drug back in my veins.

The room was unfamiliar, with no windows. A bare bulb hung above me, its pull string emitting a tinny clink as it swayed. It felt like someone cracked open my skull and filled it with hot, shifting sand. I tasted blood and realized my lips were chapped and split. Where was I? What day was it? I didn't know.

"Shay."

It took me a minute to find him in that too-bright room. Bram shifted his messenger bag and took out a bottle of water. "You thirsty? Hey, don't be scared. We know each other. Remember, Shay?"

150

"—support the family business our entire careers, and Jasper swoops in and starts derailing all our work."

"What?" I blinked, and Bebe's face swam into view, but I couldn't process her words. Meditation. That's what Carson would prescribe at a time like this. *See these anxious thoughts, acknowledge what they're doing to my body, and zero in on my breathing.* Give the brain an object to focus on. Quiet that jumpy monkey mind.

"I *said* Jasper's already tried to sabotage Sinclair Fabrics," said Bebe, "and now he's moved on to sabotaging our private lives."

Mindfulness. Awareness. A crazy woman in my face. *Snap out of it, Shay.* "Just . . . slow down."

"Try to keep up," Bebe said with a roll of her eyes.

"What she's saying," said Miles, studying me with an expression of concern, "is Jasper isn't following Flynn and Bebe's rules and they're pissed as hell."

He'd hardly spoken a word since we sat down. Miles obviously expected me to glean some information from Bebe's account. Either she wasn't getting there fast enough for him, or he was starting to worry she wouldn't get there at all. "What she's not telling you," he said, "is without Jasper the business would already be sunk."

Bebe looked aghast. "That's a lie."

"It's really not."

"Business isn't going well?" I said, finally coming around.

"We've had our ups and downs. At the moment we're down. It won't last." Bebe retrieved her coffee. Took a sip, made a face, put it back on the table.

"I thought Jasper's marketing campaign was working. Ned's a big star on social media, right? That must be good exposure for your brand," I said.

"Ned's good at what he does," said Bebe.

"Can't be that good if the company's tanking." If I wanted to get anywhere with her, I couldn't go easy anymore. My cut-to-the-chase strategy inspired a reaction, at least. Bebe shot me a venomous look.

"Come on, Bebe," said Miles, "you think she won't find this out for herself?" He turned to me and squared his shoulders. "Sinclair Fabrics is on the brink of bankruptcy. The problem is the competition. The Sinclairs are getting crushed."

Bebe's mouth dropped open in shock. "They're a flash in the pan. It's dumb luck. They don't have the selection we do, or the expertise."

"She's talking about Attitude," said Miles. "They're a new fabric retailer in the Garment District. They have a partnership with a reality-TV show, and every episode the contestants shop at the store for their fabrics. Attitude signage is front and center. Their sales are through the roof."

A competing business muscling in on the Sinclairs' turf. Jasper's area of expertise was marketing and PR. "Is that why Jasper joined the company when he did?"

"Bebe and Flynn tried to stop the bleeding on their own. Tried and failed," said Miles. "Jasper thought he could save the day, and he boosted sales by a lot, but the company's too far gone. Not even Ned's gorgeous face can pull it back from the brink now. Such a shame."

Flynn hadn't mentioned any of this, but neither sibling seemed the type to admit failure, especially if their little brother came out ahead. How had Camilla described it? *Things come more easily to Jasper than the others. It puts a strain on their relationship.*

Bebe and Flynn may have needed help, but I couldn't imagine they'd be thrilled to get it from their faultless little brother.

"But that didn't stop you from showing Ned how much you appreciate his help," Miles said, facing his wife once more. With a lewd expression he added, "Ned's just so *good* at what he does."

"Shut up," said Bebe. "You shut your mouth."

"She may not be worried about Jasper," said Miles, "but I am, and my daughter is, too. There could be a killer in this house, and I'm not going to sit around and wait for another attack. You had your chance, Bebe. You should have told them the second they got here. And if you won't, I will."

My eyes narrowed as I listened to Miles rant. A few minutes ago he'd suggested Jasper's abduction was on par, stress-wise, with moving house. Now there was a murderer hiding in the curtains, and he and Jade were quaking with fear.

"Stop it," Bebe said, digging her fingernails into her knees. "I'm warning you, Miles."

"Christ, Bebe, you couldn't wait until you were back in the city? You had to do it here, in full view of the house with your whole family watching? Honestly, you'd think a person who's fucking her brother's boyfriend would try to be a little more discreet."

"You bastard," said Bebe. "You absolute *beast*."

"Was that part of the fun? Did you get off on the risk? She *saw* you. Jade saw you with Ned."

Jade's bedroom window with the view of the shed. *I know what she did.* Jade was talking about Bebe.

When Bebe shook her head, strands of hair stuck to her forehead. She was sweating. Afraid. And Miles wasn't done yet.

"You know what else Jade saw? She saw Jasper, out on the lawn. You saw him, too, didn't you? You and Ned. And Ned couldn't have him knowing. He couldn't take the chance that Jas would run off and tell Flynn."

Watching Bebe was mesmerizing. Her eyes got enormous while every muscle in her face went slack. "Ned would never hurt anyone. Never."

"What about Flynn? What would he do if he found out about you two? Oh, I'm sure he suspects—your trip up here together, the way you're always fawning over Ned. But what would he do if he knew for sure? Flynn's not great at controlling his temper, is he? You know how he feels about Ned, how afraid he is of losing him. He'd rip you both apart."

"You'd be finished at the company, of course," Miles went on. "The business can't afford a scandal, not with Attitude nipping at your heels. You and Ned would both be out so fast it would make your heads spin. I'm sure Ned doesn't care. He's leaving anyway. But your reputation would be obliterated, and Ned knows it. Did he tell you he'd protect you from all of that? Did he explain Jas would have to die, or did he leave that up to your imagination?"

I didn't know what type of law Miles practiced, but I'd have bet money he had experience as a litigation attorney. He watched Bebe closely while awaiting her response. He had her trapped, and he knew it.

"So you see why I'm worried," said Miles as he crossed one leg over the other. "In the past twenty-four hours, Jasper witnessed his best friend banging his sister and then promptly disappeared. I'd say that's cause for concern, wouldn't you?"

"Ned would never hurt Jasper," Bebe repeated weakly. She looked ill.

"You're sure about that?" I asked, taking Miles's lead. "Your feelings for Ned might be skewing your perception of things. Right now you two are happy. You've got each other's backs. But soon the sparkle will wear off, and when it does do you want me wondering whether you, Mrs. Sinclair, are involved in your brother's disappearance, too?"

"You can't seriously tell me you're going to listen to *him*," Bebe said. "This is a setup! You want to talk about feelings getting in the way? Miles is angry with me, and his solution is to frame Ned for murder. We're through—not because of Ned, by the way, but because Miles is a selfish bastard who only married me for my money."

"What money?" said Miles, deadpan.

Another vibration. Another text. I was starting to get worried. If McIntyre had news she'd shoot me a message asking if I was free to talk—just one. Something was up, but I couldn't hit pause on Bebe and Miles. What I was witnessing was better than all those episodes of *Geraldo* I watched with my mom as a kid, and it was getting me closer to where I needed to be.

"This is insane," Bebe said. "If you insist on treating this as a suspicious situation, the person you should be questioning is Abby, or Bella, or whoever she is. Jasper barely knows her and she's about to get kicked out of the country. She has nothing to lose."

"Jasper must know her better than you think," I said, "considering he's about to propose."

Bebe and Miles traded a glance. The act was automatic. They hadn't been on the outs for long. "Who told you that?" said Bebe.

"I believe that news came from Jade."

The room was plunged into silence. That told me everything I needed to know. Jade had the inside track on Jasper's life, and it was common knowledge in the family. The mention of her name was confirmation enough for Bebe. Jasper and Jade were friends, and he confided in her. Jasper did plan to propose to the girl who now sat in the parlor with his blood all over her. When Jasper divulged his secret, Jade immediately turned around and told Ned. Why didn't Ned pass the news along to Bebe? Where exactly did Ned's loyalties lie? I wondered the same about Jade. Of all the people in the house she could have told, she didn't go to a family member but a man she hardly knew.

Something else occurred to me that complicated things further. According to Miles, Jade told him she saw Bebe and Ned sneaking into the shed. If Jade and Jasper were so close that he'd revealed his plans to propose, surely Jade talked to Jasper about the dirt she had on Bebe and Ned. It wasn't Jasper in that raincoat, peeking through the shed window. But Jasper had to know what was going on.

Dusk was falling on the island. Night was a few hours away still, but the leaden light beyond the window had dimmed. Moments earlier I could see Bebe clearly, but now she sat in shadow. I wanted to flick on a lamp to get a better look at her expression, but I didn't dare. I didn't move.

"So who did it?" I said into the void. "I think we all know Jasper didn't stage that grisly scene up there as a prank. Someone inflicted the wound that resulted in that bloodstain. So was it Ned, or was it Abella? Or"—I looked to Bebe—"was it you?"

She let out a startled laugh. "You can sit here and devise ridiculous theories all night long for all I care. I'm leaving."

As she stood and turned to go, Bebe knocked my full mug of coffee to the floor. The mottled liquid spread and darkened the antique rug.

"Nana's going to love that," said Miles. "Better add it to your list of confessions."

Bebe's head whipped around and a look of sheer horror came over her face. "Don't even think about it. Don't you dare."

"It's not like it would make a difference. She despises you already."

I watched them carefully, trying to read between the lines. From one second to the next Bebe had changed. Her vigor drained away. Now she looked at Miles with desperation in her eyes. "Please, Miles, you can't. Tell Flynn, I don't care. Just don't tell Nana."

I was missing something. Camilla wouldn't approve of the affair, but Bebe wasn't close to her like Jasper was. What was the worst that could happen if Camilla found out? "Mrs. Sinclair," I said slowly. "I should warn you, in the course of this investigation your relationship with Mr. Yeboah may well come out to your grandmother."

She spun around to face me. "No. I won't allow it. It would be too much for her. Jasper, and that blood . . . it's all too much."

I pictured Camilla. Her gaunt face. The wig. The realization hit me like a stream of icy water. "Camilla's sick."

"Cancer," Bebe said, nodding. "She has a few weeks at most. My poor, poor grandmother." She ratcheted up the sadness in her eyes.

Camilla was dying. That's why Jasper brought Abella to the island, and why Camilla insisted everyone else come, too. She might have hoped for reconciliation, but based on what I knew about Camilla's grandchildren, it was more likely she knew the most she could hope for was that they pretend. It explained why Miles and Jade were present even though he and Bebe were splitting up. They'd all come together, because Camilla asked them to.

Bebe didn't want to upset her grandmother. Or was it that she didn't want Camilla angry? Bebe and Flynn didn't spend time with Camilla in the city like Jasper did, but Bebe wished she had come to the island earlier, and was adamant that we suppress her affair. Flynn visited Camilla when he first got to Tern, too. Now that she was dying, it seemed to me they were both trying awfully hard to stay on their nana's good side.

"Jasper's gone, Bebe," Miles said evenly. "It's all going to come out eventually. It always does."

As I reached into my pocket to grab my phone, I hoped to God he was right.

SEVENTEEN

Gone. That word means something different to me than to most. That's partly because of my job. Homicide victims are gone forever. I'll never know them, and I can't change that; all I can do is try to keep the same thing from happening to someone else. Death is fast and finite. A hawk plucks a pigeon from the sky in a flurry of feathers. One goes while the other stays behind, wearing a shit-eating grin.

There's more to it, though, because I was gone, too. As far as my family, the media, even the police were concerned, I was as gone as gone can be. The only difference between me and other victims is that I came back.

It was clear Miles believed Jasper was dead, and his case against Ned was strong. The stories I'd been told by Abella and

Miles about the previous day, from Flynn's temper to the tryst in the shed, lined up.

That only generated more doubt. Ned and Bebe's secret had the capacity to tear apart an already unstable family. It was the kind of thing a person might go to great lengths to bury. So who wielded the shovel? It wouldn't go well for Ned if Flynn found out about the affair; one conversation with Jasper's brother was all I needed to see that. But what about Bebe? She had just as much reason to panic, and plenty of excuses for why Jasper was gone. This woman who cheated with her brother's partner while he worked nearby might be capable of anything.

I wasn't ready to give up on Flynn either. According to Abella, he routinely abused Jasper. If he was angry about Jasper's comparably successful efforts to save the family business, or even something as trivial as Jasper's happy relationship, Flynn might snap. He was quick to pin Jasper's disappearance on Abella. If he'd done the deed, framing her for murder would serve him well.

It was after four by the time Miles and Bebe left the library and I was finally able to gather my thoughts and check my phone. I'd started hoping McIntyre's messages contained a bombshell revelation about Ned Yeboah, the ambitious bisexual New York YouTuber who needed Bebe so urgently he threw her over a sawhorse in a freezing-cold shed. To my surprise it was Carson's name, not Maureen McIntyre's, I saw on the screen.

There were times, especially lately, when Carson made me feel like a child under a parent's watchful gaze. He'd say it was for my own good—and maybe it was—but it concerned me that he was reaching out in the middle of a case. He'd made his position clear. What good would it do to keep reminding me I might lose my shit? Couldn't he at least give me a chance to prove him wrong?

Cut him some slack, Shay. Whenever Carson's micromanaging annoyed me, I reminded myself what he'd done. Carson saved me. In a way, I owed him my life. Quelling my frustration, I scrolled through his messages.

Been thinking about Tim, his first text read. *You're right about the wedding. We shouldn't invite him.*

It's a bad idea, Carson went on. *It's tradition for friends of the groom to drudge up old stories. Roast them or whatever.*

We have history. Tim would love to embarrass me.

There's some jealousy there.

He's that type.

That's where Carson ended it. I puzzled over the texts. Why the sudden change of heart? I couldn't imagine Tim telling embarrassing stories about Carson. As far as I knew, Carson and Tim hadn't hung out in years. Get up in front of a hundred people to roast a guy Tim hadn't been close with for decades? No way.

I didn't expect Carson to answer when I texted my reply. It was ages since his last message came through. *OK then he's off the list,* I wrote, even though he'd never been on it. I didn't have it in me to solve this mystery, too. Today of all days, I needed my mind in the game.

When I hit the send button, his response was instantaneous.

Good, Carson wrote. *Watch out for him. He might try to turn you against me.*

I'd been prepared to end the conversation, but that stopped me short.

What? Why the hell would he do that? I was more proficient with the tiny keyboard than Carson, and the dead time between my text and his response was agony. Finally, his reply appeared.

Jealousy, like I said. It was always him who got punished for the shit we pulled as kids. And look at us now.

Meaning you're rich and important and he's a lowly cop? I thought. What I wrote was, *Tim doesn't care about that.* As I typed, it struck me I wasn't sure whether Tim's lack of wealth bothered him. It didn't look like Tim was blowing his paycheck on designer clothes and fancy cars, but he was visibly impressed by the Sinclairs and their estate. He knew a lot about how families like this one spent their fortunes. Maybe it did grate on him that Carson made it big in the city while he never got out of A-Bay.

I get that he's your colleague and you want this to work, Carson wrote back, *but he's not a good person. I'm sorry, I'll explain when you get home, but please believe me. It's the truth.*

Not a good person? Ten hours ago Carson was Timmy's biggest fan, petitioning for his inclusion in the most meaningful day of our lives. I'd only known Tim a few months, but Carson's left-field claim didn't mesh with what I'd seen firsthand. Or maybe I just hadn't been paying attention. Hearing Carson, my fiancé, talk about him that way turned my stomach. I *did* want our partnership to work. Was it possible I'd been misreading Tim all this time?

Just be careful, Carson wrote, for the second time that day. *Promise me. You might feel like you're in control out on that island, but remember what you've been through.*

"Typically," Carson had said thirteen months ago on the day we met, "adult victims of this kind of trauma experience one of two reactions. An emotional response—shock, disassociation, hopelessness—often tops the list, but there may also be social repercussions. Despite having been isolated from society during their confinement, victims often withdraw from others after they're freed, even their closest family and friends. You may experience intense feelings of loneliness, even when you're not alone. I know that doesn't make much sense, but it's textbook for this kind of psychological condition. You're going to feel lost. Abandoned. Adrift."

I walked out of Dr. Carson Gates's Junction Boulevard office with my brain reduced to mush. I'd gone in expecting to be picked apart, but I was still disheartened when, after listening attentively to my story and promising not to give up on me, Dr. Gates said I was in for a lifetime of pain. I remember thinking, *Great, this pretty police psychologist's going to turn the ordeal I barely survived into a case study.* Before I even got back to the subway I was convinced he'd already decided which psychology journal was most likely to give him the cover.

I was all set to call it quits and fight through that pain on my own—go *through the motions, my ass*—when Carson did something surprising. After our first meeting he called me to apologize. It was too much too fast, he conceded. Of course I felt overwhelmed.

As we talked, I realized it wasn't his diagnosis that left me feeling beaten down, but the implication that it wouldn't go away. I needed to work, couldn't imagine a life without the force once my leave of absence came to an end. Dr. Gates said the damage was done. My trauma was too great. I could no longer separate good from evil, not even when evil stared me in the face. He recommended a desk job, and tasks that were "professionally gratifying, but far removed from violence." It was the last thing I wanted to hear. So I refused to hear it.

But I didn't quit. Week after week I begrudgingly continued those mandatory visits, and every time I argued my case. I could get over the ordeal, I told him. I'd find a way to move on. When he saw how determined I was, he made me a promise. He'd work with me until I was ready to go back, no matter how long it took.

I showed up for our sessions with new energy and resolve. For his part, Carson went out of his way to schedule extra meetings and check in with me via phone calls and texts in between. Before long we were seeing each other outside of the office—a coffee on a Saturday morning, a drink when he finished work. In all the ways I felt weak, Carson was strong. He insisted the horrible things I'd done for Bram were forgivable.

It felt like ages before our relationship progressed beyond a friendship. The more time I spent with Carson, the more convinced I became that only a psychologist trained in trauma therapy for police officers would ever be able to understand the person I'd become. The day he told me he could no longer be my therapist because our connection felt too personal, I knew there was no going back. It didn't seem to matter that dating him was unethical and unwise, not to mention a criminal offense. When I stumbled out of that basement with blood on my hands, I was utterly alone. Until I found Carson.

"Detective Merchant?"

"Jesus." I brought my bandaged hand to my heart. Norton had a way of sneaking up on me that made me want to jump out of my skin. He was standing in the hall. Over his shoulder I saw Ned crouched next to Abella, murmuring gently in her ear. Watching them together yanked at my gut. Three friends with a lifetime ahead of them, now down to two.

"Didn't mean to scare you," Norton said, "but I was wondering if you noticed the time."

Putting away my phone, I said, "Got someplace you need to be?"

He flushed, all the way from his neck to the tips of his ears.

"'Course not, I just meant it's almost cocktail hour. After that there'll be dinner and dessert—"

"I'm familiar with how meals work." I was tetchy. Carson's messages had gotten to me.

"I have to get cooking, yeah?" Norton said. "We're a lot of people. It's gonna take time."

Once again this man was asking if he could disappear into the kitchen. Out of sight. At that point I'd questioned nearly everyone, and all had their share of problems. Abella was unemployed, weeks away from being deported. Flynn's lover was cheating on him. Bebe and Ned were engaged in an affair that, when exposed, would wreak havoc on their lives. Jade was losing Jasper to a fiancée. What about Philip Norton? He'd been working for these people for twenty years. It seemed unlikely their profound dysfunction hadn't worn off on him.

"Hang back a minute," I said.

"Is there something you need?" His gaze fell to the spilled coffee on the library rug and he set his jaw. "I should clean that up before—"

"Sure, sure. I've just got a couple more questions first."

"Oh?"

I motioned for him to sit down. "You said you only work here during the summer?"

"During the season," he corrected. "April through October. I'll be shuttering the house for the winter next week."

"And you come whether Mrs. Sinclair visits or not?"

"There's a lot to be done on an island."

"Where do you spend the rest of the year?"

"A-Bay." He smiled. "Same as you."

"Getting some well-earned rest, I imagine. You went to a lot of trouble this weekend. Must be exhausting," I said.

"It's a special occasion. Jasper never brought a lady out here to meet Cam—Mrs. Sinclair—before."

It was the second time I'd caught him calling Camilla by her first name. I remembered Abella watching them in the parlor. I needed to talk to her again, not just to hear what she wanted to tell me but to ask what she knew about Norton and Camilla's friendship. "I guess that means it's serious," I said. "Can't see him bringing a girl all the way out here otherwise."

"Mrs. Sinclair hopes so. She'd like to see him married soon."

"Because she's ill."

Norton's eyes widened. "Who told you?"

"Bebe. Cancer, huh?"

He dropped his gaze and nodded.

"I'm sorry," I said. "She talks about you like you're family. Got any family of your own around here?"

"Not locally."

"Never been married?"

"Nope."

"No kids?"

Norton shifted his weight around in his seat. "I didn't say that."

"I saw a picture in your bedroom. You and a little boy."

He nodded. "That's my son. His mama and I were real young when he was born. He doesn't live around here. Never did."

"Ah." It was a tale of woe I'd heard a million times before, and it instantly changed the way I felt about Philip Norton. I pictured him in his teens, telling his baby mama he couldn't raise a kid because he was still a kid himself. "This place must feel like home to you, then."

"Two decades is a long time." The whites of his eyes were alarmingly bright surrounded by all that pink skin. "I've seen some things over these years, you know?"

"Have you?"

"You wouldn't believe it. One spring? I got out here and found a deer and her fawn." He said it fondly. The memory made Norton smile.

"On the island?" I remembered the long ride from the mainland. "But how?"

"They swam! I had to chase 'em off, of course. Can't have a deer invasion. But it was something, watching those deer swim back to shore."

I waited for Camilla to factor into the story, but she didn't. "Will you stay on, do you think? When Mrs. Sinclair passes?"

Norton seemed unsure how to answer. "With the grandchildren, who knows what'll happen. It's not the place it used to be, never will be again. And I guess I'll need to retire one of these days."

"Got enough money saved up for that?"

"She's always paid me well. I should be all right." Again Norton rapped the wooden doorframe with his knuckles for luck. "What about that trapper? You get anywhere with him?"

"Sounds like he's got an alibi."

Norton grunted. "Guess I should get started on that dinner."

"Right," I said, watching him go, feeling my gaze pull magnet-like back to Ned, and the girlfriend Jasper left behind.

EIGHTEEN

ack in the parlor, I took a minute to read the room. The fug that hung over the guests earlier was gone, replaced with a kinetic buzz. They spoke in pairs with low voices, flicking furtive glances my way.

Tim wasn't getting the same treatment. Sitting quietly on an ottoman in the corner, he'd managed to make them comfortable with his presence. Soon our witnesses might even forget he was there. As I watched him smiling passively at the room, I thought about what Carson said. *Not a good person.* Huh. Tim had a knack for blending in, and he wasn't big on socializing. I really didn't know much about him at all.

Ned pulled a chair next to Abella, who had given in to her despair and was weeping softly into her hands. Miles and Jade were still on the couch, while Bebe and Flynn stood by the fire,

their backs to the room. With every hour that passed, our witnesses were growing more restless. Lines were being drawn, alli-
ances established—or maybe that was all an illusion. Maybe on
this forsaken island it was every man for himself.

I took a step toward Ned. He was whispering to Abella again,
and I heard him say, "We'll find him, baby. Hush, now. I'm here."
At the sound of his voice, Bebe swiveled her head and watched
from the corner of one smoky eye as Ned stroked the girl's matted
hair. Ned was the only person I hadn't interviewed, the only one
left. It was a matter of convenience and timing, but now that I took
stock of the way his gaze darted from face to face, his mechanical
movements, I feared I'd made a mistake. Ned was a wild card. He'd
caught a ride into the family with Jasper, found a permanent place
with Flynn, and traded him for Bebe. The Sinclair siblings were
flavors of ice cream and Ned was working his way through the
freezer. No matter how Jasper felt about his older brother and
sister, I didn't think he'd approve. If Ned thought Jasper knew he'd
swapped lovers, he might have been scared yesterday. And fear's
right up there with anger and jealousy as the emotions that cause
people to kill.

"Mr. Yeboah," I said casually, like I was looking for a friendly
chat. Fear also turns men into liars, and I didn't want to alarm
Ned, not yet.

There was wariness in his eyes all the same. It turned the hon-
eyed irises black. As he rose from his seat Abella did the same, the
two of them twin puppets on a string. She looked up at his face,
imploring him to stay. Abella was being truthful when she said she
and Ned were close. Both were outsiders trying to navigate a family that doubled as an active minefield.

I have a method, as all investigators do, for interrogating

witnesses. Rarely do I get straight to the point. I've learned it's better to ease in and look for ways to make connections that coerce an interviewee into sharing everything. Back at the academy, someone once showed me the transcript from a police interview with Robert Pickton, the pig farmer turned serial killer who murdered dozens of women in western Canada. The detective spent hours chatting with Pickton in an effort to eke out the truth. The endurance that investigator displayed was a thing of beauty.

Right off the bat I could see that's what it would take to get Ned to talk. He knew he was the last person to visit the library, and that put him on edge. I had to gain his confidence, but this posed a problem. The more I hacked away at the family's tangled lives, the more rot I turned up. Everyone on the island was guilty of something, to the point where I didn't know which trail to follow. And then there was Carson. I'd always thought of him as a touchstone for my sanity, but what he'd said about Tim and the way he said it threw me off. If I could sense Ned's anxiety, he could surely feel mine.

The coffee stain was still conspicuously present on the library rug. It must have killed Norton that I sent him back to the parlor without allowing him to assess the damage. When the doors were closed behind me, I turned to Ned.

I started by asking about his family, steering as far from Jasper as I could. Ned was born in Ghana but grew up in the South Bronx, in a working-class family of six that still lived in the same two-bedroom Prospect Avenue apartment they'd rented upon their arrival. All the money Ned made stocking shelves at the bodega downstairs went toward paying a monthly rent that could have gotten the Yeboahs a four-bedroom new construction in Accra. When he wasn't staying at Flynn's place, Ned lived with his family even now. On the weekends, Ned told me, he still made time to volunteer at an animal rescue in Brooklyn. I couldn't picture this buffed and polished man de-fleaing mutts and hosing down cages, but the skin around his eyes relaxed when he told me about the dogs he cared for, and I took him at his word.

Ned hadn't been an especially good student, but he knew how to entertain and he got involved with a friend's YouTube channel at a young age. Soon Ned had a channel of his own and was amassing a fan base by sharing fashion tutorials and lifestyle tips.

It was a shock when Ned realized he could make more from the ads associated with his videos than he could earn at the bodega, and even more of a surprise when a talent agency came knocking. The next thing he knew, his agent had received a message from Jasper Sinclair. An exclusive contract with the company would establish Ned as a major influencer. He didn't hesitate to take it, and before long, he and Jasper were friends.

"We're a lot alike," Ned said of Jasper. "I'm sure you don't believe that, but it's true."

"No, I get it. He may not have to worry about paying the rent, but he suffered in his own way. It isn't easy losing your parents at a young age. At least he has a brother and sister to lean on."

"Whatever," Ned said with a shrug.

"Are they not close?" I said, feigning confusion.

"I'm not the person to answer that."

Though the library was chilly, Ned's forehead shone with sweat. He'd dressed as any respectable fashion vlogger would for a weekend getaway to a luxurious rustic home: woolen plaid shirt, thick tan pants, suede slip-ons in a fetching shade of loden green. Several of his shirt buttons were undone and I could see sweat on his breastbone, too. I'd arranged the overstuffed chairs across from each other so we were knee to knee. It's how I used to sit with Carson in his office when we talked about Bram. Carson said it was conducive to sharing and created a balance of power that helped people relax. With Ned, the arrangement made me apprehensive. We were a mirror image of each other, our feet firmly planted on the soiled rug, and in that moment Ned and I were equals. So why did I feel so unstable? Nothing I knew about him indicated he was violent, yet I didn't like being alone with Ned. As I watched him joggle one knee and then the other I realized it wasn't the man I feared, but the possibility he'd bolt.

Holding him in my gaze, I leaned forward and pushed a piece of hair from my brow. I was so close I could see Ned's pulse in his neck. His eyes moved to the scar on my cheek, widened at the faint stitch marks that gave it a centipede look, and cut away. "You and Jasper are pals," I said.

"That's right."

"For his sake, help me figure this out. Something happened here yesterday. We both know it involves his family."

I was throwing it all out there, hoping to gain purchase. Now Ned's hands were twitching, too. As he rubbed his palms up and down his muscled thighs I saw his nails were polished to a high shine.

"I don't know what you're talking about." He wouldn't look at me.

"You and Flynn haven't been getting along."

"Flynn's a salty bastard. We argue. So what?"

"My fiancé and I argue, too. Sometimes those arguments escalate, make us say and do crazy things. Has that ever happened with you and Flynn?"

"Have we ever argued and ended up killing someone? Nah," he said, "we usually stick to armed robbery."

"If Flynn's such an asshole, why did you get together with him at all?" I couldn't conceive of a more unlikely match, or understand what anyone could see in Flynn that had the potency to spark romantic attraction, let alone sexual desire.

"Domineering brutes are my type."

"Are they?" I said. "Just men, or women, too?"

"What business is it of yours?" Ned dragged a hand across his forehead with a sound like sandpaper on wood. "Look, Flynn wasn't always this way. He treated me like royalty. I cared about him, okay?"

"You realize I've spoken with everyone but you. There are some disadvantages to being last. The others already had their chance to shape the story. Do you get what I'm saying, Ned? Whatever you aren't telling me, the secret you think you're hiding? I already know."

"Jesus Christ, it doesn't fucking matter. We should be looking for Jasper! What if he's still on the island, hurt or . . ." His voice trailed off. "What if he needs help?"

My visions of Jasper out there in the storm . . . Ned saw them, too. They stretched his mouth into the shape of a scream. He wasn't wrong with those *what-ifs*. I'd searched bits and pieces of the three-acre island alone. I could easily have missed something. Jasper might still be shivering in the mud while his blood turned the yellow leaves black. Knowing Ned was thinking the same thing softened me, but only a little. As he spoke Ned folded his arms across his chest, a demonstration of his refusal to tip his hand.

"What do you think I'm trying to do?" I said with frustration.

"Everything matters—every act, every look, every word. We're not going to find Jasper until we know who hurt him. He could be dying out there." *He could be dead.*

Ned ground the heels of his hands into his eyes. "There was a fight," he said in a tight voice. "Last night."

"Right. Upstairs." *Loud voices after midnight.*

His forehead puckered. "No. That was Miles and Bebe."

It was the first time he'd spoken her name. I watched carefully but his expression didn't change. "Miles and Bebe?"

"Arguing in their room."

"Are you saying there was another fight? Somewhere else?"

"Outside." Ned cocked his head. "You didn't know?"

I felt my cheeks get hot. I'd told him I knew everything worth knowing.

"I thought," Ned said, "maybe Flynn . . ."

"Lucky you. You get to be the one to fill me in. Who was involved in this fight?" I said. "You and Flynn?"

"No. Flynn and Jasper."

Remembering Flynn's knuckles, battered and bruised, made my chest seize up. *Got in a fight with his brother and took off.* Hadn't that been Tim's theory from the start? "What happened?"

Ned's face went from pained to resolute. Somewhere in the span of a few seconds he'd made the decision to betray someone. In the gloomy half-light of the room there was a cruel curl to his lip. "Abby wasn't the only one who had too much to drink last night. Flynn got lit and laid into Jas. He hit him."

"Flynn physically assaulted his brother last night." I blinked at Ned. "I've talked to every person in this house and not one of them mentioned this."

Ned lowered his voice another notch. "That's because they

don't know. It was after dinner, late. Everyone was in bed. The only person we saw afterward was Norton. He was in the kitchen when we came inside. I told him Jas tripped in the yard."

"Why?" I asked. "Did Jasper ask you to cover it up? Or were you trying to protect Flynn?"

"Neither," he said, and looked away. Earlier, when I'd interviewed Bebe and Miles, I'd caught them exchanging a conspiratorial glance. Old habits die hard, and I suspected that maxim applied to Ned's loyalty to Flynn as well.

"Okay," I said, wondering if Ned could hear the light-speed rhythm of my heart. "Back up. Walk me through this."

He exhaled and wiped his brow. "Dinner was over. We went out back to smoke a joint and Flynn followed us. Started in on Jasper."

It would have been pouring by then. That explained the dried mud on Flynn's, Ned's, and Jasper's shoes. Before long, I had enough details to envision the scene. Jasper and his older brother breathing hard, locked in a struggle in the storm. Ned forcing his way between them, but not before Flynn split open Jasper's lower lip. When Ned got to that part of the narrative, my mind jumped back to our crime scene. There was no way a split lip could have caused the stain on the mattress, but it did clarify the source of the blood on Jasper's pillowcase.

Abella went to sleep early, drunk and alone. She didn't wake when Jasper came to bed, so she didn't know about his bloody lip or the fight. The only other person who did was Flynn, and he'd deliberately hidden his knuckles from me. Flynn wasn't stupid. If he'd told me from the start that he gave his brother a thrashing mere hours before Jasper went missing, the day would have gone a lot differently for him.

I asked Ned where Flynn went after the fight, but he didn't know. "I slept down here last night." He nodded at the library's leather couch. "I didn't want to see him."

"You haven't told me what they were fighting about."

"Money. It's always money with Flynn. He told Jasper he can forget about Abby coming to work for the company, no matter what Camilla says. There isn't enough to pay her. Hell, there's barely enough to pay me."

"That's why you're leaving. Better opportunities, bigger paychecks."

"I'm leaving," said Ned irritably, "because I know I'm about to get hosed."

"But Flynn wants you to stay."

"Flynn doesn't give a shit about anyone but himself. He thinks I'll work for nothing. 'I'll support you,' he says. 'I'll take care of you'." Ned balled his hands. "I'm not his fucking pet."

I could see how Camilla's suggestion that Sinclair Fabrics should hire Abella would leave Flynn enraged. His boyfriend was leaving because the business offered no long-term prospects, but Jasper's girlfriend was deserving of a corner office? Sinclair Fabrics was floundering, and Flynn was at serious risk of losing Ned. Throw in a few glasses of scotch and Flynn had to be out of his mind. "What else did Flynn say?"

Again Ned rubbed his thighs. There was always a beat of hesitation before he spoke, as if he was grappling with what to divulge. "That Jas isn't doing his part."

"How could he not be doing his part? Didn't Jasper come up with a whole new marketing plan?"

"A plan they didn't ask for that spent money they don't have.

They hate that he's around now, and they hate that he's trying to help them."

"If Flynn and Bebe don't want his help, what do they want?"

Ned looked at me like I was a moron. "His money," he said. "Flynn and Bebe are vultures, and they think Jasper's an easy meal."

Where there's money, there's someone reaching for the pot. What I'd told Camilla was true. She and Norton thought a ransom note was on the way . . . but what if this attempt at extortion was an inside job? Jasper was careful with his finances, and according to his grandmother, he had savings to spare. But all three siblings had received an inheritance just two years ago. It didn't add up.

"Why would they need Jasper's money?"

"I told you, the company's tanking."

"Bebe implied it's a temporary slump."

"She's lying. After Baldwin and Rachel died, Flynn found out the company was deep in debt. He had to pay off a bunch of suppliers and creditors. Bebe pitched in, but it wasn't enough. Flynn's trying to keep it quiet, but I'm pretty sure they're gonna declare bankruptcy. Long story short, they're screwed."

The Sinclairs' wealth, the posh apartments in the city, their status as the heads of an iconic Garment District institution, the family legacy . . . all of it hinged on keeping Sinclair Fabrics afloat, and by Ned's account, it was sinking fast. They were the picture of prosperity, among the Thousand Islands' most elite residents, on par with railroad tycoon George Pullman and Isaac Singer with his sewing machines—according to Tim. I couldn't imagine them losing it all. Or how desperate they must be to keep it.

I looked around the library I'd spent so many hours in. With its rich wood built-ins and enormous collection of hardback books, the room was stunning. The whole island was. "There has to be more family money than that. This place must be worth a fortune."

"Sure it is. It's a goddamn gold mine. But Tern belongs to Camilla."

"Can't she loan Flynn and Bebe the money to get the business back on its feet?"

He flinched and said, "How should I know?"

Camilla. The previous day, when Jasper and Abella planned to play cards with Camilla, it was Ned they'd chosen to round out the game. In his interview, Flynn told me Ned encouraged him to drop in on Camilla. Ned knew she'd been waiting for Flynn to arrive at the island. That meant Ned had spent time with her already.

"I know Camilla's sick," I said. "There'll be an inheritance soon. Why would Flynn and Bebe need Jasper's savings if they have more money coming to them?"

"Not my family, not my problem. Look, that's all I know." Ned leaned back in his chair and tried to look confident. "We done?"

I'd gone into the interview believing Ned Yeboah was pivotal to the case. He'd been disingenuous with Flynn, and his behavior on the island was troublesome. Yes, he'd shown loyalty to Jasper and Abella, his besties from the city. As for Bebe, the woman he was sleeping with, he'd just called her a liar.

I wanted to believe Ned was an honorable person. I don't know any hardened criminals who voluntarily spend their weekends cleaning up dog poop. I had to admit, though: the man was starting to piss me off. I'd waited all day to talk to him, and while he'd given me more to work with than the others, he was still holding out. Flynn, Bebe, Abella, Miles . . . every road led back to Ned.

"You wanna be done?" I said. "Okay, let's finish with a recap. Jasper's been missing for hours and that's blood up there on his sheets, a lot of it. He was here last night, and now he's not. This house is filled with his closest family and friends. I have a hard time believing not one of you knows what happened here."

I tented my fingers and studied his face. "It's been a long day, Ned, and I've conducted a lot of interviews. Would you care to know what I found when I grilled the others? I found you. You and Bebe." I nodded at the window. "Out there, in that shed."

Ned's face opened up in surprise, and I felt a prickle of fear. Was it possible I was wrong? "You're having an affair with her," I said, pushing harder. "You're sleeping with Bebe behind Flynn's and Jasper's backs, and yesterday somebody caught you. There was no mistaking what they saw. I have to tell you, Ned, it's been suggested you might not have been so sorry to wake up and find Jasper gone. That maybe you had something to do with our missing person and his blood."

"That's bullshit. Who said that?"

"You say Jasper's a good friend, but it looks to me like you used him to get to Flynn and now Bebe."

"That's not true. I didn't do that." Ned's long fingers clawed at his knees.

I was wired and my senses hummed—my questions were getting to him, at last. "You put Abby's boyfriend's life at risk when you went out to that shed."

"Don't you talk about her," he said in a fierce voice. "Don't you say her name."

"How do you think she felt when she saw you fucking Jasper's sister? Because she did see, Ned. It was Abby out there, not him."

In a flurry of movement Ned got to his feet—and I reached for my gun. The burn, the gauze, the pain, none of it mattered when my fingers made contact with the pistol grip. In a fraction of a second I was looking down the barrel at Ned.

"Fuck! Don't shoot!" cried Ned. "I was just gonna leave, that's all!"

What the hell? I'd drawn my weapon. Why had I drawn my weapon? My heart was in my throat and Ned's hands were in the air, his face scrunched up in fear. The man towered over me, but he was unarmed and obviously scared, and there I was ready to splatter his brains all over the library wall.

"Sit," I said, my head hot with shame and my 9mm bouncing all over the place. I holstered the gun. *Pull yourself together, Shay, my God.* It was the pressure of the day, I told myself. I was off my game. But what if it was something else, too?

"I'm all out of patience," I said.

Ned sat down hard. He was shaking, and he couldn't get control of his hands. "Okay! Okay. Last year, Bebe and Flynn met with Camilla in the city. They wanted to borrow some money."

"How much money?"

"Five million."

My mouth dropped open. "Did she give it to them?"

"Yeah. It was supposed to be part of their inheritance. She doled it out early, even sold the boat to pad the check. But they spent it all on the business."

"Five million," I repeated. "Just . . . gone."

Ned's Adam's apple wriggled down his throat. "And they still needed more. On July fourth weekend they asked to see her again. Here, on the island. Jas and I came, too, and Miles brought Jade. We all knew how sick she was by then. I honestly thought they wanted to say good-bye. But instead Flynn and Bebe asked for more money. This time, Camilla turned them down."

I drew in a breath. "So they asked Jasper." I was on the edge of my chair again, my eyes unblinking and dry. "But Jasper refused."

"It's not that he doesn't care about the company," Ned said. "He's working damn hard to turn things around. But now Flynn and Bebe are practically broke, and Jas doesn't want the same thing to happen to him. He was planning on quitting. He was done with them."

Past tense. There it was.

"All the money Camilla has left goes to Jasper now."

Unless Jasper's not around to take it. "You should have told me this hours ago," I said through gritted teeth. Ned Yeboah had been sitting on the motive that explained almost everything, and he'd done it because he didn't want to upset his lover. But it wasn't Ned who was causing anger to thrum in my veins. This was the missing piece I'd been hunting for. I'd interrogated everyone else on Tern Island. I should have managed to expose this critical data point long ago.

"If Bebe's involved in Jasper's disappearance, you can't protect her," I said. "She—"

"Protect *her*?" Ned's laugh was chilling. "I'm not protecting that bitch. She used me to make herself feel young. Begged me to tell her how sexy she is." He said it with revulsion. "Don't you see? Bebe's my *way out*. I made the worst mistake of my life getting together with Flynn, and he refuses to accept it's over. He texts me in the middle of the night freaking about some picture of me and a friend he saw on Instagram. Two weeks ago he followed me to my parents' place and yelled up at my window like a fucking psychopath. Those two can go to hell together, for all I care—and I swear, if they did something to Jasper? I'll send them there myself."

NINETEEN

The case came down to money: Jasper had it, and his siblings needed it. At least, that's what Ned wanted me to believe. He'd taken his time with the big reveal, and I was uncomfortable with that, but numerous aspects of his story rang true. Between the delicate state of Camilla's health and Jasper's forthcoming engagement, what remained of the Sinclair family fortune was about to be redistributed, and Flynn and Bebe didn't stand to profit. If they hoped to save the business, they needed another influx of funds. It was now or never. Their last chance to make a change.

It was a believable motive, but did Jasper's siblings really have it in them to kill their kid brother? I didn't subscribe to Tim's utopian ideals—there are bad people everywhere, an island paradise included—but this was an especially heinous crime, one that took grit and a heart cold as a river stone. To pull it off, Flynn and Bebe had to work together. But Bebe was sleeping with Ned, and I had a hunch she didn't know she was being used. The idea of her partnering up with her brother boggled my mind, as did the notion that Flynn could control his anger long enough to tiptoe while butchering the man he loathed in a full house in the dead of night.

Alone in the library, I took a minute to text Tim the latest news: another witness statement, another motive, this time supported by physical assault. I recapped everything Ned had said. Tim was my investigator, but it was my idea to drag him out here, and I owed it to him to keep him informed. Still, I made a point of leaving out the incident with the gun.

If Tim had been with me when Ned gave his statement, he would have found a way to argue that Jasper survived. There was an element of willful ignorance to Tim's attitude. I knew he'd draw a different, much less dramatic conclusion, like that Jas knew what was coming and took off while he still could. If he did, I'd tell Tim he was wrong. Why leave Abella behind? Jasper was about to propose to the girl, yet he'd abandoned her in a house with two greedy, angry, unscrupulous people who were out of options. And if Ned was such good friends with Jasper, why did he wait all day to reveal critical information that could help us solve this case?

The text I'd been waiting for from McIntyre finally came while I was finishing my message to Tim. I didn't waste any time calling her back.

"What'd you find?"

"No 'hi, Maureen'? No 'how's tricks?'"

I laughed. "Sorry. Eager beaver, I guess."

"As you should be. I've got news."

Sheriff McIntyre had done extensive digging. Some of the facts she reported I'd already unearthed for myself, and to my dismay nothing she added pointed a big foam finger at any one of our witnesses. Nobody had a criminal record, and aside from Miles's divorce from Jade's mother, there was nothing unexpected in the way of publicly recorded relationships. In keeping with their respective accounts, all the guests lived in Manhattan. Abella was newly unemployed, but her LinkedIn updates suggested she was actively looking for a job. If she was counting on Jasper for financial help, she was at least smart enough to have a backup plan.

The transfer of power at Sinclair Fabrics from Baldwin and Rachel to Bebe and Flynn also checked out, and it appeared Ned's description of the business's financial health was bang on. By poking around on Twitter, Mac discovered Sinclair Fabrics was soon to be the subject of a magazine feature. A freelance reporter had bombarded the company's Twitter account with inflammatory questions about Attitude and the increasingly competitive textile industry. Domestic suppliers were mostly doing well, and a push on the part of the federal government to buy American meant products like the Sinclairs' were in high demand. Even considering the competition there should have been enough business to go around, so the reporter wanted to know why the company wasn't capitalizing on the opportunity. McIntyre got the sense the piece wouldn't be favorable. The writer's attempts to snag a quote from a Sinclair heir ended with the company ignoring her requests, but that didn't mean a story wasn't imminent. Just one more source of pressure for Bebe and Flynn.

Like Ned said, Camilla Sinclair sold her boat—a "gorgeous 46-foot 2005 Riviera 40 Flybridge," whatever that was—the previous year for close to $600,000. McIntyre tracked Miles to a law office in Midtown, where he provided general counsel to companies without in-house lawyers. From what McInytre could tell, he'd never worked for Sinclair Fabrics.

As for Philip Norton, it was true he'd been with the family for close to twenty years. He had accounts with the local market, hardware store, and fishmonger on the Sinclairs' behalf, and when he wasn't on the island he rented an apartment in a small complex in Alexandria Bay. Everything our witnesses said about their everyday lives looked to be accurate. Unfortunately for me, the real value lay in what they were keeping back.

"Your turn," McIntyre said when she was through.

"God, where do I start? Jasper's sister is sleeping with his brother's lover, and they think Jasper caught on to the affair yesterday afternoon. Jasper's brother has a history of treating him like garbage and busted his lip last night. Jasper planned to propose to his girlfriend, but his sister's husband's daughter has a thing for him that's not exactly aboveboard for a teenage girl. We've got a terminally ill grandmother sitting on a fortune, and a longtime caretaker about to be out of a job. But right now my money's on the siblings. They're trying to save the family business, and Jasper's due for a big inheritance when his grandma dies. If he's not around, it could go to them instead."

"So just your average open-and-shut case." She snorted. "What does Tim think?"

The question made me hesitate. In the parlor, Tim had looked utterly at ease. Had nothing we'd learned over the course of the day changed his mind about the magnitude of Jasper's disappearing act? "The blood indicates assault, but last I checked, Tim thinks Jasper left the island on his own."

"Okay, what am I missing?" I could hear the confusion in McIntyre's voice. It sounded much like my own.

"Bebe says Jasper gets a kick out of messing with her and Flynn. I guess it's possible he could have staged this, but everything about that feels wrong. Tim's hoping we'll find him in Canada, or back in the city."

"Tim's always been the optimistic type," said Mac. I got the sense she didn't think the personality trait was all that useful. "For what it's worth, I talked to the manager at Jasper's building. He checked the apartment for me. All clear, no indication of anything unseemly."

I nodded to myself. Figured as much.

"I called the hospitals, around here and in Kingston, too," she said. "Jasper hasn't turned up and they've got no John Does that fit his description, dead or alive. If he did leave on his own, he couldn't get back to Tern now if he wanted to."

The storm, she explained, had gotten worse. The National Weather Service was predicting it would rage all night, with gale-force winds and more flooding. Waves were breaking records, and there were fallen trees and downed power lines all over the mainland. An apartment building had caught fire, and the flooding displaced a half-dozen families from their homes. Since I last spoke with Mac, A-Bay had gone from a town quietly shouldering a bit of rough October weather to a community in full-on panic mode. With the trooper boat out of commission, she'd been working on another way to get help to the island. There were available patrol boats a couple towns over, but McIntyre hesitated to dispatch them in such rough waters.

"So," she said after a beat. "How do you feel?"

"I don't know. A little peckish?"

"Shay."

"What? It's been a while since lunch." McIntyre went silent, and eventually I sighed. The truth was, I didn't feel great. There was still no infallible evidence of a murder on the island to validate my gut instinct. Every time I thought I had the case figured out, something happened to make me question my lead. I was sinking deeper and deeper into the family's dark and convoluted lives, and I was running out of air.

How would I have handled this situation a year ago, before Bram and Carson and everything that came with them? I was definitely more suspicious now. Less self-assured. When I pressed him on it, Carson said Bram would make me stronger in the long run, both as a person and a cop, but he made sure to add that I wasn't there yet. I couldn't even use Tim as a barometer to measure how well I was doing my job, not now that Carson had me doubting him. I hated that Carson didn't trust Tim, but I couldn't ignore his warning. There was a reason why my fiancé said what he did.

I used to be a good judge of character. Separating the heroes from the villains was my specialty. It was all so simple back then— get the bad guys, avenge the good. As I listened to McIntyre try to convince me I could count on Tim's help all over again, I thought about how Tim had behaved since arriving on Tern Island. Despite evidence to the contrary, he refused to believe Jasper was dead. I'd relayed every bit of what I'd gleaned from our witnesses. Tim ignored it and stuck to his sunshine-and-rainbows theory that all was well.

Tim knew the islands, and he knew the Sinclairs. At least, he knew *of* them. He seemed relaxed around the family. Like his guard was down. I thought it was an act, his way of getting on their good side, but what if there was more to it? Was it possible he'd met the Sinclairs before? Could it be Tim was concealing something? A relationship of some kind with our witnesses?

I trusted that Tim was a competent investigator, but nothing about his behavior today buoyed my confidence about his ability to help solve this unusual case. He'd tried to incriminate Abella with a ridiculous theory about the blood in the bed. He'd allowed Jade to wander off on her own in the middle of our investigation. When Abella came to me asking to talk, at the exact moment I needed her to break, Tim sent her packing.

Like everyone else in the house, Tim wanted to convince me his account of the situation was the gospel truth. Now, when I pictured him, all I saw were the smiles he'd traded with the Sinclairs and their guests over lunch. How quick he'd been to let me take the reins, and satisfied he was to fade into the background. His confidence on the water and on these islands. The muscles that strained against his clothes.

I thanked McIntyre for her concern and reiterated that I was in full control.

Then I closed my eyes and counted the heartbeats resonating in my hollow chest.

TWENTY

Trust is a trickster. A con man. A shark. We think we know it. We tell ourselves it's a simple emotion. Either it's present or it's not.

Before Bram took me, I trusted in myself. I knew where I came from and where I was going. I was sure about my life. If not for him, I'd still be in full possession of the mettle I once prided myself on. I'd never have drawn my weapon during an interview with a witness. And I would know with certainty whether Carson's warning about Tim was a harbinger of dangers to come.

Bram changed everything.

It was a Friday, and after a week of long hours collaborating with the Seventh Precinct on the murders of Becca, Lanie, and Jess, I was spent. I'd followed a breadcrumb trail of eyewitness accounts, had spoken with everyone from the missing women's friends and loved ones to bar patrons and strangers on the street. I felt duty bound to find the guy. The fact that he claimed to be from Swanton made me feel connected to him. I had an obligation to figure out how my hometown could have produced such a monster. I needed to know who he was.

I should have gone home to a hot shower and a cold glass of wine, but instead I walked to Tompkins Square Park. Bram's most recent victim had been found across the street at a construction site. I wanted to take another look around to see if there was something I missed.

I wandered the park for twenty minutes before it started to rain. There was an Irish pub down the block, its picture window emitting a warm and welcoming glow. A beer. That's what I needed. A few minutes to clear my head.

Scanning the bustling pub from the threshold, I shook off my coat and took a seat at the bar. The bartender, a freckled brunette like me, smiled and said, "What'll you have?"

A lucky break, I thought. *A sign.* There was a theory going around the precinct that Bram lived in the neighborhood. Sooner or later someone would recognize him. His days of ensnaring victims through the dating app were over. The papers had reported on the murders, the women of the East Village were on high alert, and we were monitoring IP addresses associated with user bios on the site. Bram would be crazy to go that route again, but I wasn't convinced that meant he was done. Call it intuition, but I knew he was still out there. I just didn't know where to look.

The pub received a steady stream of off-duty office workers looking for shelter from the cold September drizzle and a well-deserved

Friday drink. A group of women with flat-ironed hair came in and went straight to the bar. I heard them debating cocktail options to kick off their night.

"Fair warning," the bartender said as they settled in a few seats down from me, "this lot's going to keep me busy awhile." I ordered an Irish cream ale and thanked her for her candor. I could have used something stronger, but I wanted to stay sharp. The bartender filled my glass and rolled her eyes while heading off to take a drink order she clearly thought belonged in a dance club in Bushwick.

The creamy froth atop my beer gave way to liquid the color of rust. The effect was like fast-moving storm clouds, and then the beer was empty and I could see straight through the glass. What did I know that could help me find Bram? His victims all met him at a bar, according to the friends they'd left behind, but never the same place twice. His dating-app profile painted the picture of a good guy from a small town—a safe choice for a city girl on the hunt for a husband. The more I thought about it, the surer I felt that Swanton was the key.

When I initially heard about Bram, the first thing I did was call my mother. Dad's newer to Swanton, but Mom's a born-and-raised townie who'd spent decades collecting local gossip. Like any small, working-class town, Swanton had a few shady characters and an underbelly smeared with dirt. Domestic disputes and drugs weren't uncommon. Some of its troubles hit close to home. My mom's family had its share of black sheep. When I was thirteen a cousin was missing for days until the cops found her by a creek in the woods with her head bashed in. She tested positive for meth and was never the same again. But the police didn't manage to establish who hurt her, and Mom said she couldn't think of a single person who could possibly grow up to be a serial killer, not even when, with a wiggle in her voice, she mentioned how I got my scar.

Again and again, the pub door swung open. Crammed with bodies, the place was starting to heat up. I took a swallow of beer and returned my attention to the case. We'd circulated Bram's profile photo around the neighborhood but got nowhere with that. There were dozens of men like him roaming the streets—attractive enough, easy to forget. Often the nastiest people are the ones you'd never suspect, the sweet neighbors and pleasant coworkers. They put on a mask and move among us so we don't notice when they start to circle their prey.

I heard an explosion of laughter nearby and took another sip of beer. The throng of bodies that had formed behind me shifted, and as the rim of the glass touched my bottom teeth a stray elbow made contact with my lower back. The shove pitched me forward against the bar. When I pulled myself up, all I was left with was a half-empty pint and a cold, wet sweater that clung uncomfortably to my skin.

A face appeared beside me. "Crap, I'm sorry, are you—"

"Drenched? Yes, I am."

"That was a good beer you had, too."

"It was."

"That's not right. That beer was just minding its own business. Christ, can't a beer sit at a bar and be left alone?"

I was using stiff little napkins to draw the liquid from my top, and when I finally looked up at the guy who'd wasted my pint, I saw his face was crinkled with amusement. There was something familiar about that face, tenuous as a long-forgotten memory. He had an average build and bangs long enough to flip back the way men his age like to do. The color of his eyes was startling, like snow in the moonlight or ice on a creek. I waited for the grimace I knew would come. Up close my scar looks like a long seam holding together my jaw and my cheek. It's not especially gruesome, not anymore, but it sends a message—*something awful happened here*. People think my bad luck's going to wear off on them. Most aren't willing to take that chance.

The guy's eyes met mine. Somehow in the midst of our banter he'd ordered me a fresh beer. He slid it toward me and smiled.

"God," he said, "these places. Why do I come?"

"For the scenery?" I nodded at the bar babes.

Ignoring them, he held my gaze. "You might be right. I'm Seth, and I'm sorry."

"I'm Shay, and it's okay."

It was easy for us from the start. We were actors in a play, effortlessly lobbing lines back and forth as if we'd rehearsed the moment for months. There were no awkward pauses, no discouraging lulls. I've done some research into mental manipulation, the kind of stuff psychics with their neon signs and crystal balls use to fool people into thinking they're real. The man I met that night relied on a technique called the Barnum Statement. His insights were so surface level and vague they could have applied to anyone. He told me I seemed like the independent type and guessed I had a lot on my mind. Sitting alone at the bar, preoccupied with the case, I convinced myself he'd nailed it. The pub filled and emptied, patrons flowing in and out like water in a tide pool. We talked until closing time.

"Last call," the bartender said. There was a chorus of groans from the end of the bar and one of the women drinking cocktails hiccuped loudly. Only then did I realized I, too, was drunk. When I pushed back my stool to stand, my head felt like an hourglass filling with sand. I made a sound of surprise and listed sideways.

The edge of the bar felt slippery, like someone coated it with oil. My eyes rolled in their sockets, two greasy marbles in the palm of a hand. Including the one that got spilled, I'd had only three pints all night. I'd gotten up to use the bathroom just once, timing my departure with the bottom of my pint. I knew better than to trust a strange man around my drink. So why couldn't my body connect with my brain?

"Let me call you an Uber, 'kay, love?"

The bartender's voice sounded far away. My head swiveled toward it but I couldn't find her.

"On it," said my new friend, and took out his phone. I tried to focus on his thumb skating across the surface of the screen. That, too, was a blur.

"We have a protocol for this." The bartender again. A phone rang somewhere in the pub, the landline kind. "I have to be the one to do it, nothing against you, yeah? It's the rules."

"Oh yeah, of course. What a sad thing, needing to have a rule like that. I'll wait with her. Is that okay? If I just wait with her outside?"

"She'll need to stay with me," the bartender said, and I thought, *They're talking about me like I'm not even here.* "I'm sorry, rules are rules—O'Dwyer's, hello? Hel*lo*? Ah, shite." She turned her attention from the phone behind the bar to the women she'd filled with cocktails. One of them was vomiting onto the floor.

"No worries, I see it, it's here." His voice was close to my ear. I tried to speak but my lips wouldn't cooperate. Quickly, he steered me toward the door. The wet fall air was a smack in the face, but I still couldn't get the words out. Sand filled every crevice of my brain. Then, suddenly, I wasn't in the bar anymore. I was nowhere.

And I knew I'd found Bram.

TWENTY-ONE

"Drinks in the parlor, everyone!"

Philip Norton's voice rang out through the hall, and all at once they were on the move. Bebe, Flynn, Miles, and Jade made for the staircase. Ned snaked an arm around Abella's waist and they followed reluctantly, like they suspected what was happening was outrageous but didn't know how to resist.

I raised my hands. "Whoa, where the hell do you think you're going?"

"To dress for dinner," said Bebe, as if it was the stupidest question on earth. Abella, in her bloody pajamas, went crimson. The skin under her eyes was marbled with veins.

Cocktail hour. The thought of it pulled my mouth into a grim line. With tensions high, the last thing we needed was to introduce alcohol into the mix. The circumstances surrounding this island-bound case were unorthodox, sure, but no way would I consider allowing a group of sketchy witnesses to have a few rounds. I didn't like the idea of them scattering either.

I glanced at Tim and felt my nerves go taut. *What happens next decides it.* If he was the investigator I thought he was, he'd agree with me on both counts. Tim would back my decision completely.

In response, my associate adjusted his belt and made a noncommittal sound with his teeth.

"We need you to stay in the parlor," I said. "No one's changing. Nobody's having a drink."

"No drinks?" Bebe's expression was halfway manic.

"A change of clothes and a glass of scotch. We're talking basic human needs, here," said Flynn. "What's wrong, detective? You worried I've got a knife under my mattress?"

"Flynn," Ned said weakly. "Don't."

"No, Ned, this is bullshit." Flynn faced me once more. "All day we've done what you asked. We played along with your pointless interviews, and where did it get us? I told you who's responsible for all this hours ago." Flynn's gaze slid from me to Abella. "Why haven't you pressed charges against her? Why haven't you hauled her ass to prison? The fact that she's still here and my brother's not, it makes me fucking *sick*. Get her out of here!" Flynn roared. "What the hell are you waiting for?"

All the color drained from Abella's face. She broke away from Ned and backed up unsteadily until she reached the staircase banister, where, without a word, she threw up on the lustrous floor.

"Jesus," Flynn muttered with loathing as Norton rushed off to get his cleaning supplies. "I'm done following your orders. This is *our house*."

Not yet it's not. "This is an active investigation, so you *will* follow my orders, Mr. Sinclair."

"You're not going to allow this, are you, Wellington?" said Bebe, and one by one every person in the hall transferred their gaze to Tim.

There were no dirty looks for Timmy Wellington. All day long he'd been developing relationships with the family and their guests. They had camaraderie; as far as the Sinclairs were concerned, Tim was on their side. I'd assumed his efforts were strategic, another impressive trick up his sleeve. I wasn't so sure anymore.

"That's enough," I said to Bebe and Flynn before Tim could reply. That's when Norton cleared his throat.

In one hand, Philip Norton held a bucket. The other clutched a bottle of wine. Fresh from the fridge, it glistened with condensation. Tim wrinkled his brow as he looked from the bottle back to Norton's face.

"Are you sure?" Norton said. "Won't you reconsider, given the day they've had?"

They, not we. I didn't expect Norton to clink glasses with the others, but considering how upset he'd been that morning and how well he knew Jasper, it was a strange choice of words. They suggested he alone was free of emotion. Distanced him from the family.

"It's tradition," he went on. "The cocktails, the formal attire. It might seem trivial to you, but I know it would mean a lot to Mrs. Sinclair to be doing something normal with the family. It's a comfort, if you know what I mean."

I didn't bother pointing out that Camilla, still resting upstairs, hadn't been with her family for hours. I was too busy wondering why Norton was dead set on plying the family with drinks. "I'm sorry," I said, "but it isn't appropriate."

Suddenly, Flynn was in my face. "I thought I made myself clear. You don't tell us what to do."

Tim pushed his way between us. "Cool it, Mr. Sinclair. Relax. He's fine."

That last part, Tim meant for me. I wasn't sure why, at first. Then I felt an explosion of pain and realized with a start my hand was once again on my gun.

I wouldn't be where I am today if I had a problem with self-control. I have a remarkable ability to stay calm, even when the situation's dire. That's what Carson called it when I told him what I'd been through: *a remarkable ability to remain calm.* Cops who can't keep their shit together don't stay alive. Some of it's muscle memory, sure. We're trained to react. Nibble your nails, think it through, and you'll have a bullet in your neck long before you make a call. There's a time and place for a freak-out, and it isn't while you're on the job.

What I experienced in that hallway was different. I had no recollection of pulling my weapon on Ned in the library until the muzzle was inches from his face, and couldn't have been more surprised to find it there than if it flew through the window on wings. Now I'd nearly done the same thing with Flynn. My arm trembled. Flynn wasn't backing down. His breath, hot on my face, reeked of stale coffee, but I couldn't move out of its path. I couldn't take my hand off my weapon either. My fingers were welded in place.

"Bebe's right," said Flynn. "You small-town detectives are pathetic. I should never have let Norton call you. You can't help us find Jasper. You can't even find your own ass."

I wanted to tell him to back off, that he was asking for trouble, but the bulk of my energy went toward keeping my hand on my weapon. Flynn was losing it, and if he moved on me I couldn't be sure what I'd do.

"Don't you get it?" Like paper in the blades of a shredder, Flynn drove the words through his teeth. A trail of spittle swung from his lower lip, and as he shouted it splattered, warm and wet, on my cheek. "We invited you to this island, this *private island.* It's time for you to go."

"You think you *invited* us here?" My voice was high, my ears under pressure. I swallowed to clear them, but no dice. I felt like I was underwater.

"That's not how this works," Tim said. His hands were up like he was miming the act of holding us back. Tim had more than enough muscle to contain Flynn, but he just stood there doing nothing. *Small-town detectives are pathetic.*

"Your brother's gone," I said. "All that's left of him is a bloodstain the size of a goddamn garden pond."

"Watch your mouth," said Bebe, "you're in the presence of an innocent child." She tried to wrap a protective arm around Jade's shoulder. The kid recoiled from her touch.

"That *child* dumped boiling water on my hand for her own entertainment." Even before the words left my mouth, I was sure. The spill was deliberate, and Jade was as sadistic as the rest of them. "Jade's a long way from innocent. Are you aware she's obsessed with her uncle? Or that her gossiping may have gotten him killed?"

"Shana," Tim muttered, startling me. He'd broken character, undermined me by using my first name. I ignored him and blinked hard. The walls of the hallway were closing in.

"How *dare* you," Bebe shouted as Jade's eyes filled with tears. "I'll have you fired for this!"

Something happened to her then. As I watched, Bebe Sinclair changed. Her features became a collection of bloated, oversized parts. I knew it was an illusion, a quadrant of my brain adjusting her face to match the person I now knew her to be, but the effect was alarming. *Breathe*, I told myself. *Let these images go and connect with the breath.* But my mind was a zoo with the gates flung open, my thoughts stampeding like underfed beasts. There were skeletons in every closet here, hidden by people who shuffled grudges like playing cards, their diamonds with edges like blades. In the game this family played, the only hearts dealt out were bloodied and beaten until there wasn't a beat left. In that moment, my perspective shifted. These people all looked like monsters to me.

I listened to Carson's voice inside my head.

In your case, Shay, I believe you're under extreme psychological stress. What happened with Bram, it messed with your mind. To put it simply, you're no longer able to separate fact from fiction. We call this cognitive dissonance. Your beliefs are in conflict, fighting against each other, and that impacts your ability to make value judgments. You can't trust yourself to know right from wrong. You'll feel fear when you're safe, see a threat where there's none. And you'll experience the aftereffects of this debilitating condition for a long, long time to come.

"Was it you?" I scrutinized Bebe's hideous face. "Did you hold a pillow over his mouth when you stabbed him, or did you jump at the chance to watch him die?"

She gasped. Near the stairs, Abella wiped her mouth on her sleeve and swayed in place. My chest constricted under my shirt. No, not my shirt—Camilla's. A million ants zigzagged over my arms, and when I clawed at the fabric I swear I felt their globular bodies pop and ooze under my nails. Hours and hours I'd been on the island. The incubation period was almost up. These people were sick, I was at risk of contamination, and nothing, not even my clothing, felt safe. Under the gauze my hand throbbed. *They did this to me*, I thought. *They caused all of this.*

"This is outrageous!" Flynn strained against Tim to reach me. His voice was deafening.

"Or was it you?" I said, staring up at him. I had to know. I needed to hear I wasn't insane, that Jasper was dead and they'd killed him. "How does it feel to know you'll never have to compete with your perfect little brother again? I'll find Jasper like Camilla asked me to, don't you worry. He's in the river, Mr. Sinclair. Right where you put him."

Several things happened at once. Flynn shoved Tim aside and lunged at me. One of the women screamed. Before I could stop myself I drew my weapon, found my target, and squeezed the trigger.

The sound of the gunshot in the hall was tremendous. There was a moment of silence, and then all hell broke loose. Flynn's body hit the hardwood with a mighty thud. There were cries and wails. Tim, on the floor next to him, shouted orders. His hands were already streaked with blood such a vibrant shade of red it hurt my eyes.

Without thinking, I ran. Down the hall.

Out the front door.

Into the storm.

TWENTY-TWO

Flynn was dead, I was sure of it. I was trained to make a shot count. The bullet had ripped through the man's thick chest, just as I'd intended.

Flynn's a suspect, I told myself. *He's dangerous. I had no choice.*

You have no proof he killed Jasper. You don't even know if Jasper's dead.

I had no destination. All I wanted was to escape from the house, and everyone in it. Outside, a row of exterior lights illuminated a winding pathway to the steep stairs that led down to the water, a vast black hole at the base of the hill. That's where I headed, taking the slick steps two at a time and praying my boots would find traction on the rocky treads. Without my raincoat, which still hung in the mudroom, Camilla's shirt was soaked through in seconds. The way it clung to my skin made me want to scream.

Far below me a wave crashed against the stone wall and exploded with a sound like thunder. McIntyre was wrong to trust me with this job. Why didn't I just listen to Carson? I should have known I couldn't trust myself after I drew my weapon on Ned. I saw a killer in every face, a motive in every story. I wasn't just a mess, I was a menace. What made me think I could recover from what Bram did to me? He'd rearranged my instincts and emotions like a kid tossing a puzzle in the air and laughing as the pieces rained down around him. He might as well have killed me in that cellar. The person I used to be—competent, steadfast, true—was dead.

By the time I got to the boathouse, my face was numb and the bandage on my hand was drenched. I stopped to unwrap the gauze. The last layer had fused itself to my seeping skin, but I ripped it off anyway. Savored the intensity of the pain.

The shirt came off next. I tore it open, struggled out, and threw the ball of wet fabric onto the rocks. I wanted to rid myself of everything belonging to the Sinclairs, but it wasn't as easy as ditching Norton's bandage and Camilla's borrowed clothes. Just like Bram, they'd found a way inside my head. My only escape from the madness was to get off Tern Island.

The boathouse was dark. Even through the rain I picked up the rank smell of rotted fish abandoned by minks that couldn't be trapped. I didn't have the keys to the police boat and couldn't have driven it if I did, but I didn't think about any of that when, standing in my wet bra, I groped at the rough interior wall for the light.

"Shana!"

Tim's voice was barely audible over the rumble of the river and torrential rain. He moved faster than he should have been able to on those irregular, rainwashed steps. How had he caught up with me so quickly? Tim didn't have his jacket either. His wet shirt was molded to the contours of his chest.

When he reached me he planted his hands on his knees and took a series of long, wheezy breaths. "What the hell, Shana?" he gasped. *"What the fuck?"*

"You have to take me back to the mainland." It didn't seem like an unreasonable request. Whatever Tim's association with the family, he should want me gone as much as the others. It was leave now or wait for backup to haul me away in cuffs. Tim would have to answer for his offenses—whatever arrangement he had with the family would come out in the end—but it was me who'd take the heat for this case going to shit. The Sinclairs would sue. No paid desk duty for me; I'd be charged with involuntary manslaughter. Would Carson wait for me while I was in prison? All he'd asked was that I leave police work behind so we could be a normal, happy couple like everyone else. Well, he didn't have to worry about me working ever again, and I'd have plenty of free time to plan the wedding. The irony of the situation was almost enough to make me laugh.

"I'll turn myself in when we get there. Just take me back." My voice was steadier than I'd expected. I took some comfort in that.

"What in God's name are you talking about?"

"I killed a witness. Was he your friend? Did I kill your friend, Tim?"

"Have you lost your fucking mind?" Tim looked down at my chest and saw the rain coursing over my near-naked breasts. His eyes got very round. "Where the hell is your shirt?"

"You were right. There isn't a shred of proof out here that

Jasper Sinclair was murdered. But you knew that from the start, didn't you? I bet you know exactly where he is."

Tim reached for my bare arm, but I yanked it away. "What's wrong with you?" he said, voice rising. "Can't you see I'm trying to help?"

"You can help by getting me out of here. Nothing's wrong," I said. "I finally get it."

"No, you don't. For starters, Flynn's not dead."

"What?"

"Lucky for you, your burn fucked up your aim."

No. I'd seen the blood. The shot was true. "You're lying."

"You grazed his shoulder. He'll be fine." He paused and gave me a hard look. "It was self-defense."

Flynn was angry and verbally abusive, but I didn't remember him threatening me. I'd had no cause to draw my weapon, none at all. "But—"

"I'll testify to that."

Why would Tim defend me? It was a trap, it had to be. "Is this the part where you throw me in the river? How much are they paying you to cover up their crimes?"

"Shana," said Tim, sounding exhausted. "Please."

"Carson tried to warn me about you. God, I wish I'd listened."

"Carson what?" Tim's tone changed then. I couldn't discern what that meant. "That makes perfect sense, actually." He said it with a bitter laugh. "How does he manage to fuck me over even when he's not around?"

"Carson's just the messenger. You brought this on yourself."

"For the love of Pete, Shana, help me understand. What is it that you think I did?"

My mouth worked ineffectually. "The Sinclairs," I stammered. "You know them. They trust you."

"I know *of* them," said Tim. "Everybody around here does. And if they trust me, then I did my job. Earlier, while you were interviewing Bebe and Miles? Jade told me her grandmother lived here—right here, in A-Bay—before moving to New York. Doesn't that strike you as a weird coincidence? And while you were talking to Ned, Bebe said Jasper used to beg to go to Antigua with his dad but he always refused to take the kids. Baldwin never even took Rachel until their last trip, the one they didn't make it home from alive."

I couldn't concentrate on what he was saying. All the evidence I'd gathered against Tim flooded my mind. "But you let Jade leave the parlor. You were supposed to watch them."

"The kid said she had to pee. How was I to know she's a lying little shit?"

"Abella was about to tell me something about Jasper. You sent her away."

"I was worried about you! You disappeared for almost an hour, and when you showed up again your hand was wrapped up like a mummy. I wanted to make sure you were okay." Tim dropped to his haunches, head in his hands. "I don't know what this is. I thought we trusted each other. What happened, Shane?"

Hearing the nickname, his way of ribbing me like a friend, left me gutted. Again I reached inside the boathouse in search of the switch. I couldn't stand to be this close to him, couldn't bear the look of disappointment in his eyes. "Nothing happened," I said as I fumbled for the light. "You just don't know me. Not at all."

He stood up. "You're goddamn right I don't. Man, to think I

actually considered trying to talk you out of marrying Carson Gates. I get it now. You two deserve each other."

"What the hell does that mean?"

"It means you're as crazy as he is."

I dropped my hand to my side. "Carson's a psychologist. He's dedicated his life to helping people who've endured unspeakable things, suffered in ways you can't imagine."

"How long have you known him?"

"Long enough," I said.

"Long enough to know Carson's favorite pastime as a kid was pinning all his transgressions on me?" Tim's body went rigid and he closed his eyes. When they opened he fixed me with a cold stare. "When Carson stole money from my mom's purse, I got the blame. He egged the school, and I got suspended. I was with him when he set a porta potty on fire just for kicks. As luck would have it, a cop drove by. When we ran, Carson tripped me so I'd be the one who got caught."

I thought back to breakfast, Carson laughing at that same memory. Except it wasn't the same, not at all.

Tim's hands were fists, his knuckles white. Even sheltered as he was by the overhang of the boathouse roof, his wet clothes whipped in the wind. "The town tried to charge me with second-degree arson. My parents had to hire an attorney. They spent half their savings to get me off the hook, and if they hadn't there's no way I could have joined the force. Carson tried to ruin my life, and almost succeeded. And the crazy thing is he acted like nothing happened, like we were still best buds. My parents had the school put me in a different class. I worked my ass off avoiding him all through high school, couldn't wait until graduation. The day I heard he was moving to New York was one of the happiest of my life, because I thought I'd never have to see that shithead ever again."

I told myself the nausea I felt was due to the smell, all those fish left to rot. Carson's family had told me stories about his childhood. Everyone described him as a good kid who loved to help others, a healer to the core. "That's ridiculous. You and Carson were friends."

"I *thought* we were friends. I wanted us to be. I didn't have a lot of them back then. He was a conniving jerk, and I was a tool. Carson's a user, Shana. You're lucky he hasn't done the same to you."

He's not a good person. Please believe me. It's the truth. "But he wanted to invite you to our wedding," I said, still refusing to accept it, still fighting. "It was his idea."

"Of course it was. He's still playing mind games, even now. If there's a way to humiliate me, he'll find it." The toe of Tim's boot made contact with a stone and he sent it flying toward the river. It disappeared into the mist. "He called me when he moved back to town, you know that? 'Heard you're a cop,' he said. He told me he was marrying a detective from the city, made sure to stress how inconsequential my life is compared to his. 'My girl left the NYPD for me,' he said, 'but hey, don't worry, Timmy, maybe you'll find a lonely cashier and settle down in a nice backcountry trailer park.'"

My legs felt weak. Tim gave me a pitying look. "All of this comes as a complete shock, doesn't it? Classic Carson."

I pictured Carson the way he'd looked that morning. Thought back to our early days together, when he was my appointed therapist. We'd been dating less than a year, but I knew him, didn't I? I couldn't imagine him concealing this from me.

Can't you? I asked myself. *What about the secret you've been keeping from him?*

"You want proof?" Tim said. "Talk to the other kids in our class. Interview my parents, for all I care—and when you get home, be sure to ask Carson about Moonshine Phil."

"What are you talking about?"

"Just another person Carson screwed over. I finally realized where I know Norton from. When I saw him with that wine bottle, I remembered. Back in high school Carson used to filch booze from my folks. They found out, they hid the bottles, I lost my driving privileges—but Carson wasn't about to give up. He found a new supplier, a guy who worked at the liquor store in town. Moonshine Phil—that's what Carson used to call him. He thought Norton was a dumb hick and saw his chance to take advantage."

"Are you trying to tell me you've known Norton since you were a kid?"

"I wouldn't say I knew him. He and Carson had a business relationship. I was just the errand boy. Carson threw him a few extra bucks, Norton sold us cheap liquor through the back door— but Carson realized he could turn around and sell it to our friends at a markup. It wasn't long before Norton's boss found out and he got canned. Guess we know where he went to work after that."

I felt stunned and sick to my stomach. The person Tim was describing sounded nothing like the Carson I knew. Tim's childhood friend was manipulative and cruel. Carson couldn't be that person now . . . could he?

"Look," Tim said with a sigh, "I don't expect you to side with me on this. Think whatever you want. But right now we're working this case together, and we have to finish it."

"I can't." Hike back up to the house to face that family? The idea was unbearable. I needed time to process what Tim said, to make sense of the huge warning sign he just slapped on my future. "If you want to stay, stay. I'm going home."

"And how do you plan to do that? You don't know how to drive the boat. You couldn't get back in the best of weather, let alone this."

"The thing is, Tim, I don't need your permission. Give me the keys."

"The hell I will."

Again I felt along the wall for the light I knew must be there. Tim reached for my arm, and this time he caught it.

"That scene up there?" He nodded at the house and water flew from his hair in a perfect arc. "That was not okay. Pulling a weapon on a witness? Walking out on a roomful of volatile people? You need to tell me what's going on with you, Shana, or you're going to get us both killed."

I was shaking so hard my teeth hurt. Tim unbuttoned his shirt, pulled it off to reveal a white undershirt, and handed it to me. Robotically, I slipped in my arms and folded the shirt over my bare chest. Even sopping wet, it was warm against my skin.

"Tell me what's going on. You owe me that. And if you still want to leave afterward," he said, "I'll take you back to shore myself."

Tim Wellington stepped past me into the doorway of the boathouse. I knew what he was doing. Setting my flight into motion was his way of proving I could trust him on his word. But he didn't understand what he was asking of me.

With no effort at all, Tim located the switch I'd failed to find and the interior of the barnlike building was bathed in light. All the while he held my gaze. That meant I was first to see what lay beyond him in the slips. He watched in confusion as my face twisted in horror. Only then did he turn around to see it for himself.

The boathouse was empty. Our police boat, and the Sinclairs' skiff, were gone.

Tim thrust his hair out of his eyes. "What the . . . did you—"

"No! So who . . ." Under my skin my blood felt like water, fast flowing and cold. "Someone was here, on the island. The trapper?"

Tim's eyes darted from the hydraulic door to the brass cleats on the decking. Norton had used them to tie up both boats earlier. Now they were bare. "No. The door's closed. Norton said there's no remote. Someone opened it from the inside, and closed it the same way. Whoever got rid of the boats was already here on the island."

All day long we'd been stranded on Tern, but this? This was different. A deliberate attempt to rob us of what little power we had. To trap us all. And here we stood while our suspects wandered freely out of sight.

In unison, we turned our wet and sallow faces to the hill.

TWENTY-THREE

Tim took the stairs at a run, and I followed. Halfway up, I slipped and cracked my kneecap against a stone tread, but I got back to my feet and, muddy and sore, limped after him. I tried not to dwell on where we were going, or that there was no chance of escape. No time for those thoughts now.

When we got to the porch, Tim stopped. The front door stood wide open, the hall empty. The entryway floor was plastered with wet leaves, and the mess almost felt like as much of an affront as the bloodstains on Jasper's bedsheets. Like the people inside it, the house's pretense of perfection was in ruin.

The scream reached me in stages, carried by the wind. This time when I drew my gun the act was deliberate. I had no qualms about putting my finger on the trigger, or the pain it caused. Tim motioned with his weapon, and I shadowed him down the hall.

The house was eerily silent. Tim made for the library while I went right, to the parlor. That's where I found Flynn.

Twenty minutes. That's how long we were gone. In that time someone had thrown another log on the fire and Flynn had positioned himself next to it with a glass of scotch, now nearly empty, in his hand. He was shirtless, his hairy chest on display, and I could see the bandage on his upper arm was soaked with blood. Somehow he'd managed to secure a cigarette. Maybe he bummed it from Jade. It was tucked neatly behind his ear. He was alone.

Flynn looked up with a start. He eyeballed my shirt—Tim's shirt—and the mud on my pants, and his expression darkened. Even with my weapon drawn, Flynn made me wary. All the things he'd done to Jasper were fresh in my mind—and what had Jasper done to deserve them? I'd planned to be long gone by now, halfway to the mainland. Instead I was face-to-face with a man who was hemorrhaging from a hole I'd put in his arm.

"Been working hard to find my brother, I see." I could hear both innuendo and the onset of a drunken slur in Flynn's voice.

"Someone screamed. What happened?"

"Is that right?" He reached for the bottle and topped off his drink, never breaking eye contact. "Didn't notice. I've been sitting here all this time. Thinking of you."

I felt my insides spasm. Flynn's eyes glittered black as he held my gaze. The lights in the parlor flickered.

"Shana."

I startled at the sound of Tim's voice. "Did you see that?" I said. I was worried my eyes were playing tricks on me again, but Tim gave a stern nod. Above our heads, a floorboard creaked. Tim looked up at the ceiling.

"Upstairs," he said; then to Flynn, "Stay here."

"I'm not going anywhere," Flynn said as he glared at Tim in his damp undershirt. "I can promise you that."

I led the way out of the parlor and into the hall, where we ran into Norton coming out of the kitchen. "What's going on?" he said anxiously. "I thought I heard a scream." There was a dish towel slung over his shoulder and he smelled of raw garlic and lemon. Not even Flynn's gunshot wound could stop this man from doing his duty for Camilla Sinclair.

"Wait here," Tim said, and by the look on Norton's face he was more than happy to oblige. The treads of the stairs groaned under our boots as we ascended. Halfway up, Tim's eyebrows rose. Bebe Sinclair's face stared down at us from the second-floor landing.

"Thank God you're back," she said, a long pearl necklace dangling from her throat into the abyss. I hadn't noticed that necklace before, and as we continued to climb I saw she had pearl earrings to match. She'd changed the rest of her outfit, too. Now she wore a tight black skirt and matching mohair sweater. Her mourning clothes. "You," she growled at me. "You'll pay for what you did to my brother."

"We heard a scream," Tim said. "What's going on?"

"Nothing good," Bebe replied. "As usual."

Miles and Jade were in the second-floor hallway, near the room I'd identified earlier as a bathroom. Jade had her face buried in his chest. The bathroom door stood ajar and a light was on inside, but father and daughter blocked my view.

"You better take a look in there," said Miles. He'd put on a fresh dress shirt he hadn't had time to button, along with a tweed sport jacket. "It was Ned who found her, just a minute ago."

My stomach clenched. Who was missing? Camilla. Camilla and . . .

"Out of the way." Tim gestured for them to move, and at the sight of our weapons they took a step back. We had a clear path.

We were in.

Under United States law there are two degrees of murder, but those aren't the only ways to classify a killing. There's voluntary manslaughter, like a crime of passion, and involuntary manslaughter, like what I thought I faced after shooting Flynn. When I'd accepted McIntyre's job offer in the tiny town of Alexandria Bay, I hadn't thought Tim and I would ever do more than investigate a break-in at the local dive bar. Like he said, violent crime wasn't common in these parts.

Over the past few months I'd convinced myself what happened with Bram was irrelevant, nobody's business but my own. My past was separate from my present reality. You might even say it was an island. There was no need to tell Tim about Bram, because Bram was one in a million. It was a convenient excuse that allowed me to keep my misery to myself.

But the islands in the St. Lawrence River weren't immune to sin.

Abella Beaudry lay sprawled on the black-and-white checkerboard tile floor. In the too-bright light from the vanity fixture her face was violet, eyes bloated and blank. The rope that killed her was still looped around her throat, and the ring it left was deep and red and raw. Her wounds were fresh, but lethal. There was no saving the girl. Dressed in her pajamas, staggered by the loss of her soon-to-be fiancé, she'd followed this twisted family upstairs to her death.

Ned crouched next to her body mumbling garbled half words as if he were trapped in a nightmare, talking in his sleep. Tim got down next to him and put a hand on Ned's shoulder. The act woke him from his trance.

"Wait in the hall," I told Ned. "Don't go anywhere. You understand?"

"No," Ned whimpered. "No, no, no."

"Go, Ned," Tim said softly when the man didn't move. Only then did Ned stand and walk zombie-like out the door.

"Son of a bitch." Tim's open palm smacked the tile floor so hard I swear I felt the sting. I was too hot, too cold, too everything as I leaned in close to Abella and touched her still-warm arm.

"Look at her fingers," I said. "Rope burns there, too. Someone snuck up on her from behind." I pictured her clawing at the rope as it tightened around her neck. My legs felt wobbly.

"They came up here to change. We were only gone a few minutes. That means . . ."

"Someone's been waiting for their chance to get to her. Norton was downstairs. Flynn, too. But . . ."

"Yeah. But," said Tim. "And what about Ned? Miles, Bebe, Jade . . ." He blinked at me. "I shouldn't have left. No matter what, I should have stayed. Jesus, of all the stupid things to do." He clasped his head in his hands. "This is on me."

"No. She wanted to tell me something. She tried, but I didn't let her. I never went back to find her. Abella was afraid of Jasper's family—I saw it during lunch. She and Jasper had an argument last night. I think he told her something that worried her, or she figured it out for herself. All she wanted was to get away from them. And I left her here alone."

I drew in a shaky breath. People kept dying. I couldn't keep them alive. I didn't stab those three women in New York. It wasn't me who took a coil of rope from the Sinclairs' shed and wound it tight around Abella's neck. But it might as well have been.

Beyond the bathroom door, I could sense the murderer's body

relax. Keen eyes swept the hall, lingering on the others' faces. This is easy, the killer thought with glee. Easier and easier. Child's play. There was no question about it anymore. Abella's murder confirmed what I'd known in my heart to be true. Jasper was dead, and his murderer had killed again. I'd provided a crucial ingredient without which the perpetrator's formula could never have proved toxic. I provided opportunity.

And the killer took it.

TWENTY-FOUR

In the parlor, the scene was otherworldly. Firelight gave the air a Christmasy glimmer, and the room was so hot we all had a ruddy glow. This time I didn't argue about the drinks. It hardly mattered now. Wineglasses were claimed, grips tightened. The atmosphere might have been festive, were it not for two bedraggled investigators and a woman's lifeless body on the upstairs bathroom floor.

I took a breath to calm my jangled nerves and scrutinized the others' faces, hunting for a clue. In mystery novels, the up-all-night-under-the-covers kind I used to love, guilty people don't give themselves away until the end. Real-life criminals are rarely that clever. Over the years, criminologists studying serial killers identified several traits the bad guys tend to share. They can be manipulative, egotistical, charming . . . but underneath it all, they're human. Their palms moisten and their necks go red. They reveal nervous ticks they didn't even know they had.

I used to rely on these kinds of tells to suss out criminals. I was good at it with everyone except for Bram, when it counted most. As I examined our suspects' faces, I felt just as inept. All of them looked guilty to me. Each had his or her own breed of suspicious mannerisms, from Flynn's barefaced disinterest to Bebe's over-the-top expression of horror and Ned's sudden weak-kneed demeanor, an about-face from how he'd been in the parlor when he threatened Bebe and Flynn. Miles buttoned his shirt with unsteady hands, maintaining a respectable level of distress. Red-eyed, Jade shuddered and yawned uncontrollably into her fist, but as genuine as her nerve-numbing exhaustion appeared to be, I didn't totally buy it. Even Camilla had that oddly timed full face of makeup (had she reapplied lipstick after her nap?) to keep me on my toes. Among all our witnesses, Abella was the only one I felt sure I understood. She'd been constant in her normalcy.

No wonder she was gone.

"I have some very upsetting news," Tim said.

"Don't tell me we've run out of booze." Flynn reached for the scotch and topped off his glass.

A muscle shifted in Tim's jaw. "It was strangulation. Abella Beaudry is dead."

Reporting a death is never easy. It's the part of the job every investigator hates. There's a wide spectrum of misery in the reactions you get from friends and next of kin, and though we always try not to, we absorb some of their pain. Tim didn't need to feign heartbreak to keep up the everyman act. All day he'd defended these people. And they'd failed him in the worst way.

They had to know what was up before Tim opened his mouth

to speak. Abella no longer sat among them. They were all aware that Ned went into that bathroom to check on his friend and came back out alone. But when Tim said what he said, Camilla let out a small cry anyway. Jade's scream had brought her back downstairs, but her energy was fading, the air around her flat. "That poor girl," she croaked. "That innocent young thing."

Flynn threw back the scotch in his glass in one gulp. "Innocent, my ass. She hung herself. Phil, can I get a light?"

Norton moved stiffly toward the matchbox on the mantel. Nearby, Ned flexed his fingers in his lap. His voice, when he spoke, came from the back of his throat. "You're a fucking prick, you know that, Flynn?" Ned said.

Ned was with Bebe in the shed. Either one of them could have grabbed that rope. Ned seemed genuinely upset over the loss of his friend, but he was sweating again. His skin appeared as clammy as it had during our interview, when he'd hidden what he knew about Flynn and the fight.

"I call it like I see it." Flynn accepted the matchbox from Norton and lit up. "Right now all I see is selfish whores."

He looked straight at me as he said it. Fueled by booze, Flynn's anger was mounting. Tim didn't seem to notice. He was focused on Norton, who walked around the room filling wineglasses to the brim. Just as in Flynn's account of the previous night, Jade held up a glass for her share. This time, Miles didn't protest. I figured he thought his daughter could use something to calm her nerves. Or maybe Miles only disapproved of Jade's drinking when Jasper was doing the pushing.

Across the room, Bebe glared at Flynn. "You know Nana hates it when you smoke indoors. I'm sorry, Nana. Flynn's a thoughtless pig."

"Extenuating circumstances." Smoke flowed freely from the sides of Flynn's smiling mouth. "That bitch killed my brother and then hung herself. You'll excuse me if I'm a little stressed."

Camilla's expression hardened. The skin around her hollow eyes was the color of an old bruise. "Stop it, Flynn. My Jasper's alive. Whatever happened here doesn't change that. My God," she said, clutching her throat. "This is my house—my *home*. Every summer of my son's life was spent here. Yours, too," she said to her remaining grandchildren. "How could something like this happen?"

"It isn't right," said Miles. "I feel for that girl, I really do, but suicide? Here? It's reprehensible."

"It's *homicide*," I said. "In case you haven't connected the dots, that means someone here's guilty of murder."

There was a collective gasp. These people had skills. Every one of them managed to look shocked.

"You're no longer witnesses to Jasper Sinclair's disappearance. All of you are now suspects in a violent murder." Pacing as I spoke, I looked them each in the eyes. "Someone in this room stole that young woman's life." I laid it on thick, giving them my best Poirot. "Waited for their chance to attack, and wasted no time doing it. We have yet to confirm it, but Wellington and I strongly suspect whoever killed Abella is also responsible for Jasper's disappearance. One or more of you will be charged with voluntary manslaughter. If it turns out whoever did this planned these killings in advance, that's first-degree murder. Under New York penal law we're talking a minimum twenty years. Max sentence is life without parole."

Jade squealed and Miles looked at her in alarm. "Detectives," he said, pulling his startled daughter to her feet, "I'd like to request that we be excused. This isn't good for Jade—for Christ's sake, she's just a kid. I'd like your permission to take her back to town."

"There's no getting to the mainland right now," said Tim.

"Screw the storm!" said Miles. "Norton knows how to drive a boat in bad weather. You two made it here this morning, didn't you? Norton will take us. We'll be fine."

"I want to go with Philip," Jade said. She looked up at Norton with huge, wet eyes. "You'll take us, right?"

Norton smiled. "'Course I will, honey."

"If they're leaving," said Bebe, "then so am I."

"Me too," said Ned. "We've got two boats. We're only nine people now." He paused to swallow the lump in his throat. "Get me the hell off this island."

"I'm telling you, that's not an option at this time," said Tim. "Earlier, when Senior Investigator Merchant left the house, she had the foresight to check the boathouse. Both your skiff and the boat we used to get here are gone. It looks to us like someone willfully let them go."

Tim had covered for me. *Of course he did*, I thought. *He can't have them knowing I lost my mind.*

Miles looked from Tim's face to mine in confusion. "Are you telling me there are no boats here at all?"

"No boats, no way off the island until another police vessel makes it out," I said.

In the sliver of silence that followed, the wind picked up. Even in the shelter of the parlor the storm sounded fierce. Again the lights in the room flickered.

"I want to go home," Jade cried, louder than was necessary, as she nuzzled her father's sport jacket.

"Soon, baby, soon—and we don't ever have to come back here again. Well?" Miles said, raising his voice. "Who was the idiot who sent our only hope of getting out of here into the channel?"

"Phil," Ned said abruptly. "You handle the boats. You're the one who helped us dock when we got here."

Norton gave a start and shook his head. "It wasn't me! I don't . . . the trapper! He must have come back."

Bebe said, "Ned's right. It's Norton who should have checked them. Maybe he did." She pivoted to face the caretaker. "Maybe you're the one who let them go."

"Don't be ridiculous," said Camilla. "Philip would never do such a thing. How could you even suggest it?"

"You heard them," said Bebe. "Someone in this room is a killer, and I refuse to believe it's a Sinclair. My God, we're not animals."

"I've got a dead body that suggests otherwise," I said.

Bebe ignored me. "How can you defend him, Nana? Philip's not even family!"

Camilla's eyes flashed. "He's family to me."

A violent flush crept up Norton's bare neck. "I swear it, to all of you. It wasn't me."

I was inclined to believe him, but there was no denying Norton was in a unique position on the island. He had the freedom to wander off without anyone batting an eye. It was his job to be invisible, to live on the fringe of this miniature society, and he spent more time alone than any of them. He wasn't part of the family in the same way as the others, regardless of his relationship with Camilla. Norton had no reason I could see for wanting to hurt Jasper or Abella. That didn't make him innocent.

"Ned's not family either," Miles pointed out.

"Neither are you, Miles," said Ned.

"Ned and Abby were friends. Ned and Jasper, too," said Bebe, keen to protect her lover. "If someone let the boats go that means someone wants us stranded here. But *why*?"

Flynn began to laugh. It started as a chortle, the intensity building until his voice boomed through the room. When he was done he wiped his eyes and tapped the ashes from his cigarette onto the coffee table. "Guilty," he said with a shrug. "It was me. I let the boats go free."

Tim and I swapped glances. We hadn't been back to the boathouse all day. The boats could have disappeared hours ago. Other than Norton, Flynn alone hadn't come to the parlor when Tim asked him to that morning. He could have slipped outside while I conducted my search of the house. He had plenty of time to make it to the boats and back.

"Care to explain?" Tim said.

"It's simple. My boyfriend was threatening to leave me," Flynn said. "He abandoned me in the city yesterday morning, and when I finally caught up with him here, he completely blew me off. I knew the next time Ned went somewhere without me he wasn't coming back, and I had a hunch it wasn't going to be all snuggles by the fire this weekend. Obviously, I was right—and it worked out perfectly, because now there's plenty of time to explain why he's fucking my sister."

My eyes went straight to Camilla. Bebe's desperate pleas to Miles in the library made it sound as if learning about the affair would kill Camilla on the spot. We didn't need another dead body on our hands. If Camilla heard what Flynn said, it didn't register. Quiet now, she stared absently at the blackened embers in the hearth.

In fact, no one spoke as Flynn's eyes traveled the room. "Ahh," he said slowly. "I see how it is. Everyone knew but me."

Standing in the doorway, I tapped the toe of my wet boot on the floor. After talking to Ned I'd been fairly sure Flynn was our man. He and Bebe might have collaborated on the plan, but Flynn did all the heavy lifting. If he was the killer, though, why rob himself of his only escape from Tern Island? A visit to the boathouse earlier meant he could have taken off before we even knew he existed. Why stick around?

The man was entirely focused on outing Bebe and Ned. It was obvious he knew about the affair—but how? Flynn's analysis appeared to be right; based on their reaction, everyone save maybe Camilla was already aware of Bebe's tryst. So how had Flynn discovered it, and when?

It had been ages since that first interview in Flynn's bedroom, but I probed my memory for a sign he'd known then. The conversation Flynn had with Ned when he got to the island suggested he had his suspicions. He'd questioned Ned's decision to travel with Bebe, and noted his lover's evasive response. Now, though, he was certain. Between yesterday and today something settled it.

On Flynn's neck ropy veins rose up from the skin, bloated to bursting with fury and humiliation. This discovery was fresh, his emotions unprocessed. Someone had told him recently. Possibly within the hour.

I scanned the faces in the room. Next to her father, Jade was doing her best to hide hers. It was she who disclosed Jasper's proposal plan to Ned. She'd told Miles, and possibly also Jasper, about seeing Ned and Bebe enter the shed. There was little for a girl Jade's age to do in a place like this, especially during a storm. She hadn't been texting or calling her friends, which meant that something else had occupied her time during the countless hours she'd spent in the parlor with her father's wife's eccentric family. And now Flynn was smoking one of her cigarettes.

I had to wonder whether Jade could even begin to comprehend the enormity of what she'd done. In a way, it was a shame Miles was leaving Bebe. When it came to the Sinclairs, Jade fit right in.

"Flynn," Bebe said, glancing at Camilla once more. "Not now. Not like this."

"How then, Bebe? Back in the city? At work? Does everyone there know, too? The irony is perfection, and you don't even see it. I'm guilty," he said. "And not just of releasing a couple of boats. But you know what, sis? So are you."

"Don't listen to him," Bebe said quickly, to no one and everyone. "He's out of his mind. My brother would never hurt Jasper."

"Hurt him? I *ruined* him," said Flynn. "Jasper, Nana, even you."

It wasn't a confession of murder, but Flynn was admitting to something. Looking at the shirtless brute reclining in his buttery navy moccasins made me furious. "Spill it," I said. "If you were involved in what happened to Jasper, or Abella, or anything else linked to this investigation, tell us. Right now."

"Flynn," Bebe said. Her tone was dangerous, but it made Flynn smile. He liked watching her suffer. Enjoyed the suspense. This was his big moment, and he relished it.

"My darling sister. What I'm guilty of is tax evasion on a scale you couldn't possibly imagine." Flynn watched as Bebe went pale. Tipped back his dark head, and laughed some more. "We've got dear old Dad to thank for laying the groundwork for us. He was hiding money in the Caribbean. That's why he was always in

227

Antigua. He kept a bank account down there, fattened it up real nice. It's not enough to bail us out, unfortunately. Not even close."

Bebe's skin had turned the color of raw river fish. "No. No, I would have known. It isn't true."

"Don't feel bad you didn't spot it, you were a little distracted," said Flynn. Ned, when Flynn looked at him, pressed his lips together and said nothing. "I couldn't pay the taxes, you see, not without tipping off the IRS, so I kept doing what Dad did, thinking I could fix it in time. Well, guess what? Time's up. I got a call the other day. There's going to be an audit. It's all coming out. Not paying our employees? All those bills you've been ignoring? That was nothing. This is so much worse."

Bebe shook her head. "But I didn't know."

"You're the fucking CEO. I didn't report it. But neither did you. We're in this together—as far as the IRS is concerned, you're just as guilty as me. I'm going to jail. And I'm taking you with me."

Dumbfounded, Bebe stammered, "But I'm your sister."

"Yes. Yes, you are. But what does that mean, really? Family's just a collection of people who happen to be bound by blood. I don't owe you anything. Not you, and not anyone else."

"Jasper," I said. "Did he know?"

"He knew enough not to hand over his inheritance when we asked for it. If he had, it would be long gone by now." Flynn nodded in his grandmother's direction. "Nana's money, too. That bastard always was smarter than me. I hope he burns in hell."

Flynn's hair had fallen into his eyes. He threw back his head the way Bram used to and jutted out his chin, one last-ditch attempt at pride. The similarity between them in that moment sickened me, but it also made my limbs rigid and ready. "Sinclair Fabrics would have been seventy-five years old next year, did you know that?" Flynn said. "We were going to have a party. It was Nana's idea—wasn't it, Nana? Picked a date and everything. I hope to God you die soon," he said under his breath, his gaze on his grandmother and his mouth on the rim of his glass. "I'd really hate to disappoint you."

I felt no empathy for Flynn, none at all. I didn't pity him for the terrible situation his father left him in. It meant nothing that Flynn and Bebe's attempts to take Camilla's and Jasper's money were fueled by a desire to keep the family's legacy alive. Yes, they'd invested years of their lives in the business, while Jasper's entire career to date had gone to ensuring some other company's success. None of that justified how they treated their brother, or their grandmother, or anyone else. Their hardships didn't make the be havior these sick siblings exhibited forgivable. Jasper was gone. He was gone and his girlfriend lay dead on the floor.

"Philip," Bebe said with a quiver in her voice, "take Nana to the library so she can lie down." Camilla, it seemed, had entered some sort of trance. A puddle of drool glistened at the corner of her mouth and her wineglass hung precariously from her fingers. Norton wasted no time in carrying out the request. With a few soothing words he coaxed Camilla up, took her hands in his, and guided her from the room. My eyes lingered on her glass, the wine it contained was paler than the chardonnay the others guzzled around her.

"She doesn't look good." I heard Camilla's shallow, labored breathing as she passed, and I stopped them at the door. "Mrs. Sinclair," I said, "are you all right?"

The old woman's lips fluttered. Her breath smelled oddly sweet.

"It's the medication," said Norton. "It makes her tired. She just needs to rest."

"Should she be drinking while she's undergoing treatment? You've been serving her wine."

"What, that? It's watered down. There's hardly any wine in it at all."

"You mix it in the kitchen?"

"Easier that way."

"How often does she take them?" I watched his face. "The drugs."

"Two . . . no, three times a day." Nobody in the room challenged him. No one said a word. I doubted they had a clue what her cancer treatment entailed. Only Jasper would have bothered to ask.

"We should keep an eye on her," I said, stepping aside to let them pass.

Norton nodded as he led Camilla into the hall and then the library, where he settled her on the couch and covered her with a blanket. Lying on her back, the old woman looked like a corpse.

In the parlor Flynn's cigarette was down to the filter. Again the lights flickered. I hadn't thought to ask Norton if the house had a generator.

Flynn said, "How about a little Q and A?" His face was red and he was sweating heavily. The man was plainly drunk. "I came clean, now it's Ned's turn. Tell me, sweetheart, what's so enticing about my sister? Is it her delicate features? Her sweet-natured personality? It sure isn't her money. God knows she's got none of that."

I glanced at Bebe, who was looking at her brother goggle-eyed. She wasn't over the shock of Flynn's bombshell news, and in her delayed response her soon-to-be ex-husband saw an opening.

"I have a question, too," Miles said from his chair. "Mine's for Bebe. What drew you to our good friend Ned? At first I thought this was some kind of charity project—fuck a dirt-poor African kid, feel like a million bucks—but Ned's bank account is a lot bigger than yours these days, so now I'm not so sure."

"Whoa," I said, leaning into the balls of my feet. Across the room Tim did the same, preparing to dive into the brawl that was surely seconds from breaking out. Ned's face was creased with fury, teeth clamped and nostrils wide, but he didn't move or utter a single word.

In more than a decade working with the police in the city, I'd heard so much offensive language I could write a dictionary of abominable slang—but Miles's racist remark was shocking in its cruelty. I couldn't fathom why Ned didn't have him up against the wall. His restraint revealed a lot. Ned was accustomed to this kind of treatment from Flynn, who used and abused him every chance he got, but I didn't get the sense that Ned was a pushover either. Then I remembered there was a child in the room around the age of Ned's youngest sibling.

"My turn," I said, capitalizing on the chaos. For the moment our suspects' attentions were diverted, but I knew that wouldn't last. "Who killed Abella? Come on, guys, think of it as family bonding. Free therapy."

Bebe's face was violet with rage. "All of you can go to hell."

"Already there," said Flynn.

"Enough. Goddammit," said Tim, "that's enough. Listen up, all of you. New rules. From now on, nobody leaves our sight."

Despite facing the prospect of being under house arrest all over again, the group emitted no further signs of dissonance. Score another win for Tim's social skills. He was still the good cop in their eyes. They trusted him, and my nonsensical behavior had probably contributed to that. It was the one and only perk to acting batshit crazy on a case.

There was another reason our suspects didn't object. Nobody was accustomed to being in physical danger on a dark and stormy night. Sitting in a room with a single exit and two BCI investigators at the door was the only safe place on Tern Island, and the best scenario they were going to get.

"In a minute," Tim said, "Merchant here is going to make a call to the sheriff."

At that, Bebe let out a snort. Sheriffs were another trapping of the small-town life she looked down her nose at from her penthouse in Manhattan.

"The sheriff," Tim went on, "will immediately dispatch a team of officers to transport you to the mainland. You'll be questioned at the police station in Alexandria Bay, at which point you'll be free to contact an attorney." Tim glanced at Miles. The only attorney in the room seemed to have no problem with Tim's instructions.

The relief I felt at hearing them was vast and cool as a lake. Since the moment we found Abella Beaudry's body I'd been racking my brain over what to do. Our six remaining suspects—I'd long since ruled out brittle and sickly Camilla—were unpredictable and cruel, but they were also human. At some point they'd need to eat again, or use the bathroom. Even burdened by the memory of what happened the last time they went to bed, they'd eventually need to sleep.

All the bedroom doors featured the same antique lock and key as Jasper's, which meant Tim and I could lock everyone in. There'd be no way for them to get from the second-story windows down to ground level without breaking some bones, and no way to get through a locked door without breaking it down. I'd been having visions of a long, abysmal Agatha Christie–style night spent watching those doors and waiting out the storm. But help was finally coming, and not a moment too soon. We were getting off the island at last.

Bebe drained what was left of her wine. Ned nibbled at the skin around his flawless nails. When Tim was satisfied they'd comply with his orders, he nodded at me to follow him into the hall.

"Okay, Shana," he said, out of earshot of the others, "start talking."

I was determined to be professional about the situation. Everything Tim had said about Carson could wait. I wasn't prepared to make a call about our killer, but I had some ideas. "It's all about the money," I told him. "Flynn and Bebe don't have any, but Jasper does, and he's in line to get more when Camilla's gone. If Jasper's not around to take it, there's a good chance it goes to them.

"That explains Jasper's disappearance, and Abella's, too. She either knew who killed him or why. Something happened over the course of the day that tipped her off, because she hadn't caught on this morning when I interviewed her, I'm sure of that. That's why she wanted to talk to me. She had a lead on the killer, based on some behavior she saw in here, or some realization she had about her argument with Jasper. And the killer knew it.

"Now, who can we eliminate?" I went on. "Camilla, for one. She's way too weak, and she's got no motive. As for Jade . . . Jade's trouble, and I'd be willing to bet she's furious with Jasper *and* the girlfriend who took him from her. Could she move Jasper's body? No—at least not alone—but she may not be entirely blameless."

"That all sounds pretty reasonable," Tim said, interrupting me. "A second round of interviews could get us closer, remove a couple more people from the equation. But this isn't why I brought you out here."

It took a second for me to catch on. "What," I said. "Now?" I sounded like Bebe in the library, trapped and desperate to wriggle away, but I couldn't help it. "Shouldn't I be calling McIntyre?"

Tim glanced back at the parlor. We were shoulder to shoulder with clear sight lines, just a few feet from the door, but even that amount of distance from our suspects made me deeply uncomfortable, and I could tell Tim shared my apprehension. "You know how I feel about this case," he said. "I never tried to hide it. I believed we'd find Jasper alive. I don't anymore." His gaze moved up the stairs toward the crime scenes, the second room we'd locked to preserve what we could. "These people are dangerous. Whatever's going on with you, you need to tell me. I have to know you're capable of doing this."

No way, I thought. *Not now, not like this.* "The deception, the lies," I said, "it's what I've been trying to warn you about all day. The trapper's in the clear, and there's nobody but us on the island. The killer's right there, in that room. So maybe this isn't the time for a chat. Look, when we get back to the station later I'll spring for a coffee—the good stuff, not office crap—and spill my guts, okay? All you need right now is my assurance I can make it another hour until help comes, and you've got that. I swear, Tim, I'm fine."

And I was. An hour, I could do. Minutes from now this depraved, perverted family would be in my past.

"You're new to these parts. I get that," he said. "But you can't seriously still think the cavalry's coming."

"What? But you said—"

"You want them knowing we're on our own indefinitely? I sure don't. Call McIntyre, by all means. Tell her what happened. Maybe skip the part about shooting Flynn. But understand, it's just you and me out here tonight, on an island with one skilled killer—maybe more—who won't hesitate to slit our throats. They have the numbers." The trace of alarm in Tim's eyes belied the steadiness of his voice. "They might hate each other, but who do you think they'll side with if it comes down to family or the cops? These people are angry and scared. They'll turn on us in a heartbeat, and as you demonstrated earlier, you're a lousy shot. We've got to have trust, Shane. I have to be able to rely on you a hundred and fifty percent, because you were right, okay? It's us against them. So tell me why you freaked out back there so we can make sure it doesn't happen again."

Us against them. Hearing my own words thrown back at me had a paralyzing, hornet-sting effect. No one was coming. It was just us.

I'd never seen Tim take a firm stance on anything—the man hated making decisions, would happily defer to someone else on everything from his sandwich order to where to park the car—and here he was making the biggest demand of all. It was the ultimate trust exercise, and I didn't know if I could do it. Tim would judge me. Who wouldn't? No amount of compassion can turn off that mean little instinct. It's inborn, even in guys like Tim, who claim people are fundamentally good. Once he knew the truth, he'd understand how badly I'd failed, and he'd never look at me the same way again.

"It'll change things. The way you see me. It won't be the same."

"You don't know that. Give me a chance."

There was another possibility, I thought as I regarded him. Maybe Tim and I didn't see eye to eye about Jasper because I was looking through a filthy lens. My point of view was tainted by what happened with Bram—but Tim's wasn't. Tim was still pure. If I could explain myself, maybe we could help each other. Solve this case together, the way we were supposed to.

I listened to the angry moan of the wind as it grappled with branches that wouldn't give in. I took a breath and felt my throat sting in a way that was terribly familiar.

"A year and a half ago, I was abducted." The words hung in the air like black smoke with no visible source. Part of me wished they would scare him away, but Tim didn't move. Behind me in the parlor I heard a hard clink as the mouth of a wine bottle met the rim of a glass. The sound shot up my spine, but I focused on Tim's eyes and pushed onward.

"The guy who did it stabbed three women and then came after me," I said.

"I should have been his fourth."

TWENTY-FIVE

I woke up reeking of beer. Ran my hands down my body in search of pain. The room was dark with a seam of light visible under the door. I crawled to it and rattled the handle. Locked.

Then came Bram. He carried an oil-soaked sack of takeout, set it on the dirty cement floor, and flicked on the light. From his messenger bag he pulled a water bottle that dripped with condensation. My mouth was cotton-dry and tasted vile. I wanted that water so bad I could feel it splash over my tongue and numb my teeth, but one at a time the memories scrambled to the surface. Our banter. The drinks. He'd drugged me. Bram drugged them all.

"You hungry?" he said, sitting cross-legged on the floor. The smell wafting from the paper bag provoked a gut-twisting reaction in me, a feeling dangerously close to carnal. He knew I'd be starving and had picked the most fragrant dishes he could think of, so the part of my brain wired for survival would compel me to eat. What if he'd drugged the food, too?

"Don't be scared, Shay."

Without a second's hesitation, I lunged. Threw my weight into the strike and landed it on his jaw. I'd trained for this, hours upon hours of self-defense and martial arts. No sooner did I feel my knuckles connect than he was on me, his hands tight around my throat.

"That was uncalled for," he said as he pulled me down to his level. I hit the floor with a thud and a groan. "Don't you ever fucking do that again. We know each other, remember?" He knelt beside me, and his finger traced my scar. "Soon we'll know each other better." Bram sat back down and cracked his jaw. "Here, look, I'll start. I love Thai food and long walks in the park. Your turn. Where are you from?"

The Ninth Precinct, you fucker, and my squad's going to tear you apart. "Vermont," I croaked, my throat agonizingly raw. "Swanton." I searched his face for something recognizable that went beyond our time at the pub. I tried to see past his features, to parse the characteristics he couldn't easily alter and compare those to the high school boys I'd known back home. Looking at Bram lifted the hair on my neck. I felt it when we met at O'Dwyer's, and here it was again. No question about it. I knew him.

"Swanton. What do you know," he said evenly. "That's where I'm from, too."

Careful, Shay. This was early days, no telling what he'd do. He had issues with women, that was a safe bet. But what, if anything, did those other girls do to set him off? What if I did the same thing? It was dawning on me, what this meant. I'd been taken on a Friday night and wasn't due back at work until Monday. I didn't have a boyfriend or a roommate and talked to my folks only once a week. Bram had time enough to act out whatever sick fantasy he had planned. Monday was way too late.

Keep him talking, I thought frantically.

Make him forget why he brought you here.

"You're from Swanton?" I said it with as much surprise as I could muster. Recalling our conversation at the bar repulsed me. A little attention from an attractive man was all it took for me to let down my guard. I'd been the easiest of targets.

"You said we know each other. Did we meet at school?" I asked.

"No." He smiled a little. "I wasn't in town for long, but I don't see how you could forget me."

"You moved?"

"I left."

"Oh." Did I know any runaways from my childhood? The question quickened my pulse.

"Why did you leave?"

"I had to. My mother wouldn't let me stay."

It was ludicrous, talking like we were still at the bar swapping stories and smiles, but the detective in me was desperate to figure him out. If I got away, I could weaponize his candor. Prosecute and put the bastard where he belonged. For the time being, my body was free of harm; I had the luxury of skin without lacerations, bruises, pain. When the moment was right, I'd try again. Next time, I'd thrust my thumbs into his eye sockets and press until he crumpled to the ground. One way or another, I'd get out.

But I wasn't just a detective anymore; I was a victim—of kidnapping right now, but later maybe something worse. I couldn't let that side of me take over. One weak moment, one more failed attempt, and I'd be added to his list. *Becca. Lanie. Jess.*

Shay.

"I don't recognize your name." *Blake Bram.* Was it an arbitrary choice? A reference to someone or someplace in town? What?

Bram chuckled. "That's okay. I recognized yours."

Hours upon hours I'd spent leafing through reports about those three dead women, looking for a pattern I could leverage. They were in their late twenties or early thirties, and all used that dating site, but jobs, leisure activities, the way they looked—those couldn't be more dissimilar. I'd long since concluded that Blake Bram dropped a lure and took whatever he could reel in. But I was no random selection. A year ago my sergeant put everyone's names and photos on the precinct website. He thought it would help create a sense of community. I was the only detective in Nine, and Jess was found on my turf. Bram knew it would be me on the case and what was on my mind when I sat down, wiped and frustrated, at that bar. All he had to do was follow me from the station house, to the park, to the pub. By stopping in there alone, I'd given him the opening he was waiting for.

"Not school, then," I said, and his smile stretched wider. Bram was enjoying this game. I had to keep it going. "Were we neighbors?"

"We were way more than that."

A frisson shot up my backbone. In a way, the realization of what he was saying was worse than any I'd had so far. This psycho wasn't just a random person from my hometown. We had history. Again I scrutinized his face and Bram watched me with amusement as I flipped through decades-old images in my brain. I rarely thought about my high school days, didn't keep in touch with old friends. After I left for the city, I left Swanton behind.

When I took too long to speak again Bram said, "I'm hurt. You really don't remember?"

"I'm sorry," I said, swallowing a hot gob of bile.

His expression darkened as he leaned toward me. "That's too bad, because you're going to have to figure this out, Shay. Who I am. Why you're here. Why I did what I did to those girls. It's the only way to make me stop."

I was backed into the corner, nowhere left to go. If Bram killed me, it wouldn't just be my parents and brother who'd suffer. Bram would hurt others, too. He wanted something from me. Whatever relationship he thought we had, it was the key to everything. There was no guarantee I'd figure it out, but if I did, maybe I could stop him from taking more innocent lives.

Bram picked up the bottle and rolled it toward me. It wobbled as it crossed the floor, the water inside sloshing like waves, and came to rest by my foot.

And when it did, I took it.

TWENTY-SIX

gave Tim only what he needed, but I didn't spare the details. He listened silently while I talked. I swear he was holding his breath.

After I was found, I saw a video of my abduction. Footage from the security camera mounted behind the bar caught Bram as he dropped the Rohypnol in my beer with expert stealth, his pinkie peeling back quick as a wink while he diverted my attention to the drunk girls nearby. He couldn't have wished for a better distraction. The bartender swore she'd never seen him in the pub before, or since. Every newspaper in the city splashed his picture on page one, but it was all too easy for Bram to change his look again and melt into the masses.

I told Tim about Bram's stories, too. Each time he came to the cellar, Bram brought another memory to share. He didn't have a white-picket childhood. Didn't often get new things. As a kid, toys still sealed in plasticized boxes elicited nothing but panic. When he brought home a rare gift from a teacher or a birthday present from a friend, his mother yanked it from his small hands. She'd pry a tire off a Hot Wheels car. Twist an arm off his action figure. As she inflicted these flaws, she told him perfection was dangerous. It was his defects, Bram's mother said, that would keep him safe.

He was bullied mercilessly at school, but still preferred it to being at home, where Mom—crippled by an anxiety disorder and left to raise two kids alone—cut Bram's hair with a paring knife and forbade him from brushing his teeth. Once, he got up the courage to go looking for his estranged father at the manufacturing company where he worked, only to be told his dad had quit and left town. Bram dragged his cousin along on that adventure, and when he got home again his mother hit him with a jug of expired milk. For eight days I was Bram's captive and his confidante. I hoarded those glimpses into his past and prayed I'd live long enough to use them against him.

"I read about that case," Tim said, his voice flat as farmland. "It made the news here. Everywhere, I guess."

"The NYPD petitioned to keep me anonymous. The articles never used my name."

"Did he . . . hurt you?"

I shook my head. "Not like you think."

His eyes traveled to my scar.

"No," I said. "That was something else. A long time ago."

I saw the bewilderment in Tim's face and knew what he was thinking. Eight days was a long time. Bram killed those other girls within hours of taking them. Why didn't he do the same to me? Mercifully he didn't ask. Instead, he said, "I remember a cop found you. That's how you got out?"

I nodded. "A rookie who shouldn't have been there. One day a tenant wandered downstairs looking for Bram to help her unclog a sink—Bram worked in the building, that's how he had access to the cellar. She heard him talking to me, and between his new hair color and his evasiveness, she got suspicious and grabbed the first cop she could find on the street. Jay Lopez was his name. His partner was getting them coffees. Lopez went into the basement alone.

"I'm sure he didn't expect to find anything down there. Must have been the shock of his life to round the corner and see Bram closing the door on a stunned, unwashed woman crouching on the floor. Lopez tried to draw his weapon, but Bram was faster. He took the guy down. There was a struggle. Then I heard the shots."

Tim swallowed, and I went on. "Lopez took two bullets to the stomach at close range from his own Glock 17. He had a wife and three kids at home, was up for a promotion. He shouldn't have been down there, but he was. Because of me."

Tim's anger surprised me. "You didn't ask to be taken. Nothing about this is your fault."

"There's a lot of stuff those news stories left out, Tim. Like that after Bram shot Lopez and made sure he was dead, right before he realized he was screwed and had no choice but to leave me, he came back into my cell. Like the fact that I held his bloody hands in mine."

"What?"

"He put the gun down right next to me." I splayed the fingers of my good hand and swiped at the air. "It was *right there*."

"You were traumatized, out of your mind. I'm sure—"

"I could have ended it. That man killed three women and a cop. I could have restrained him, and I didn't." I felt queasy, but I needed to finish. Get it all out. "Stockholm syndrome. Terror-bonding. Whatever you want to call it, that was the diagnosis." God, how I hated those terms. They were go-tos for the press, just what the reporters who covered my story needed to romanticize my trauma and turn nightmares into content that sells online ads. "He could have killed me, but day after day he let me live. I guess some part of me was grateful for that.

"At first, it was just about staying on his good side," I said. "He could have easily left me there to starve. I depended on him to keep me alive, so I had to behave. But I also kept track of the hours and looked for patterns in his behavior and actions—anything I could use to my advantage when the time was right. Sometimes he showed up sweaty and smelling like synthetic lemons. I figured out Bram was the building's janitor, and that he only worked part-time. He had less patience for me on the days he smelled, and I learned to be cautious when he jangled with keys. I'm sure he knew I was reading him. Once he asked if I was enjoying myself, trying to get inside his head. I told him I monitored his moods because I wanted him to be happy. I oozed obedience. Out in the world my precinct was killing themselves trying to find me, but I wasn't holding my breath. There was the bartender's eyewitness account and video footage of Bram, but nobody had his real name. He paid with cash the night he took me, and without a criminal record, his picture wasn't in the database. If I wanted to live, I couldn't count on anyone but myself.

"After a while I stopped thinking of Bram as the killer we were looking for. We were both from the same town. There was no defense for what he did. But my emotions took over, and not a day goes by that I don't hate myself for that. The bottom line is I let him go. And someone else is going to die because of it."

"You don't know that."

"No, Tim, I do. Bram had his reasons for what he did to those women, and for taking me. He wanted something from me that he didn't get."

"But, Shana—"

"I made a choice. I wasn't in my right mind, but I made it all the same." I laughed a little. "You aren't the first person to say this isn't my fault. When the diagnosis came in, the NYPD absolved me of responsibility. There was no investigation into my conduct in that basement, but I resigned from the force anyway. I shouldn't be here, Tim. This is the last place I should be."

We both fell silent. *There it is. Take it. I'm done.*

He searched my eyes. "I'm so sorry. I had no idea."

"McIntyre's the only one who does." I thought of all the conversations I'd had with her over the past few months, including our talk that day. "She's been pushing me to tell you. She's convinced that would make a difference somehow." I paused. "I took a psych screening when I applied for this job. I want you to know that."

"I'm sure Mac just wanted to make sure you were okay to work."

"I didn't do it for her. There's a standard protocol for PTSD. It's minimal—a debriefing, a mental health screening, and you're done. I kept up with therapy way longer than I needed to. Technically, I was cleared to go back to work months ago. I *wanted* to take the test. Mac said it wasn't necessary, but I insisted. I wanted to make sure. But I worry that deep down she's still scared I'm going to lose it. I'm scared of that possibility, too. I have no business being here right now. What you saw before?" I said. "That was the memories rearing up. The fear. How do I know I'll be able to tell the good guys from the bad? You saw what I did to Flynn.

What if I hurt an innocent person because for a split second I look at them and see Bram? When flashbacks happen, I react. I don't know if I can control it."

"What happened doesn't erase who you are. You've got years of experience and instinct and skills to protect you. But if you thought you might lose it, why didn't you tell me?"

"*This* is why. Because of what you're thinking right now. Because of that look on your face. I don't know how to trust anyone anymore. Not them, and not you."

I broke eye contact, but he caught my chin and lifted my face level with his. "You may not trust me, but I trust you," Tim said. "I didn't know any of this, and yeah, it's alarming. But we've been working together for months. You're a good person, and a good investigator. But you have to trust yourself. Why do you think those psych screenings exist? There are thousands of officers who've been through traumatic situations. They get the help they need, and they move on. You can, too."

"My situation is different."

His expression was indecipherable. "Who told you that?"

"It just *is*. I was taken. Locked in a room for a week and—"

"The therapy you got after it happened," Tim said, interrupting me. He was still looking at me, but his gaze was unfocused. "It was from Carson, wasn't it?"

"He was doing his job. I stopped seeing him professionally before we started dating." I couldn't keep the defensiveness out of my voice. I wore what Carson told me after we met like a brand on my skin, how Bram went from enemy to ally in my mind because without his help my basic needs wouldn't be met. Carson said that's why I couldn't see him for the criminal he was. There was more to it than that, but I couldn't deny he was right. "Carson helped me figure things out. It was his idea to move up here. Get away from the bad memories."

"Was it his idea for you to go back to work?"

I hesitated. "He knew I would eventually."

"Did he? Does he support what you're doing, Shana? Or is he still telling you you're unbalanced so you'll be the dutiful wife he always wanted? *That's* why you didn't tell me," Tim said. "Carson has you so convinced you're crazy you couldn't even tell your closest colleague about the most significant event of your life."

Closest colleague. Tim wasn't wrong about that, but even though his words were sparse and sounded bureaucratic I found them strangely touching. I could see the struggle in his deep-set eyes. He took my injured hand in his and moved his callused thumb along the edges of my burn. "I can't understand what you've been through, and because I respect you, I won't pretend I do. But whatever happened, whatever's happening now, we'll figure it out together."

It was so completely different from how I'd imagined the conversation would go that when it was done, shock glued my feet to the floor. Tim's hand was warm and dry and covered mine completely in a way that left me feeling protected. Safe.

I won't deny my devotion to Carson was tied to the fact that he'd freed me. I came out of that basement feeling shame more profound than I'd ever thought possible, and Carson rationalized my depraved behavior. If it hadn't been for him in those early days after my release, God only knows where I'd be.

Something unexpected happened during my time with him, though. Despite his insistence that I was still broken, I began to heal. I was a long way from being whole, but I wasn't adrift anymore—at least not all the time, the way I used to be. There

were consequences to Carson's warnings I don't think he antici-
pated. He hadn't known the me who lived before the day I disappeared. To him I was a victim to the core. But I didn't want to be
a victim anymore. It took until that moment with Tim for me to
understand why I'd been delaying the wedding and biting Carson's
head off every time he reminded me I was too fragile, too shaky,
too weak.

Tim was proof that McIntyre's faith in me wasn't a fluke. Here
he was, offering the same kind of support that made the sheriff
and me grow so close so fast. I was sure I'd squandered my chances
of ever having mutual trust with another officer again, but Tim
made me feel separation from my trauma was possible. That maybe
even the most terrifying of my evocations could be overcome.

I hadn't forgotten about Jasper and Abella, but for a second I
felt a lightness in my chest I hadn't experienced in a long time.
McIntyre was right. I needed to come clean—and clean was what
I felt. It was a temporary fix, but it felt so good I allowed myself
to enjoy it, if only for a little while.

Neither of us spoke for a long time. Eventually Tim let go of
my hand.

"I'll call McIntyre," I said quickly. "I know you're right about
the storm, but things are different now. This is an active murder
investigation. There has to be a way." I checked my watch. "At six
on a Saturday night she's usually walking her dog or eating fried
perch at the Thousand Islands Inn." I'd joined her for both of those
activities on multiple occasions, and on one especially nice night
in early fall we'd combined them, taking her Maltipoo to the Clay-
ton restaurant with us for takeout and eating while watching tankers glide through the channel. "With this rain, though," I added,
"who knows."

"Perch." Tim stuck out his tongue. "Don't know if I could do it after being in that boathouse."

I inclined my head, thinking about what he'd said. As Tim walked away I mumbled, "We'll never think of fish the same way again."

I didn't want to call McIntyre from the hall. The last time I stormed out of the house, a woman wound up dead, and even with Tim watching over the others now, that course of action didn't feel safe. Camilla was asleep in the library. As far as main-floor rooms out of earshot of the parlor went, there was the sun-room, Norton's bedroom, and the kitchen. The kitchen was closest, and it smelled of roasting chicken. I pulled out my phone and dialed McIntyre's office as I followed the mouthwatering scent. With the weather such as it was, I guessed she was still managing storm-incited mayhem.

"Sorry I haven't been in touch," I said when she answered. "We've got a situation out here."

Explaining Abella was dead, Flynn was injured, and we were trapped on the island took surprisingly little time. I suppose that's because I heeded Tim's advice and gave the details of the shooting a wide berth.

"Christ on a bike, in all my years," said Mac. "Think you can keep them under control?"

"We don't have a choice," I said. Then I asked her to check into one more lead. I could tell she found my request puzzling, but she agreed all the same.

"I'm not going to give up on that boat," she told me. "In the meantime, I've got something new that might prove useful."

Like Tim, McIntyre was a local with deep Thousand Islands roots. She'd asked around and discovered someone else had been doing the same. Two months ago, the real estate office in Alexandria Bay received several calls from a man inquiring about selling an island. He wanted to know what a three-acre private estate and immaculate vintage six-bedroom house would fetch. The property the man described matched Tern to a T.

If the caller was one of our men—Flynn, Miles, Norton, Ned, or Jasper—it would go a long way toward validating my theory about the killer being after Camilla's money. "Anything else to go on?" I asked.

"No notable accent," she said.

"That rules out Ned. He was born in Ghana. His accent's faint, but it's there."

With fondness in her voice that warmed me like broth in my belly, McIntyre said, "Getting closer, kid. One more thing, nearly forgot. Carson called."

I never used to be an anxious person. If my parents were an hour late coming home from date night, I didn't assume they'd been in a terrible accident, I just squeezed out a few extra minutes of TV. When McIntyre said Carson's name, though, my stomach dropped. They'd met before, but Carson and Mac weren't in the habit of gabbing on the phone. Given the way he felt about me going back to work, I'd partitioned off my fiancé from the force. If he called her, something was up.

"Apparently," she said, "he's concerned about your health."

"My health?"

"Your mental health. He thinks I should pull you from the case and send you straight home to Daddy."

"Jesus Christ."

"Look, you've been nothing but honest with me," Mac said. "But you know I was a tad uncertain when you came to me about this job."

Again my gut twisted. "I was, too. That's why I volunteered to be screened. I'm not going to lie, Maureen, I've had a few iffy moments out here." What would she say when she found out about Flynn's gunshot wound? I tried not to think about it. "But I talked to Tim."

"Ah. That's good." She paused. "Isn't it?"

"It is. You were right, as usual. He was amazing. *Is* amazing." I said it with a smile. "I think I can do this, I really do. Carson doesn't have a clue what's happening right now. He doesn't want me here, and whatever he said to you is just his way of trying to pull me back."

On the other end of the line I heard a door click shut. "I haven't told you this," McIntyre said, "but I dated someone like Carson once. Controlling. Paranoid. I'd be at work and get these phone calls accusing me of cheating. In the same breath he'd tell me I wasn't good enough for him."

McIntyre didn't gush about her personal life. She'd never once mentioned an ex. *Controlling and paranoid.* These were the words my friend selected to describe my fiancé. I'd never thought of Carson like that, but the endless questions about Tim, the accusations against him, the ceaseless efforts to convince me I was defenseless . . . it added up.

"What did you do about it?" I didn't feel totally comfortable asking, but McIntyre had brought it up for a reason.

"I left," she said. "It wasn't as simple as it sounds. I broke the rules. Me leaving him was the ultimate act of disobedience, and he wasn't about to sit back and wish me well. But that's a longer story, and you've got work to do."

"Right, yeah," I droned absently, mulling over what she'd said.

"I'm not going to tell you what to do, but I will say this. You might want to step back and analyze the situation before the wedding day rolls around."

I hung up and stood in the kitchen, stunned into a state of inertia as I thought about what Maureen McIntyre had said. *Broke the rules.* It was a good way to describe what I'd done, too.

And I wasn't done yet.

TWENTY-SEVEN

People are simpler than we give them credit for. We imagine our species is composed of complex beings with extensive wants and needs, but we really only yearn for two things: to feel safe and to feel loved. It sounds elementary—but there's a problem. If we're deprived of these things long enough, it gets to the point where we can't take it. We're desperate, and desperation activates our survival instinct. Makes us do inconceivable things.

When I remembered Carson on that first day, wearing his kitten socks and smelling of fresh sage, I had to fight with myself to stay angry. I'd found safety and love with him at a time when I thought I'd never have either again. In return, he tried to turn me against Tim; hell, he'd called my boss mid-case to convince her I was hanging on by a thread. By no means was I back to my old self, but I needed to believe I could get there. Until McIntyre took me in, my career was DOA, and I'd always blamed Bram. But Carson was equally guilty of killing it.

I understood why he did it, didn't doubt his motivation for a second. It was just like McIntyre said. He was always distant and dismissive when I brought up work. Even the texts we'd exchanged hours earlier were rife with admonitions. My fiancé had embarked on a full-fledged crusade to remove me from the force, and there was a whole lot more to it than fearing for my mental health.

I was back out in the world now. No more sitting at home waiting for him to psychoanalyze me. I'd dared to stray outside the neat parameters of his life. Carson needed to dominate me, and whether because I didn't trust my own judgment enough to question his behavior, or because I needed to relinquish control of the life I'd let spin off its axis, I'd let him. Tapping my deepest fears and summoning my demons was his pet pursuit.

I'd been a fascinating hobby for him at first. He quickly recognized that damaged, docile Shana would make an obedient wife. He'd doled out his diagnosis then, used my condition to keep me right where he wanted me. I felt like an idiot for not spotting Carson's trickery sooner. Caught up in my own thoughts and actions, I didn't think to monitor his.

What really got me, though, was how Carson looked straight at my face and lied. Dozens of times I'd heard him say it's a bad idea for people who have suffered psychological trauma to put themselves in high-stress situations. He made his professional feelings about that known whenever he read about a cop who'd done something insane, like gun down a kid in the street or sexually assault a witness. Carson always chalked it up to the officer's mental state. In the same breath, he'd tell me I was different. The second he saw how determined I was to go back to my job despite the horrors of a homicide detective's daily life, he swore to me I could, and would, prevail. He'd figured out what I needed to hear and was clever enough to oblige. I clung to his insistence that one day I'd be a good detective again. Banked on his pledge to help. But from denigrating my condition to proposing Thai food for dinner, it was all just a strategy designed to strip down my self-reliance and make me question whether I'd survive.

When I thought back to Tim's account of his childhood with Carson, I felt an overwhelming urge to toss my engagement ring in the river and bring up my lunch on the shore. Carson's behavior as a kid proved McIntyre's point. Power was my fiancé's favorite high. My dynamic with him wasn't so different from Tim's: doctor and patient, enabler and pawn. And that filled me with a boiling, bottomless rage.

Down the hall I heard the others talking, and through the kitchen door I spied Tim pacing nervously just outside the parlor. Time was running out, and we both knew it. Without the boats, the perp was trapped, and when people feel trapped, they panic. Fear had already killed Abella. I worried it was about to strike again.

An empty wine bottle in hand, Norton stepped up to Tim and pointed in my direction. A few seconds later he was walking toward me under Tim's watchful gaze.

"Jade's hungry," Norton said. "I thought I'd put out some appetizers. Detective Wellington said I could make a plate if you stay with me."

My watch read half past six. Tim and I had been on the island for almost nine hours. Maybe what my brain needed was a hard reset. A quick, invigorating swim in the frigid river should do it. It'd be worth the risk to my life if it helped me see things clearly.

I blinked my dry, bloodshot eyes and told Norton to be my guest.

He crisscrossed the kitchen, opening cupboard doors and pulling ingredients from the fridge. Despite his prep work earlier, the counters were spotless. The few dishes he'd used were already washed and left to dry by the sink. I leaned back against the counter and revisited everything I knew about "Moonshine Phil." He'd been short on money twenty years ago, fired from his dead-end job at the liquor store. Then Camilla brought him to Tern Island and his life changed for the better. He'd put his previous boss at risk of being charged with selling alcohol to minors, but to Camilla he was a loyal employee, a compassionate caregiver, a friend.

Camilla wasn't the only person in the house Norton seemed to like more than the others. I'd noticed it throughout the day, and it nettled me even now.

"Spend much time with kids?" I asked.

He was arranging cold roasted vegetables on a platter at the kitchen island and folding slices of cured meat and cheese. My question made him fumble a sliver of salami. "Sorry?"

"I was just thinking about Jade. You're very attentive to her needs. You made her favorite soup today."

"Everyone enjoys that soup. I make it because it's not hard on Mrs. Sinclair's stomach. But I am fond of that girl. She hasn't had it easy. Until Bebe, Jade didn't have a mother around—and between you and me, Bebe isn't exactly the mothering type."

"At least Jade's got Miles."

Norton smiled. "That she does."

"There are going to be a lot of changes around here now. After Miles leaves Bebe, he and Jade won't be visiting anymore. I wonder if anyone will. With Abella's death and Jasper disappearing the way he did, how can the Sinclairs keep the property? Some horrible things have happened here."

Norton opened a drawer and took out a paring knife. It glinted under the bright pendant lights above him. "Maybe they won't," he said. "But to be honest, that's no concern of mine. It's almost time for me to move on. When Camilla leaves this place, so do I." He shook his head sadly. "I hate to say it, but sometimes I think this family is cursed. Baldwin's and Rachel's deaths, their business troubles, Camilla's illness, Jasper . . ."

"That's quite a string of bad luck."

Norton opened a bag of radishes and started carving them into elaborate edible flowers. My eyes followed the blade's every movement. His knife skills were precise and lightning quick. "Flynn and Bebe . . . they're very negative people, and negative people attract negative energy. Trust me, I know. I made my share of mistakes as a younger man, some I'll regret for the rest of my life. But I turned things around. Coming here changed everything. We've all got to make our own destiny."

His speech reminded me of what Camilla said upstairs, about the importance of forging your own path. "I'd love to know how to do that," I said, and meant it.

He looked up from his knife. "What I do, see, is I picture myself where I want to be. In the future I want to have. That's what helps me get there."

I felt my cell phone buzz twice in quick succession, two messages coming in at once. Excusing myself, I glanced at the display. McIntyre had made an interesting discovery related to my request. I filed it away in the back of my mind. The next message was from Tim. *Miles and Jade want to talk to you.*

I raised an eyebrow. Typed *Send them in.*

"Ah," Norton said when he saw them coming down the hall. "I'll leave you all alone."

"No need," I said quickly. "Please. Stay and finish up."

Norton gave a reluctant nod and went back to work.

"Not the happy hour you're used to, I guess," I said when Miles and Jade stepped into the room.

"Please don't," said Miles.

"Don't what?"

Jade snatched a piece of salami from the plate. When Norton smiled at her, his cheeks plumped up and his eyes turned into crescent moons. Miles said, "Say it like that. Lump us together with *them*."

I wrinkled my brow. "You've been part of the family for how long now?"

"Long enough to know it's a bad thing to be. We're leaving. I already told you that."

"You did. But for the moment you're still here, and as long as you're on this island, you're as much a part of this as they are. Now, what can I do for you two?"

Neither his fresh shirt nor his smart tweed jacket could make Miles look composed anymore. "I have a request," he said, and I thought, *Again?* His voice quavered and he cleared his throat. "I want your assurance you can keep my daughter safe. I want you to protect her. No matter what."

"What exactly are you expecting to happen?"

"You saw what went on in there. They're all crazy, literally out of their minds. She's a child," he said. "Promise me."

I turned to Jade, nibbling mouselike at the meat in her hands, and felt my annoyance with the girl ebb. The skin around her eyes was puffy and red. She *was* a child, and for the first time since I'd met her, she actually looked it. "I promise," I told her directly. "This is going to be tough on you, huh? I know you and Jasper were close. It may not feel like it now, but you'll be okay."

Jade said, "It's not like I didn't know."

Norton's bald head snapped up. "Excuse me?" I said, equally startled.

"Daddy told me, like, a month ago? And I'll still be able to see him. We all live in the city. Jas and I can still hang out."

I glanced sidelong at Miles. Discomfort issued from his body like a heat haze. "I don't—" I began, but he cut me off.

"She's talking about the divorce. I wanted to give her plenty of time to get used to the idea. That's important with children this age. You can't spring things on them. It's very upsetting."

"Jade, I'm not sure you understand," I said. "A horrific thing happened here tonight, and Jasper's still missing. There's evidence he was seriously hurt. I'm sorry to have to tell you this"—*why hasn't Miles told her?*—"but there's a chance Jasper's not coming back."

"Um, no, you're wrong," Jade said, but there was uncertainty in her tone. She might not have confided in her girlfriends, but she was still a typical teenager. She wanted to believe what she was saying, but wasn't wholly convinced.

"I hope I am wrong." I turned back to Miles. "You've known you were leaving Bebe for a month?"

"It wasn't a snap decision."

"It's no big secret," said Jade. "They fight all the time. They were fighting last night."

"There's a child involved," Miles was quick to remind me. "My main concern is making sure Jade's okay."

I said, "I got the impression you'd only just found out about . . . you know."

"You can be blunt. Jade's well aware of her stepmother's indiscretions." Miles snorted. "Everyone is."

"Everyone except Flynn. Up until an hour ago he had no idea. It sounds like *you* did, though. So if you knew about the affair before today, why didn't you leave Bebe sooner?"

"You aren't paying attention. For all intents and purposes Bebe and I have been separated for weeks."

"So she's been sleeping with Ned for weeks?" I confirmed. "And you're still living together?"

"It's an arrangement of convenience. We don't even share a bed."

"What about last night?" I said. "I thought you both slept upstairs, in the room next to Jade. Did Norton put you up in the library or something?"

"Correct." Miles nodded in the caretaker's direction. "He made up a bed on the couch in the library after the others went to sleep. I didn't want to upset Camilla. We're *transitioning*, do you understand?"

"Is that true?" I asked Norton, thinking back to my interview with Ned. "Did Miles sleep in the library last night?"

Norton's head was bowed over the platter again. Leisurely, he looked up. "That's right. All set here." He grabbed a handful of cloth napkins from a drawer, hoisted up the platter of appetizers, and pasted on a smile.

"You all can go back to the parlor," I said. "And don't worry. Wellington and I are perfectly capable of keeping you safe tonight. The rest of our team will be here before you know it, and then we'll get you back to shore."

"Really?" said Miles, letting his eyes drift to the window, where the rain slapped at the glass.

"On their way," I lied, watching Miles, Jade, and Norton go. Then I took out my phone.

I was starting to understand, and this new awareness made me fear for our safety even more. I was getting close. Closing in.

But there was still something I needed to do.

TWENTY-EIGHT

I called Carson. In the kitchen. In the middle of an investigation. But I didn't do it for me. My personal life was irrelevant, my engagement immaterial. I was on a case I'd fucked up bad, determined to stanch the bleeding. And as astonishing as it was at the time, there was a chance Carson had intel I needed in order to make things right.

"Shay, thank God, do you know what time it is? I've been waiting for hours, do you have any idea how worried I've been?"

"I talked to Maureen."

He didn't miss a beat. "I also spoke with Maureen McIntyre. I had to know you were okay."

"And suggest I was mentally ill?"

"Now listen to me. You left me no choice."

"Why, Carson? Because I didn't stay home like a good little

girl? Because I wanted my career back and expected my fiancé to support me?"

"We've been over this a million times. You're not ready!"

"And you'll keep saying that forever, no matter what I think, while you make sure I continue to feel like a failure. You were never going to help me recoup my career. From day one you've been plotting to keep me at home. What was your plan, exactly—to get me fired? Tell all of Jefferson County I've got PTSD so there's nowhere left for me to go?"

"I'm trying to protect you." As hard as he worked to regulate it, I could hear the faintest trace of insecurity in Carson's voice. "You aren't in your right mind. What is it, flashbacks? That's it, isn't it? You're experiencing a sense of disassociation, like you're outside your body, losing touch with reality. Of course you are, in an environment like that—and that's just the beginning. This is exactly why I need you to come home."

He was doing it again, trying to make me distrust myself. As he spoke I imagined him in his high-priced glasses and novelty socks, clenching his jaw just enough to convey discontent. Flexing his foot to tap his toe in the irregular rhythm he knew made me jumpy. Every word Carson spoke, every movement he made, was carefully crafted to send a message. I wondered if he'd used the same tactics on Tim all those years ago.

"The flashbacks are going to keep happening. You may think you've managed to pull yourself together, but you haven't. Soon you'll shut down completely—and what will you do then? How are you going to protect yourself when you've regressed to the state you were in when we met?" Carson's voice got hard and low. "Don't ever forget how that cop looked at you when he found you in that basement, crouching over his partner's dead body while a killer ran free. Or how you felt when you saw the gun just lying there and made the conscious decision to let an unconscionable monster walk. You could have stopped him. Given the families of those poor girls some peace. But you didn't, Shay. You let him go."

My heart hammered against my ribs. "Come home," Carson said, softly now. "We'll work through this, just like we did before. I'll make it right. I always do."

The speech was exactly what I expected from Carson. If I'd been just a smidge weaker, it might have worked.

"Tell me about Moonshine Phil."

It was the question I'd been waiting to ask, and just as I'd hoped, it caught him off guard. It took longer than it should have for him to recover. "That's a name I haven't heard in a while," he said. His laugh was synthetic, a cheap simulation of the real thing. "My ears are burning. Have you and Tim been gossiping behind my back? Don't tell me you never broke the rules to have some fun."

"Sure I did. But I never made a friend break the law. Philip Norton. He's a local, like you. What do you know about his family?"

"What are you even talking about? I bought booze from the guy twenty years ago. What does any of this have to do with us? Christ," he said after a beat, "this is Tim, too, isn't it? What, is this Norton guy a suspect or something? Is Timmy trying to convince you I was friends with a criminal now?"

"You're the one who negotiated that liquor deal. Did he talk about his family or not?"

"How am I supposed to remember that? We talked one time to set things up and Tim did the rest. You ask me, Tim was nuts to go anywhere near him. The pervert had a thing for young boys."

"What? How could you know that?"

"I saw him around town a couple of times with a kid about our age. He wasn't from our school. What does it matter? Moonshine Phil was a nobody. Just like Tim."

"Tim," I repeated, livid. "You could have ruined his career, his whole fucking life." I suddenly remembered our text conversation, Carson's abrupt decision to freeze Tim out. "That's why you changed your mind about inviting him to the wedding. You're afraid of what he'll tell me about how you treated him."

"Shana." Carson loaded my name with displeasure, turned it into a reprimand. "If I was concerned about Tim Wellington, if I spent even a millisecond of my time thinking about what harebrained stories a pathetic, small-town cop might tell you about me, don't you think I'd ban him from the guest list from the start? Wouldn't I have explained myself preemptively if I thought he might try to bad-mouth me to my fiancée? You've been with the man almost every day for the past several months. If he had any power over me, believe me, he would have used it."

Tim hadn't fully understood why Carson wanted him at our wedding in the first place, but I saw now his hunch was spot on. Tim grew up to become a cop. An upstanding person who did the right thing. And Carson was afraid. The wedding invitation was a pseudo peace offering, a false message to Tim that Carson had changed. With it, virtuous boy that Tim was, he wouldn't dream of disrupting our relationship.

But introduce a high-pressure case, throw in our recent spat over taking the job—a job Carson knew McIntyre and Tim both supported—and Carson's confidence in his plan had waned. He'd spent the whole day picturing Tim and me on the island, engaged in interviews he knew would push me to the limits of my rusty capabilities. It was Carson who'd treated me, and if I lost my shit his role in my recovery was bound to come up. From his perspective, I was playing detective with a man from his past who, with enough coercion, might actually, finally, get angry enough to snap. Carson had been right to worry after all.

"I have to go." There were alarming sounds coming from the parlor, a noise like chair legs scraping the floor and raised voices, I wasn't sure whose.

"Yes. Good. McIntyre said she hopes to get a boat out to you in a matter of hours. It's about time that woman started doing her job. Until then, I want you to remember your breathing exercises and—"

"I'm not leaving the island, Carson. I'm leaving you."

Saying it out loud was easier than I thought. I didn't allow myself to think about the real-world implications—the call to my parents telling them the man they'd come to think of as their son-in-law and I were through, the e-mail to the wedding planner Carson hired explaining we wouldn't need her services after all. When I spoke those words, all I thought about was Tim in his teens. A boy who hadn't yet started to lift weights and didn't realize he possessed all the strength he'd ever need. His eyebrows would have looked even more absurd on a thinner face. They would have hovered in bewilderment over the things Carson asked him to do. Carson, who was sharp and bold and knew, even then, he had a special sway over people in this world. How Tim contained his feelings of betrayal and anger, I'll never know. What I did know was I could never marry a man who took pleasure in his power to inflict so much pain.

Carson tried to reason with me. I knew better than to listen. Just like Tim, I didn't need him anymore. The sad thing is, neither of us ever did.

I had just ended the call when the kitchen lights flickered. A sound cleaved the silence, the noise like a bolt of electricity zipping along a wire, and the lights went out for good. I spun around to face the kitchen windows. In the distance, through the rain and far off on the shore, a tiny orange flash, and then another. Transformers blowing on the mainland, knocking out the power to the village. Wherever it was, the transformer feeding electricity to Tern Island had failed, too.

More bad noises down the hall. I heard a glass shatter with spectacular force, a muffled thump. Jade screamed, then Bebe. There were shouts from the men, brayed orders and exclamations of confusion. I turned to go. That's when I felt a hand in my hair and the agony of a punch delivered with precision to my spleen.

Doubled over and breathless with pain, I reached for my gun, but it was dark and my grasp was unreliable. I was too slow. A hot, clammy hand closed over my mouth, and before I could do a thing about it someone was dragging my aching body across the slate kitchen floor.

TWENTY-NINE

H e moved quickly, towing me along like a disobedient child. For a second I thought he was taking me to the basement, felt a kick of terror to match the fire in my gut, but it was Norton's room he took me to. Then I realized. It was the closest room with a lock.

Inside, he slammed my back against the closed door, wrenched my hands above my head, and pinned his body against mine. I felt him reach behind me to find my weapon. He was trying to yank it free. I bucked under his mass, struggled with all my might, but he raked my burned hand down the wooden door. The tender boil left by the burn ruptured and my skin blazed with pain. He jabbed the muzzle of my firearm under my chin and brought his mouth close to my ear. His voice, when he spoke, was thick with rage. "You let her die," it said.

The voice belonged to Ned.

In my state of shock I struggled to catch up. It was Flynn I'd been expecting to fight in the dark. I'd shot the man, on top of which he was vicious and unstable, already facing prison time. Flynn had nothing to lose—but Ned? His friend was missing, and all day Ned remained collected. It took Abella's death to make him snap. Abella and Ned were friends, too, spent all their time together in the city. It was always the three of them there—Jasper, Abella, Ned.

Images of Ned Yeboah hurtled through my mind. Ned, overcome with grief next to Abella's lifeless body. Holding her hand at lunch, and again in the parlor. Comforting her. Stroking her hair.

Ned was a friend to Abella. But to him, I realized then, she'd been something more. When Ned described his friendship with Jasper to me, he'd omitted a critical point. It wasn't Ned's disgust with Flynn that made him desperate to get away from the Sinclairs. It was Abby.

I coughed out a warning. He'd be charged with assaulting a police officer. I wasn't the only investigator on the island. Ned would be arrested in no time, go to prison.

"You think I care? It doesn't matter. You left." Ned's hot chest heaved against mine. "She's dead. Abby's dead because of you."

"What about you?" I winced as the cold, hard barrel of my gun grazed my throat. "Where were you when she went upstairs to change?"

"I didn't lay a hand on her. She had to use the bathroom. I thought . . ."

"You thought she was safe? Yeah," I said. "Me too."

Under the weight of his fury and sorrow, I sensed Ned drop his head. In that split second I acted. Every muscle in my body coiled and released. My knee connected with his groin. He sucked in a breath and let go of my arms.

I staggered away from him, deeper into the small room. Ned still had the gun. The safety was on, and I had no reason to believe he knew what to do about that. But I'd been wrong before.

Beyond the window lightning flashed, and I caught sight of Ned's face. When he saw me it contorted with rage.

"Put it down," I said as the room was enveloped in darkness once more. "Killing me won't bring her back. Lay the gun on the floor and kick it over. Do it now, Ned. You can still turn this around."

"You don't understand. I loved her."

"Enough to hurt Jasper?"

Far off, through the thunder, I heard more shouts. Tim calling my name. *Not yet*, I pleaded wordlessly, willing Tim to get the message. *Wait*.

"What happened after the fight," I said, "when you and Jasper came back inside?"

Ned's adrenaline was fading. He was coming to his senses. "I told you. I went to bed."

"In the library." I needed to know for sure.

"Yeah."

"And then?"

"She saw us. Bebe," Ned said weakly. "Me."

I didn't understand, and then, all at once, I did. He was talking about Abella. What she'd witnessed in the shed.

Tim's calls were getting closer, more urgent. "So you wanted to talk to Abby. Explain why you did it."

Ned nodded. "I thought it was Jasper by the window, but it

wasn't. Abby told me last night. I needed to make her understand it was just one time. That it was the only way to get away from Flynn."

"One time," I repeated, confused. "You mean you and Bebe—"

"It was supposed to be Flynn who saw. He was in the library. If he saw me with Bebe . . . that would end it. He'd kick my ass, probably try to kill me, but he'd let me go. I had to do it. Jas was going to propose this weekend—today, Jade said. I was out of time." He paused to swallow and catch his breath. "I had to make Abby understand everything I did was so I could be free of Flynn. Be with *her*. She wasn't sure about Jas, did you know that? I don't think she would have said yes." The momentary hope in Ned's voice gave way to despair as he remembered how Abella felt didn't matter, not anymore. "She was talking about going to Europe, traveling for a while instead of taking a new job. I've got money and an uncle in London. I told her we could stay with him. She was into it. She was."

I almost felt sorry for Ned, listening to him describe this chimerical future with his best friend's girl. I wondered if it might have worked out between them, had she lived long enough to make her choice. It would take a tremendous amount of love to justify marrying into a family like this.

"Did you go upstairs last night? Tell me, Ned."

"I . . . thought I could wake her up."

A chill shot through me. I waited.

"I just wanted to get her away from him so we could talk. I didn't kill him, I swear on my life," Ned said. And then he told me the one and only thing that could make me believe it.

In that dark little room I felt something way down at the base of my spine, where hunches that grow into theories are born. "What time was this?"

"Around three."

"Did you see anyone else?"

"No. I went back downstairs. Walked away. I thought," he said thickly, "if Jas was gone, there'd be nothing to stop us."

"Open the door!" Tim bellowed on the other side of the wall. "Open this fucking door right now!"

"You're not a murderer," I told Ned. "Give me the gun."

The sound he made was small, but the misery it carried was something I'm not sure I'll ever forget. With a quiet clack Ned set the gun down on the nightstand, and I unlocked the bedroom door.

Tim's flashlight beam hit me square in the eyes. In seconds he had Ned against the wall.

"Don't," I said when Tim reached for his cuffs. He tilted his head in confusion, but obliged me. Left the handcuffs where they were, and grabbed Ned's arm instead.

"The power outage. Ned made a run for it. You okay?" Tim's voice was surprisingly shaky. "What did this bastard do to you?"

"I'm fine," I said. Tim's timing was perfect. "Ned just told me who killed Jasper and Abella."

THIRTY

The hallway was dim, the only light a faint orange glow emanating from the dying fire in the parlor. Tim marched Ned in front of him while I brought up the rear. The soles of my boots came down on broken glass that crackled under my weight, and I remembered the sounds I'd heard earlier. There were blade-sharp hunks of crystal all over the floor and wet spots on the hallway wall. Someone had flung their wineglass straight out the parlor door.

"What'd I miss?" I whispered as I holstered my firearm once more.

"Sibling infighting," Tim replied, unimpressed. "I swear, these brats are grounded."

As my eyes adjusted to the hazy light of the parlor I saw what remained of our group of suspects. Bebe, by the window, was now conspicuously sans wineglass. Miles and Jade sat side by side on a couch, as far away from everyone as they could get. After hours on his feet, Norton had finally given up and taken a seat, but not before lighting the candles on the mantel. The flames flickered wraithlike on the walls. And then there was Flynn, still shirtless and sweating next to the hearth.

When he saw the grip Tim had on Ned, his eyebrows shot up. "I was starting to worry about you," Flynn said. "Did you put the moves on Sherlock and get shot down? Christ, you really will screw anything with a pulse."

Tim gritted his teeth. "Mr. Yeboah just assaulted a police officer."

"Would you look at that, Ned," Flynn said. "You found a way to leave me after all."

"That's enough," I said. "We need to talk to all of you."

Tim leaned in close. "We do?"

The moment when I'm about to catch a criminal is a moment like no other. I can't explain how it makes me feel. It's the highest of highs, a thrill that's astounding in its potency. The only person I know who might understand it is Tim. *One day*, I thought, *maybe I'll ask him.*

"Let's start at the beginning," I said, resuming the position I'd taken when I first walked into the parlor all those hours before, "with the first person blamed for Jasper's murder. It was Norton, I believe, who brought the trapper to our attention." I faced the caretaker, and he instantly reddened under my gaze. "In fact, Norton was the only person to suggest it might have been a total stranger who took Jasper. He convinced Camilla the man was after her money. Told her a ransom note was on the way. But no note came, and thanks to Wellington—who was able to confirm Billy

Bloom's alibi—we eliminated the trapper from our suspect list very quickly.

"But you clung to your theory he was to blame, didn't you, Mr. Norton? You insisted he was guilty after we found Abella's body, and brought him up again when Wellington told everyone the boats were gone. You had to know we'd see the trapper's involvement as a long shot. Surely you noticed nobody else was pointing at Bloom as a suspect." I waited. Though his mouth hung open, Norton said nothing. I could see his chest rising and falling fast under his flannel shirt.

"Your story about Camilla not wanting mink under the boathouse made sense," I said. "There's no denying the smell. Honestly, if Jasper was MIA for longer we'd have torn that building apart, but there's no way a stench of decay could be traced to a person who's only been missing one day. Billy Bloom found a pile of fish guts down there. That much is true, too. According to Bloom, they were all perch." I didn't mention it was Tim's comment about never wanting to eat fried perch again that had burrowed into my ear and stayed there. I did, however, make a mental note to buy Tim a beer. "Now, I don't know much about this river, but I do know there are many more species of fish, and the odds of a mink being that particular are low. I had the sheriff make a call. What she discovered is that Norton bought several pounds of bones and butcher scraps from the local fishmonger the day before you all arrived here. I believe he planted them under the boathouse as an excuse to bring in Bloom."

According to the shop owner Mac interviewed over the phone, Norton requested a mix and wasn't too happy to hear perch was all he could get. It must have taken him hours to fake the mink infestation. The process left him so behind on his housework that he wasn't ready for the guests and had to make a last-minute trip to the market.

"The thing about deductive reasoning is that it isn't about finding big flashing arrows, but quiet attempts at diversion." *Like Carson's shifting attitude about having Tim at the wedding*, I thought. *Like Norton's insistence the trapper was bad news.* "You brought Billy Bloom out here for a reason," I said. "A distraction, maybe, or to protect someone. The question, of course, is why?"

Philip Norton didn't move and didn't breathe as he waited to hear what I'd say next.

"Now Flynn—" I pivoted to face him. "He was quick to blame Abella. She was a stranger to all of you except Ned. That makes her a convenient scapegoat. Flynn tried to persuade us Jasper was using Abby for sex, while she was using him to get a job that would allow her to stay in the States. Flynn insisted Abby found Jasper out after they arrived here, and subsequently took her revenge. But there isn't a shred of evidence to support that claim. Yes, she was in bed with Jasper last night. Yes, his blood was on her clothes. But Abella's been actively searching for a job." I glanced at Ned. "I believe she loved Jasper and wanted their relationship to work. She had no reason to kill him, and as we've already established, she didn't kill herself."

Everywhere I looked, faces stared back at me. Riveted. Afraid. "You've been trying to pull us in different directions, all of you," I said, hitting my stride. "Accusing each other of lying and cheating. Incriminating your family and so-called friends. You've all got cause to be angry with Jasper. Take Jade. She thinks she's in love with him and is furious he doesn't feel the same way. She's been spying on Jasper and Abella, and trying to get between them. That's why she told everyone he planned to propose. Her hope was she could ruin the relationship. She wanted Jasper's attention all for herself."

Jade's lips quivered as I spoke. Here was a girl who'd spread rumors about the Sinclairs for her own entertainment. Now she looked helpless and lost. What she'd done was finally sinking in. Emotionally exhausted, the girl rested a heavy head on her father's shoulder and closed her eyes.

Miles stiffened. "If you're suggesting my daughter—"

"I'm suggesting her teenage bullshit damaged this investigation. But I'm not concerned about Jade anymore. I'd rather talk about Bebe.

"Bebe," I said, "did something even more astonishing. She tried to pin a murder on the victim himself by suggesting Jasper faked the scene and fled the island. I was sure you and Flynn were in it together," I told Jasper's sister. "You need the money. Without a bailout, you're screwed. Maybe you're screwed either way—but you weren't about to let your little brother, the family golden boy, walk off with what remains of Camilla's fortune. Yes, Bebe wanted to conceal the fact that she'd slept with Ned, but it's Camilla she's trying to deceive. What you did with Ned would likely destroy any remaining possibility Camilla might leave you some money—a delusion, in my opinion," I said to the woman, "but I guess a girl can dream. I'm sure you were concerned about Flynn's reaction. You knew he'd been violent with Jasper—there's no way you didn't see that growing up in a house with them—and taking Ned from him was the most egregious of acts. But you were fully dressed when Wellington and I found you upstairs in the hall. You'd even had time to put on your pearls. That means you couldn't have strangled Abella, and you don't have the strength to get Jasper out of the house anyway.

"Flynn and Jasper got in a fight last night, outside in the yard, and Flynn hit him," I said. "All the more reason to think Flynn went upstairs to finish the job. Except he didn't. Neither of you did."

"How do you know that?" said Miles.

"We know," I said, "because of Abella. Abella wasn't a part of your family drama. She died because she found out something about last night. Something happened today that allowed her to identify the killer—and the killer knew she'd tell us what it was. Whoever murdered Jasper also killed Abby. Flynn was laid out down here, and Bebe had no reason to want Jasper's girlfriend dead."

Everyone in the room was looking increasingly alarmed, and that gave me a rush of confidence. After the day I'd had, the sensation felt so foreign it caught me unawares. I'd thought this through, examined Camilla's guests like slabs of hooked meat, and searched every part of them for signs of rot. I had finally reached a conclusion. It felt good. No, it felt great.

"That takes us to Ned." At the sound of his name, Ned recoiled. "Ned also makes an excellent suspect—don't you think, Wellington?"

"Uh, yeah, excellent," Tim said, trying to play along.

"And Ned had motive, too—just not the one you submitted to us, Miles. Jasper stood in the way of something Ned wanted. When he heard the rumor about the engagement from Jade, and realized it was Abby who saw him in the shed with Bebe, he knew he was about to lose his chance. Last night, Ned went upstairs to profess his love to Abella. But Jasper's body was already gone."

Bebe emitted a squeak of surprise, though I couldn't tell if she was reacting to the news about Ned and Abby or her brother. To his credit, Tim didn't say a word as I let the man who'd just threatened to shoot me off the hook. "Ned was able to identify the shape of the bloodstain," I said for my colleague's benefit, "in a crime scene he never set eyes on this morning. Ned's not our guy."

"You saw blood on my brother's bed last night," Flynn said to Ned, "and you walked away?" I didn't like the look in his eyes, his supreme state of calm. "You were in *love*?" Flynn went on. "With that dead little *bitch*?"

All the talk of Abella had sent Ned into a stupor, and I wondered if Flynn's words registered. Ned's apathy enraged Flynn even more. Flynn's motions were swift and decisive. One—grab the candlestick from the mantel. Two—lunge. Three—bring the object down on the side of Ned's head. It smacked flesh and bone with a sickening thud and Ned's tall, lean body crumpled to the floor.

Before anyone could blink, Tim had Flynn facedown on the rug next to Ned. From under his heavy brow Flynn stared in horror at what he'd done. His hair was wild and his mustache dripped with sweat or tears, I didn't know which. Blood, so thick it was almost black, pulsed from Ned's head.

It was the first time I found myself in close proximity to Jade's screams, and I thought my eardrums might explode. Miles pulled her up and ushered her to the door, near where Norton sat. "Nobody move!" I shouted as Bebe, too, struggled to distance herself from Ned's motionless body. "Stay where you are!"

"Oh my God," Jade managed through her sobs. "Oh my God, is he *dead*?"

"Shoot him!" Miles roared, pointing at Flynn. "That man is an animal!"

I dropped to my knees next to Ned and saw that his eyes had rolled back in his head. I found his pulse with two fingers on his neck, thought, *Thank you, Jesus*, and took a closer look at his wound. "Bebe. Grab those napkins and put pressure on this.

Hurry." I didn't like how much the cut was bleeding or the slack, gray look of Ned's skin.

In her too-tight skirt, Bebe knelt awkwardly beside me and pressed the cloth against Ned's wound. Tim fastened his cuffs around Flynn's thick wrists and ground his knee into the man's back. All the while I was acutely aware of the location of every person in that room. It didn't surprise me when I glanced up and saw Miles's expression change. I turned my head just in time to see Norton run for the door.

It was what I was counting on.

What I didn't expect was that he'd take Jade with him.

THIRTY-ONE

The terrain on the west side of the island was rough and steep, but I heard their feet crushing wet twigs down below, so I knew I was on the right course. They were both in their house shoes, while my boots at least had a suggestion of grip. If they made it to the river without fracturing a bone, I thought, they'd be lucky.

I hadn't considered Norton's familiarity with the island. While I took the cliff at an angle, picking my way down with only my flashlight to keep me from wrenching an ankle, his movements were nimble and unfaltering, and the path he forged helped Jade to keep pace. They circumvented deadly outcroppings and evaded near-invisible hollows with ease. Twenty years of caring for Tern gave Philip Norton an edge. Camilla may have owned the island, but nobody understood it like he did. Every patch of moss and goose nest, where to find the best views of the river . . . Norton

282

knew it all. This place was his home, and by the time I was halfway down the bluff, I couldn't hear them at all.

People kill out of jealousy, fear, and hate. They kill because they want what someone else has. More than anything, though, what drove Norton's actions was love. His love for Tern Island.

I can't say exactly when I realized he was covering up Jasper's murder. There were many moments when I thought, *I wonder.* As keeper of the house Norton had access to everything and excuses for anything—including hiring Billy Bloom and using him as a stooge. If forensics found Norton's DNA on Jasper's sheets, he could remind them he made the beds. He could argue his fingerprints were on Jasper's bedside table because it was he who did the dusting. Nobody would bat an eye if Norton slipped away to get more wood for the fire, or to snatch a thick, rough rope from the shed.

To his friends and grandmother Jasper was a sweetheart, but he had no love for Norton. According to Abella, Jasper was inexplicably rude to Norton on the dock. In her bedroom Camilla suggested her grandchildren should cut Norton some slack, but it was Jasper she'd been talking about. He alone was concerned with Norton's behavior. Either he didn't like how close Norton and his grandmother had become, or he sensed Norton was acting strange and got wary.

Even though she never got the chance to tell me, I think Abella sensed it, too. I'd concluded she and Jasper had argued because of the way Jasper was treating Norton. The photos Jade took of them in the hall, both with and without the caretaker, confirmed it. In spite of Abella's desire to stay on her new boyfriend's good side, she'd called him out on his discourteous behavior. It wasn't until later on, when she witnessed firsthand the level of control Norton had over Camilla, that she understood Jasper's paranoia about his Nana's trusted companion was warranted.

I knew Norton would run when he saw an opening, for the simple reason that he didn't belong in this world. It was instinct driving him now, the pure, animal need to flee—not just from Tim and me, but all the Sinclairs. I knew what that felt like. I'd run, too. But Norton was desperate, and he had Jade. She didn't hesitate to go with him. Leave her father and take off. No, Jade wasn't a hostage.

That didn't make her safe.

I reached the river's edge and wiped water from my eyes. The gun's grip felt like it was bathed in oil. I squeezed it harder. There was no tracking their footprints. The ground was the same mix of rock and wild grass as the yard up by the house, every blade pounded flat by the rain. The island was large and wooded, and looping to the right would take me nowhere. Only the boathouse lay to the left, and there was nothing there for Norton now, but it seemed the better choice. I hugged the shoreline, pushing through a cluster of trees that thrashed wildly in the high wind. The branches slashed my cheek as I passed and I felt the piercing bite of torn flesh. At the sensation, my memory flickered. I remembered a long, rusty nail gripped tight by a hand as familiar to me as my own, and gagged when I recalled how it punctured my skin and made a breakneck journey across my face. But that pain was old, and I couldn't dwell on it now. I ran on.

As I reached the outer limits of the island, I thought again about how much damage Bram and Carson had done. Norton was right in front of me all day, but I didn't trust myself enough to connect the dots. I couldn't tell good from bad until the truth was presented on a fucking platter. I can't even see a man for what he is when I look into his eyes and accept a ring.

The boathouse loomed ahead of me and I spotted Norton a few feet from the river's edge. He was pushing a battered old canoe into the water near the dock. The green tarp he'd used to camouflage it lay abandoned behind him in the brush. The boat tipped and swayed in the water, no match for the ferocious waves. Gripping a paddle, her free arm braced against the canoe's edge, Jade was already huddled inside.

"Stop right there!"

Both Jade and Norton startled and whipped their heads around. Jade wasn't wearing a lifejacket, and the canoe didn't look seaworthy in the best of weather. I trained my flashlight at Norton's face and leveled my gun at his chest. "You can't run," I hollered. "Look at the river. She'll die. You both will."

Norton squinted into the light, and his small eyes sank into his doughy face. Rain flowed in rivulets over his bald head. "I have to," he said, wading into the water. "I've got to take her home."

"I thought Tern was your home." I willed my hands to stop shaking. He appeared unarmed, but there was no way I could get off a clean shot if Norton made a move. With the rain, visibility was poor, and the harder I squeezed the more the gun's grip felt like sandpaper grating at my palm. I took three slow steps toward him. "Where's Jasper, Philip?"

He was still holding on to the canoe, trying to drag it deeper, but my question loosened his resolve and he stopped moving. Norton locked eyes with Jade. Jacketless and soaked through, she looked miserable and afraid. "I didn't think," he told her. "I didn't know . . ."

"Where is he?" I shouted.

"He's dead!" Norton's sobs were nearly drowned out by the sound of the waves, but I saw the horror in his eyes. "He's gone. In . . . in the river. I'm sorry, honey. I'm so sorry."

Jade's perfect lips formed the shape of an O. As I looked on she transformed, fragile now in the knowledge that she'd crossed from childhood to the inhumanity of adult life.

Norton let out a moan. "I'm sorry," he said again, and dropped his chin to his chest.

"Out of the boat," I told Jade as I closed the distance between us.

She looked up at Norton with confusion, but did as she was told. Jade scrambled out of the canoe, sinking her coltish legs into the water.

Fumbling the flashlight, unwilling to lower the gun, I reached into my back pocket and handed Jade her phone. "Get in the boathouse. Call 911. Tell them we've got suspects out here we're charging with domestic assault and first-degree murder. *Go*," I yelled when the girl didn't move. She hurried to the boathouse and closed the door behind her.

Several facts still needled me, slivers of treachery stuck so deep I was desperate to pinch their ends and pull them free. "I think you drugged Jasper last night," I said when Norton and I were alone. According to Ned, Norton was the only one who saw them after the fight outside. Ned told Norton Jasper had taken a fall. They'd come in through the kitchen. *The water ring on Jasper's bedside table.* "You drugged his water, didn't you? And this morning you got rid of the glass."

Norton looked at me with grave eyes and nodded.

"You did the same to Abella during last night's cocktail hour."

From the start, Tim had wondered whether drugs were involved. But Jasper wasn't the only target. "Did you spike her ice? Clever. If someone else wanted their wine extra cold and ended up knocked out like her, all the better."

"I didn't want her to see," he said feebly. "I was trying to protect her."

"And you did it again tonight, to Camilla." She was required to take pills several times daily, Norton had said. But I'd spent a whole day with the family and hadn't witnessed her take anything, and there were no pills at her bedside. Camilla had seemed tired during our conversation in her bedroom, but she was coherent—nothing like the near-comatose state she slipped into after just a few sips of wine. "You couldn't have her contributing to a conversation about the family money. Not with Flynn and Bebe in the house."

Norton brought his hands to his head and squeezed. "You don't understand! It wasn't like that!"

"No? Camilla's dying. The Sinclair fortune's dried up. All that's left now is the island. Who gets it when she's gone? Who did Camilla name as her heir? It's you, isn't it? She's leaving it all to you."

Philip Norton's shoulders collapsed and he closed his eyes.

"Jesus," I said under my breath. More than anything, I felt disappointed. Camilla seemed like such a strong lady, the only one in the family in her right mind. She'd lost her husband, her only son, and the business she'd watched her family build from nothing, but she should've had the good sense to spot Norton's ruse. If only she'd heeded the warnings of her beloved grandson, whose instincts had been on target. Instead, she listened to her friend of twenty years tell her how much Tern Island meant to him. That leaving it to Jasper would put it at risk of being snatched up and sold by Bebe and Flynn. Norton painted himself as the only logical choice. He promised to protect the priceless property until it could safely be transferred to Jasper. Jasper, who was about to disappear into the October mist.

Norton would face a colossal legal battle when Camilla's wishes were discovered. A widowed empress of New York spurns her rightful heirs and leaves a multimillion-dollar estate to its long-time caretaker? The media would go wild. With Jasper gone, though, Flynn and Bebe were the only ones left to fight for the island, and doing so would inevitably call attention to the family business. The siblings needed Tern Island sold, but if it meant the press might shine a spotlight on Sinclair Fabrics, they'd be better off mourning the tragic loss of their brother and grandmother and letting the property go. Norton must have been overjoyed to hear Flynn announce he and Bebe were corporate criminals. Both faced massive fines, possibly even jail time. There was no one left to interfere with the plan.

"You think this place is worth killing for?" I said. The injustice of what Norton had done made my trigger finger itch. "Was it a kitchen knife or a tool from the shed? Was he dead before his body hit the water, or did he writhe in pain while he drowned? Did you watch him sink to the bottom of the river? *Did you?*"

Norton clutched his head tighter and released a primal moan.

"I thought you were working alone. When I realized what you'd done—implicating Bloom, the drugs—I was sure you concocted this whole plan. But I don't think you killed Jasper anymore. No, you left that part to someone else."

I knew better than anyone, maybe even the Sinclairs, that families don't always stick together. It was like Flynn said. A blood bond doesn't guarantee loyalty.

"It's not too late to save yourself, Philip. I'll take you back to the station. You can sign a confession. Jade will be safe, I gave her my word."

Pummeled by wind and rain, Norton slumped against the edge of the canoe and let the water slosh against his knees. He was close to cracking, but not close enough. I was too late.

The storm was loud, and the ambient glow from my flashlight turned the world black and white, all gloss and shimmer, wet grass and mud—but still I felt it. He was here.

Miles Byrd's rapid breathing preceded him. I didn't need to see him in the light to know he'd taken a bad fall on his way down. There was a limp in his gait as he stumbled toward us.

"*There* you are," Miles said to Norton. "Where's Jade? It was the right decision, getting her out of there. Flynn's fucking nuts." He turned to me. "You were wrong about him, I hope that's obvious now. Flynn lost it last night, just like he did in there with Ned. Flynn killed Jas and that girl."

"Stay where you are." I said it loudly. I needed Jade to hear. Miles was wearing gloves. *Where did he get those gloves?*

"I came to get my daughter." Miles squinted against the beam of light and cracked an amiable smile. "Where is she?"

"Neither of you is going anywhere."

Miles looked at Norton, then back at me. "You can't mean . . . Philip? Come on. He's harmless! He's not the one you're looking for."

"You're right," I said as I transferred my aim and my weapon found its true target. "You are."

Miles wasn't like Norton. He wasn't afraid. The man eased back his shoulders and faced me head-on. "I'm curious, is that really how you operate? By process of elimination? Your little speech up there, about the others being innocent . . . tell me that isn't seriously how you solve a crime."

"Process of elimination is a handy tactic, Miles. It's what brought me to both of you."

Miles laughed and wiped the cold night rain from his brow. "Are you kidding me with this? You and your idiot partner, you're complete amateurs. You don't know what you're talking about." Miles didn't like where this was going. He couldn't see his daughter, and despite his bravado that made him nervous.

I clutched the grip of my gun harder and fought through the pain. "I know about the inheritance, Miles."

A few feet away from him, still knee-deep in water, Norton straightened up. There was panic in his eyes.

Miles brought a gloved hand to his heart and gave me his most earnest smile. "You're confused," he said. "That's understandable. It's a hell of a situation we're in. Tell her," Miles said. "Tell the detective she's wrong."

"You're too late. I know everything. You were smart, I'll give you that. How long have you been planning this, Miles? At what point did you realize Norton was sitting on a gold mine and decide to use him to cash in?"

It was a long game, the con so complex with so many moving parts I had to believe it was months if not years in the making. A marriage to Bebe was just the beginning. She wasn't his mark, but a means to an end that satisfied two of the man's deepest cravings: money and revenge.

"Hey." Miles tossed the word over his shoulder at Norton. "Come over here and tell this poor, confused woman what's what."

Maybe it was habit. Philip Norton was accustomed to doing

as he was told. More likely, though, the man had an all-consuming yearning to make amends. So he went to Miles. And when he got there, Miles made his move.

It was a boning knife he pulled out, lean and deadly, and Miles held it to Norton's throat. In the light of my flashlight the skin around the blade was so white it glowed. Miles had hidden the murder weapon in the pocket of his sport coat. The coat he slipped on after strangling Abella Beaudry with the rope Norton left for him in the bathroom.

"Drop it." My voice wasn't my own. "For God's sake, Miles, he's your father."

The plea sounded like a line from an insufferable melodrama, even to me—as soon as I blurted it, images of Oedipus Rex and Kylo Ren flashed through my mind. On top of that, what difference did shared DNA make in a place like this, where family members manhandled each other and themselves? But I had to take a shot, and I hoped it was enough to give the man with the knife pause.

The photo on Norton's bedside table of him with a young boy meant little to me when I first saw it that morning. Combined with Jade's offhand remark to Tim about her grandmother's Thousand Islands roots, and Miles's comment about growing up without a dad, and the way Norton doted on Jade, its significance grew. Crazy as it was, my conversation with Carson about Moonshine Phil and the unfamiliar teen in town clinched it. Philip Norton and Miles Byrd weren't just partners in crime, but father and son.

The minute I said it, I knew I'd guessed right. Norton made a gurgling sound and Miles grinned at me, all pluck as he pressed down on the blade. Pitifully, Norton croaked, "Miles . . . please . . ."

"Jade," I said, trying another tack. "She'll lose her grandfather. Think of Jade."

"Oh, I have been. That's why I married Bebe in the first place. Bebe was our safety net. There was supposed to be plenty of money." Miles glanced down at Norton with a grimace. "It was supposed to be easy. *All* of this has been for Jade—Jasper most of all. My mother was *sixteen years old* when she had me." His grip on Norton tightened as he spoke. "You refused to help her," he hissed in Norton's ear. "Got her pregnant and tossed her aside. I'll be damned if I was going to let a spoiled rich kid do the same thing to my daughter. All I wanted was to know you," Miles said, "and you wouldn't give me the fucking time of day."

"I was a kid, too," said Norton. "I had no job, no money, nothing. I tried to make it right."

"You tried? You *tried*? Soon as I got my driver's license I was up here every couple of weeks, following you around like a loyal puppy. You sent me away every time. Did you think I'd forget all about that when you finally showed up begging to be best friends?"

"Killing him won't save you, Miles."

"No?" Miles lifted his gaze to find me. "Philip bought the drugs. His name's in Camilla's will. His fingerprints and DNA are all over the knife and the rope upstairs. You've got no signed confession," he said. "No evidence to bring charges against me. No proof at all I'm involved beyond a theory shot full of holes. I'm about to kill him out of self-defense. I'll tell your boss that when you take me in—and take me, by all means. I've got enough criminal attorney friends to start a softball team, all itching to vouch for my character. Meanwhile you shot a witness today, and your incompetence got another one killed. I saw you up there with Wellington, having your little heart-to-heart. Seems to me you've got issues that need serious attention. Maybe some time off is just what you need."

His arm tensed in preparation to slit his long-lost father's throat, but the grin slid off his face. He'd heard it, too. The creak of a door.

"Go back inside, Jade," I said quickly. "Nobody else has to get hurt tonight, not your dad, not your grandfather. Just stay—"

"Daddy?" Jade sounded utterly lost. She was shaking so hard she could hardly stay upright. "What are you . . . what does she . . ."

"My God," I said, absorbing the horror on Miles's face. "She doesn't know."

"Get inside," Miles roared. "Now, Jade."

"But—"

"I wanted to tell you," said Norton. "I didn't even know about you until I tracked Miles down last year. He said we had to wait . . . wait for the right . . ."

"You didn't tell her who he is," I said. "You didn't trust Jade not to spill the secret to the Sinclairs while her grandfather robbed Camilla blind. Were you ever going to let Philip live after this weekend? Or is he just another casualty of your conspiracy to hijack a family fortune?"

Norton's anguished cry contorted his face into a mask of misery, and for the first time I saw the resemblance between these family members. Jade wore the same expression now. Her father held a knife to her grandfather's throat, and she'd just realized Miles and Norton killed the man she thought she loved.

Raking the wet hair out of her eyes, Jade let out a wail and lurched forward. With the three of us blocking her path to the house, there was nowhere for her to run. Nowhere except the flooded dock. Waves rolled over the submerged planks and the water was past her knees, but she moved too fast for me to catch her as she passed.

Miles threw Norton aside and went after his daughter while I beat a path through the waves. The boards of the dock were slippery, the current strong. I was bigger than Jade and even I had to fight not to fall. A few yards away Miles was up to his waist, and then his neck. His strokes were clean but the rain on the water created a blinding, disorienting haze, and he was soon way off track.

Up ahead a wave crashed against Jade, flinging her body sideways. Her head went under, came up slick as a seal, went under again. I saw a pale arm lift and flail, grasping at air, and then she disappeared completely into the cold, dark water.

"Jade!" The men's screams rang in my ears, but a rush of water snuffed them out as I plunged headlong into the river. The cold knocked the air from my lungs and left me breathless. I tried to keep my eyes on the place where she'd gone under, but it was all I could do to stay afloat. My aching muscles seized up almost immediately. My feet were anvils pulling me down. Inside my mouth my teeth throbbed as if I'd chewed aluminum foil. Without my flashlight everything was white froth and black water and that terrible, glacial, mind-numbing cold.

It was reckless. I wasn't a strong swimmer, didn't know the river at all. I just couldn't let another girl die. *But I have. I did.* Jade was nowhere—no Jade, no Miles. Just the river that swallowed Jasper Sinclair, and now me.

Through the rush of water in my ears and the rain and the thunder, I heard a call. When the waves around me went silver I thought it was the lightning again, a flash so bright it turned night into day, but then I saw it. A boat. It rolled and pitched, towering above me where I swam. Something fat and soft landed next to me and I reached for it. Suddenly I could float. I clenched my teeth and craned to see out of the water. What I saw was Maureen McIntyre.

Leaning over the gunwale.

Reaching for my hand.

THIRTY-TWO

S o when you left the house to go after Norton, you knew. Norton had an accomplice. The killer was Miles."

Lieutenant Jack O. Henderson folded his hands on his desk and awaited my response. My direct superior's fingers were thick, his knuckles swollen. They were hands that could crush a windpipe like a straw. I pulled my gaze away from them and looked up.

"I knew there were two people involved in Jasper's murder," I said. "Tough to get a grown man's deadweight out of the house without help. I suspected Norton early on, but narrowing down the others to find his partner was harder. Abella's death sent me back to the beginning of the day, and my dominant memories of our suspects. In those first minutes I spent on Tern Island, Norton explained how the family searched for Jasper. Flynn, Bebe, and Ned looked in the house. Norton took the grounds, with Miles.

"It was their chance to get their stories straight and confirm their game plan. Norton would point the finger at the trapper. Miles would make a case for Ned. The more suspects, the better—and they had plenty of blameworthy people to choose from. Miles must have thought he hit the jackpot when Flynn came after Abella, and again later on when Ned assaulted me and Flynn went after Ned. They all played right into Miles's hands. His plan was ambitious on every level, but so much worked in his favor." *The only thing Miles didn't account for*, I thought, *was Tim and me.*

"After everything I learned about the family's financial situation and Camilla's attitude toward Jasper and Norton, I was pretty sure Norton was in the will as the beneficiary of the island. I just didn't see him stabbing someone. As for Miles, he grated on me. He'd made numerous comments about Bebe's dubious financial state. At one point Bebe even accused him of marrying her for money. They were through well before Bebe slept with Ned, yet Miles stuck around and even came out to the island for what should have been a family affair. Miles was stalling. Waiting for something. I just didn't know what."

I wiped my palms on my pants and was startled by the fine wool twill I found covering my thighs. I'd splurged on a new outfit for my visit to the New York State Police Troop D headquarters, the command center for my county and six others. If ever there was a day when I needed to look professional, this was it.

The BCI lieutenant watched me, unblinking. "You gleaned a lot of information from stories and interactions most people would consider irrelevant."

"Women's intuition?" I offered, smiling.

He didn't laugh.

"There was something else," I said. "It was obvious Jade had a close relationship with Jasper. The prior day, during cocktail hour, Miles watched Jasper ply his smitten daughter with wine. When I questioned Miles in the kitchen, Jade implied she planned to continue seeing Jasper even after Miles and Bebe divorced. I don't know any father who'd be cool with his teenage daughter doling out that kind of attention to a twenty-six-year-old man, let alone one related to a wanton soon-to-be ex-wife. But Miles never said a bad word about Jasper. The man exhibited heroic restraint. That didn't sit right with me. Plus, there was the issue of where he slept."

The lieutenant raised a bristly gray eyebrow, and I went on. "Ned told me he'd bunked in the library. But when I pressed Miles about his sleeping arrangements with Bebe, he claimed he did the same thing. Miles was quick to accept my suggestion that he'd been downstairs, far away from the murder scene. He knew Norton would corroborate his story. What he didn't know was that Ned already occupied the library couch. Guess they didn't notice him when they moved Jasper's body out of the house in the dark. Once I concluded Norton and Miles were covering for each other, I put the rest—their past, their relationship—together from there."

I told Lieutenant Henderson everything I knew, including what I learned after Maureen McIntyre pulled me and Jade out of the river. Norton contacted Miles two years ago, hoping to make amends. Miles was still furious, but when he heard about the Sinclairs and Norton's life with Camilla, it got him thinking. It was easy to track Bebe down in the city. Miles couldn't compete with her wealth, but a lawyer with a beautiful teenage daughter was a respectable choice for a middle-aged woman who'd never been married, and Bebe bit. Miles convinced Norton it was better not to tell Jade who he was until she got older. *Best not to upset the child. Let her get to know you first*, he said.

Miles and Jade fit right into the Sinclair family. Jade got close to Jasper, who treated her like a peer and not the child she was, while Norton got to know his granddaughter after years of estrangement. Miles assured his father all was forgiven. But it didn't take Miles long to discover Sinclair Fabrics wasn't the cash cow he believed it to be. He made his move when his daughter finally spilled a secret worth knowing: Jasper was worried his grandmother was too close to Norton and feared Norton would take advantage of her trust.

It never occurred to Norton to manipulate his situation with Camilla. But Miles made sure to explain how much was at stake. If the business went down, the island would go with it. As a lawyer, however, Miles could help Norton retain his access to the land. If Norton could convince Camilla to will the island to him, he could protect it from Bebe and Flynn. The place Norton treasured, which he'd come to think of as home, would be safe. Jasper was the only thing standing in their way. Norton was understandably reluctant. He told Miles he had no intention of signing up for bloodshed. But as his young granddaughter's infatuation turned into a serious obsession, it was decided. Jasper had to go.

"I know men like Miles," I said. "He used Norton's love of the island and guilt about abandoning his son to twist his thoughts. Jasper may have been a great guy, but he was still a Sinclair, and that made him everything Norton could never be—wealthy, privileged, able to provide for a family. Meanwhile, Norton had just gained a son and granddaughter. His luck had finally changed. He didn't want Jade to end up pregnant and jilted any more than Miles did. Norton isn't entirely heartless. It was his idea to hide the body so Camilla would be spared some heartache. By the time Jasper disappeared, the will had been changed. The island was his."

"I've seen that will," the lieutenant said. "It was amended on Fourth of July weekend to name Norton as sole beneficiary of the entire estate."

"Camilla trusted him. She knew he'd take care of Tern. I'm sure she had visions of life carrying on there the way it always had. Camilla thought she was doing her grandson a favor by taking the estate out of the equation. Money was tearing the family apart, and she didn't want Jasper caught in the middle."

Tap. Tap. The tip of the lieutenant's pen struck the cover of a fat manila folder on his desk. "As you know," he said, "a team of forensic analysts have been out to the island. They found ketamine in what remained of Camilla's wine, and also in Norton's belongings. We're looking into how he obtained it. Probably off some city kid who summers up there."

"Norton lived in A-Bay for a long time. I'm sure he's got connections," I said. "There are a couple of vet offices in the area, and ketamine's used as a sedative. Maybe he got it there."

My knowledge of date-rape drugs caused the lieutenant to quirk his eyebrow again. I didn't bother to explain I had a personal interest in finding out where that shit came from.

"As for the blood on the sheets," he said, glancing down at the folder, "the medical examiner collected family reference samples from Jasper's siblings. It was a match for Jasper, and your initial visual analysis was right. Based on the amount of blood found at the scene, the medical examiner believes Jasper's condition was grave. That said, we had search parties all over Tern Island, divers in the water, and found nothing."

Aside from Miles's body. He didn't say it. There was no need. Mac had been keeping me abreast of all new developments since the second we got back to shore. Miles tried to save his daughter, but it was too late for redemption. I'd heard Jade was in California now, living with her mother. With Philip Norton at the Clinton Correctional Facility, there was nothing left for the kid in New York.

In the end, it wasn't Jasper's body that intruded on my dreams in the nights after I left Tern Island, but Abella's. The girl had been so inconsequential to Miles and Norton's plan, but she'd been targeted anyway, and that made her death all the more painful to swallow. The day before I met Lieutenant Henderson to go about the painful task of explaining how a missing persons case became a double homicide, I'd pilfered the Beaudry family's phone number from the station's digital files and called Abella's parents. Their English wasn't as solid as their daughter's, but there was no misinterpreting the sentiments they wished to express to the investigator who allowed their child to die.

Surreptitiously, the lieutenant checked his watch. "Well, Merchant, that really only leaves Flynn Sinclair. Wellington says he threatened you."

There were plenty of excuses to choose from. Tim's official account made it easy to cover my ass. He'd back me up, no matter what I said. But what I said was, "I don't know why I shot him."

"I think I do." The lieutenant pursed his lips. Again his pen whacked the file—my file—resting under his large hands.

"Bet you're glad that's over."

From his place on the hard wooden bench in the hall, Tim

looks up at me, waggles his eyebrows, and smiles. He went in before me, which means he's been done with the lieutenant for hours. We made the two-hour drive south to Oneida together. When it was my turn, I left Tim outside the door of Troop D headquarters fully expecting him to wait out the grilling at a nearby coffee shop. But here he is.

"It's over, all right." *Suspended pending psychological analysis*. I don't tell Tim it's the outcome I was counting on. Instead, I sit down beside him. "Know what I need?"

Tim slides toward me until we're only inches apart. "I couldn't begin to imagine what you need right now, Shane."

"Damn," I say with a half smile. "Me either."

Aside from us, the hallway is deserted. It's so quiet I can hear Tim's watch ticking on his wrist. The corner of his lip curls into an inquisitive smile. "Buy you a drink?" says Tim.

I haven't been alone with him since it all happened. I don't know how he feels about me hijacking the investigation and going after Philip Norton and Miles alone. "You sure that's what you want?" I ask.

Tim rests his forearms on his bent knees. "I saw a YouTube video once, of a bunch of crickets chirping."

Crickets are what Tim gets in response. I angle my head as I look at him, trying to work out what he's going to say next.

"The second half of the video is what matters. It was slowed down by something like eight hundred percent. It doesn't sound like crickets anymore, but music. Like a choir of human voices. I thought that was so amazing," Tim says. "How making one change can produce a totally different outcome." He pauses. "We don't all come from the same place, you know? We've all got different backgrounds and different pasts, and that affects how we see things. Like with those crickets. Everyone on Tern Island told us what they wanted us to hear. But you heard something different."

"That doesn't guarantee it was right."

"I was willing to take that chance. We're a team." He paused to swallow. "I figured you knew what you were doing."

"You've got a lot of faith in me, under the circumstances."

"Of course I do," he says, not taking his eyes off mine. We both fall silent. Then, "How's it going with Carson?"

My fiancé and I are through, of course. Tim knows that, and he cares about how I'm taking it. It wasn't as easy as I thought it would be, upending my former life and starting over. But easy isn't something I expect from upstate New York anymore.

I study Tim's gray eyes, the strong angle of his jaw. His face is the face of a good man. I can't believe I ever doubted him. "If it wasn't for you, if you hadn't told me how Carson treated you back then . . ." My voice trails off. "Just . . . thanks. You were right. I talked to McIntyre. After Carson called her, she took it upon herself to do some research on him. All this time I thought he left New York for me, to help me heal, but that wasn't it. Carson was fired. The NYPD psych division was getting complaints about him from the people he counseled. All of them women."

"Wow." Tim's gaze falls to the floor.

"Listen," I say. "This is all wrong."

I hear his breath catch. "Oh?"

I smile. "Yeah. I'm the one who should be buying today."

The closest bar is a Mexican place three minutes away. I turn up my collar against the bracing cold as we climb into the car under an overcast sky. The drive is made in silence, and we don't talk again until we're seated at a table with menus in hand. There's no need to consult with Tim before ordering two margaritas and a platter of pork tacos to share. When I turn over the past three months in my mind, all the time we've already spent together, I realize I know him better than I thought.

The drink numbs my throat like a balm as Tim throws himself into small talk with impressive zeal. I appreciate the effort; after all the talking I've just done, I could use a break from the sound of my own damn voice.

"So," he says after a while, when we've both paused to sip at our drinks. Tim seems suddenly nervous; under the lip of the table he jiggles his knee. "I thought about what you told me."

"What I told you?"

"About Bram."

"Oh." I set down my drink too hard. The glass strikes the tabletop with a clink.

"Everything you said that day about the kidnapping, and letting him go. He's still out there," Tim says. "How do you know he's not coming back for you? What I'm saying is, I'm worried. Moving up here . . . I'm not sure it's enough."

God, what I'd give to be able to tell you everything.

"You said the police figured out who he was," Tim goes on. "A custodian in the building. So why haven't they found him?"

"He changed his name? It's not that hard. He's done it before."

"What about his ties to Swanton? Someone must have followed that lead. If he was so obsessed with the place that he risked giving himself away by telling those women where he was really from, maybe he went back there. Has anyone combed the town to see if they could figure out who Bram really is?"

I shrug. Say nothing.

Tim casts a glance around the bar. If he's picturing me sitting in a place just like it, talking to a killer, he doesn't let on. "I've been thinking about this a lot, actually," he says. "Everything you've been through. Tell me something. How much did Carson explain to you about Stockholm syndrome?" Folding his hands, he leans closer. The act reminds me of the day I met Carson, when he was still just a harmless shrink. "What I'm asking," says Tim, "is how much did you know about that condition before you went to see him?"

"Doesn't everyone know about Stockholm syndrome?"

"The concept? Sure. But the symptoms, the circumstances surrounding it, the particulars about onset and—"

"You'd make a great therapist," I say.

"I'm serious. How much did you know about that stuff?"

"What difference does it make?"

"Carson diagnosed you."

"So?"

"So do you agree with him, or was that just a convenient excuse to justify letting Bram go?"

"Excuse me?"

"You're forgetting," he says grimly. "Carson manipulated me, too. I know how persuasive he can be. He convinced everyone at the NYPD you weren't in control down there. I'm sure he was believable. I'm sure it made sense. But here's the thing, Shana. You're stronger than that. I think you suspected he was wrong, and went along with that diagnosis anyway."

"And why the hell would I do that?"

"Because you're *you*. You need to know what makes people tick. You like to get inside their heads. Look what happened on the island, the way you solved that case. The *how* isn't good enough—you have to know *why*. If you killed Bram that day, down in that basement, you'd have lost your chance to find out."

"Find out *what*?"

"Why he took those other women's lives and not yours."

Under his cartoon eyebrows, Tim's eyes are serious as death. I'll never look at his eyebrows and see a clown again.

"You're wrong," I say, because I don't know how else to play it. How can I explain without telling him the truth?

"You were afraid it would happen all over again on the island," Tim says. "That you'd let the killer escape and put other people at risk."

"Every investigator's afraid of that."

"Maybe so. But promise me you won't beat yourself up over it, Shane. You're not the one at fault."

I study Tim Wellington's face. We're colleagues, but we're friends now, too, and his need to protect me stems from that. Tim's kind and honest, and if I ever meet his family I know they'll be just like him. But Tim thinks too much of me. He's too quick to forgive and forget everything I've done. Tim doesn't just refuse to accept my demons, he refuses to acknowledge they exist. There's darkness in me he doesn't see. He doesn't want to.

When I think about Carson now, I suspect that's why I stayed with him. Deep down I knew he had a nasty side, and nasty is what I deserve. Both of us harbor secrets. Hard to say whose are worse. "*Promise*," Tim says again. And I do.

It isn't the first lie I've told him. That happened in the Sinclairs' house when he inquired about my scar. I said Bram had nothing to do with my deformity. In fact, it links us sure as a chain.

Bram wasn't lying when he declared we have history. I wish I could say his claim didn't register until after he escaped, but I was already wise to him in the belly of the East Village. It was there I cracked open his stories and inspected the cold goo inside until I found the nucleus. The heart of it all.

There's darkness in me, just like there is in Bram, but I refuse to let it take over. I owe it to my family, to A-Bay and Tim, to fight. I have skin in the game, no question, but I've got skills, too.

Enough to defend about a thousand islands.